"There's

Vic smiled. "Although I've always thought we were completely wrong for each other."

"Maybe we're actually attuned to each other in ways unimaginable?" Mimi suggested.

"Oh, I can imagine all right," he said teasingly. They continued to shift and sway as they stood there in the moonlight. Their faces close, so close to contact, but not quite.

Mimi felt giddy, felt herself tremble. "You know what they say? Opposites attract." She grabbed his finger when he pointed it at her. She felt possessive.

He looked at her hand on his. "Why'd you do that?"

Because she wanted him. "Because you shouldn't point at people," she answered instead.

"You're teaching me manners now?" He angled his head one more time and brought his lips near hers.

She angled her head the other way, but kept their mouths only an inch apart. "So, is this where you assert your manliness and kiss me?"

"Bossy, too." He put his hands on her waist. Drew her hips to his.

And that was the type of assertion she wanted from him.

Dear Reader,

When I was in college, I was a jock—not the first thing most romance writers tell you.

I was a member of the varsity women's crew at Yale University, and in my junior year was elected captain. But I also served as an undergraduate representative on the university's Title IX committee. This group of faculty, administrators and students evaluated the effects and compliance actions regarding the federal measure to ensure equal opportunity for men and women competing in intercollegiate athletics.

The head of the committee was the athletic director at that time. He was intensely loyal to Yale, and his family had a long relationship with the university. He also understood the emotional, social and historic aspects of sports, in addition to the physical benefits. Yet above all else, he valued the importance of doing the right thing.

Luckily for me, he took me under his wing, and I learned a lot about patience, kindness and the joy of life despite hardships—of which he had suffered more than a few. And because of him, I made regular pilgrimages back to my alma mater for the annual Yale-Harvard crew race on the Connecticut River. I returned for more than the race, though. I returned because I learned the importance of keeping in contact with true friends.

And, now in retrospect, I realize he was the genesis for this School Ties miniseries.

Warmest regards,

Tracy Kelleher

PS—As always, I love hearing from my readers. Reach me through my website, www.tracykelleher.com

The Company You Keep

TRACY KELLEHER

TORONTO NEW YORK LONDON
AMSTERDAM PARIS SYDNEY HAMBURG
STOCKHOLM ATHENS TOKYO MILAN MADRID
PRAGUE WARSAW BUDAPEST AUCKLAND

Recycling programs
for this product may
not exist in your area.

ISBN-13: 978-0-373-60716-7

THE COMPANY YOU KEEP

ABOUT THE AUTHOR

Tracy sold her first story to a children's magazine when she was ten years old. Writing was clearly in her blood, though fiction was put on hold while she received degrees from Yale and Cornell, traveled the world, worked in advertising, became a staff reporter and later a magazine editor. She also managed to raise a family. Is it any surprise she escapes to the world of fiction?

Books by Tracy Kelleher

HARLEQUIN SUPERROMANCE

*School Ties

Other titles by this author are available in ebook format.

Don't miss any of our special offers. Write to us at the following address for information on our newest releases.

Harlequin Reader Service
U.S.: 3010 Walden Ave., P.O. Box 1325, Buffalo, NY 14269
Canadian: P.O. Box 609, Fort Erie, Ont. L2A 5X3

I'd like to thank Audrey Zak for providing insight into training methods for the sport of water polo.

This book is dedicated in loving memory of
Delaney Kiphuth, a smart and gentle man.
You left us all much too soon.

PROLOGUE

Grantham University
Twelve years ago

"WHAT ROCK HAVE YOU BEEN living under for the past twenty-two years?" Mimi Lodge wailed. She shook her fist, the wide sleeve of her black-and-orange-pin-stripe class jacket slipping down her arm.

Grantham University, an Ivy League college in Grantham, New Jersey, had been educating future world leaders for centuries in a pristine setting of academic Gothic architecture, ornamental shrubbery and a strong sense of entitlement. And every year its senior class picked a new jacket to wear for Reunions weekend before graduation. At five-foot-nine, with wide strapping shoulders from years spent competing in water polo—and the long, sleek torso from being in top physical condition—she was one of the few who could carry off such a garment with aplomb.

Of course, maybe it was just her forthright attitude that substituted for shoulder pads. She continued to fume. "In case you didn't know it, this is the twenty-first century. Men and women are equal. Women have had the right to vote for almost one hundred years. You know the twentieth amendment?"

Vic Golinski, the object of her tirade, slowly peeled off his blue blazer. Vic was also graduating from Grantham, but he was wearing more sedate attire—or at least, *had been* wearing—until Mimi had up-ended a water pitcher all over him in a particularly heated moment. They were participating in what was supposed to be an open panel discussion.

Reunions organizers often featured panels with faculty members, administration officials and occasionally students to discuss topics of interest to returning alumni. Theirs had been anything but routine. With the subject being The Impact of Title IX on Participation in College Varsity Sports, the session had drawn a large crowd. Title IX was an amendment to the Civil Rights Act that prohibited discrimination based on sex in regards to school sports. And while the university abided by the law, there were any number of Grantham alumni from the once all-male bastion who felt it was undermining long established men's teams.

And it appeared to Mimi, these former students—meaning, old, stuck-in-the-mud type guys—were not alone. Vic Golinski might be all of twenty-two, but as captain of the football team, he appeared to be firmly stuck in the mud. How else to explain his statement, "I believe the university's football program must inevitably suffer due to siphoning off dollars to create so-called parity programs in minor sports. What's going to happen next? The call for creation of a women's football team when girls programs don't even exist in high schools around the country? That would be the height of absurdity, all in the name of so-called equality."

Whoa there. *Minor sports?* (Meaning hers, no doubt.) *Height of absurdity? So-called equality?* Talk about reaching a tipping point. Mimi had seen red. Her hand had migrated to the water jug. And upended it—all over her classmate.

"Giving women the right to vote was the nineteenth amendment," Vic corrected, his voice low as if he was trying to keep his temper in check.

Mimi stood there, barely keeping still, while Vic yanked his arm out of the sleeve of his soaking blazer… when…when she momentarily forgot her anger. Instead, she realized that when water comes in contact with a man's dress shirt, it turns the material virtually translucent. Translucent and amazingly pliable, she couldn't help noticing, as the thin cotton molded to Vic's biceps and triceps, in addition to his well-contoured pectoral muscles.

She stopped in midstride, took a deep breath and willed herself to replay what he'd just said. "Details," she scoffed in rebuttal. Vic Golinski wet might be better than any firemen's pinup calendar, but that didn't excuse his reactionary sentiments.

He loosened the knot of his orange tie and undid the top two buttons of his blue dress shirt. A few dark curls from his wet chest hair peeked out through the opening. "The devil is in the details," he responded.

Mimi gulped and turned away. She exited the building and marched away from Baldwin Gymnasium where the panel had been held. She walked a short distance along the path, before she cut between two of Grantham's Social Clubs, the university's version of coed fraternities. Ahead lay the Alexander Hamilton School of International Studies, an elite branch of the university. She had wanted to ditch Vic, but he kept up stride for stride, shoulder to shoulder—forcing her to keep acknowledging his presence.

"You deserved that soaking—and more," she muttered, her eyes focused on the uneven sidewalk. "What you said is just so infuriating...such a personal affront to me as captain of the water polo team, one of your so-called 'minor sports.'" She raised her hands and gestured with her fingers to form quotation marks. "You have no idea what you are talking about." Without bothering to look she jaywalked across Edinburgh Avenue, oblivious to the fact that she'd also crossed against the light.

Her statement was met by silence. Surprised, Mimi looked over her shoulder—and realized that Vic Golinski was waiting for the light to change and the "Walk" signal to flash. Mimi shook her head. "What's the matter with you?" she scolded him. "There's not a soul, let alone a car, in sight. Don't you believe in taking the initiative?"

The light changed, and Vic stepped off the curb. "That's no reason to disregard the rules," he said patiently.

Mimi waited with hands on hips.

He stepped up next to her, towering over her despite her above-average height. "You may have gained some satisfaction in pouring water all over me, but this is my only dress shirt—and I need it for graduation in a few days."

"I'll get it dry cleaned for you." She raised her chin.

He lowered his. "That's your solution for everything, isn't it? Throw money at it?"

Mimi didn't back down. "Well, I hope you're not expecting me to break out the ironing board."

Vic narrowed his eyes. "Spoken like someone who was born with a silver spoon in her mouth. I bet you don't even know how to iron."

He was right, dammit. Mimi whipped around and marched on. On the right was the courtyard for Allie Hammie, as the Alexander Hamilton School was affectionately known. The whole area was paved in white marble, the same stone that clad the exterior of the school with its attenuated columns and narrow arcade. A row of magnolias ran along the far side, and in the center of the courtyard was an ornamental pool out of which rose an abstract metal sculpture. Water jets splashed its rusty surfaces and droplets bounced off and rained down to the water below.

Mimi stopped by the fountain and held up her arms in exasperation before letting them fall to her sides. "Okay, I'm sorry." Her palms thwacked against her black trousers. "In hindsight, the powers-that-be never should have put us on that panel. Maybe they thought we would provide a student perspective besides the usual drivel from the administration flunky and the coaches. But *you* are clearly a throwback to some Neanderthal age."

"Just because I don't believe that there needs to be a comparable women's team for every men's athletic team, doesn't make me a caveman. And I'm sorry if it offends you, but guys who are friends of mine on the wrestling team—who work their butts off—are pissed, rightfully pissed in my estimation, that their sport is being thrown on the trash heap because there's no comparable women's sport. Following that logic, what's going to happen to the football program?"

"There's nothing wrong with being a club sport." That wasn't quite true, as Mimi knew. Club sports received only small budgets, didn't have paid coaches and didn't travel.

"Then why don't you petition for Women's Water Polo team to be a club sport instead of varsity?"

"No way! That wouldn't be fair because the men's team has varsity status. You want that to become a club sport, too?"

"Of course not." Vic ran his hand through the top of his brown wavy hair. He seemed entirely unaware that it stuck up like a lopsided Mohawk.

For someone intent on maintaining the status quo on and off the field, he looked remarkably off-kilter. Mimi had an intense desire to fluff up his hair even more, loosen him up and see what lay beneath his stuffed shirt exterior. Actually, she knew exactly what lay beneath his shirt—lots of well-developed muscles.

Vic seemed completely oblivious to Mimi's inner ruminations. "Listen, all I'm saying is, before you— or anybody else for that matter—goes jumping into things, they need to weigh the pros and cons, evaluate a program over time, consider making adjustments when necessary. I'm not saying things can't—or shouldn't—change just that why rock the boat too much? Why not take it nice and easy?" He furrowed his brow. "Doesn't that make sense?"

Raising one eyebrow, Mimi gave him a jaundiced view. "Are you always so cautious? Don't you ever believe in taking risks? Are you always so slow to make up your mind about something?" It was a taunt, and she meant it.

"What are you talking about? Risk? I've been drafted into the NFL. A career in pro football is all about risk."

Mimi waved off his question. "That's all about seizing an opportunity. Because I bet even though you're going to give the pros a chance, you have an airtight backup plan—maybe some trainee position at a bank or an acceptance to business school."

Vic rubbed the sole of his black leather loafer on the sidewalk.

"Ah-hah!" Mimi shouted triumphantly. "I was right, wasn't I?"

He shrugged. "Maybe. But some of us can't simply plan on being world-renowned international correspondents."

Mimi had voiced her post-graduation plans when she'd introduced herself at the start of the panel, minus the world-renowned part.

"We don't just take off for parts unknown on the chance that we might run into some newsworthy event or use old family connections to get interviews with generals or presidents," he continued. "Some of us need to think about things like paying back college loans and getting jobs that provide health insurance."

"Oh, please, this is not about health insurance. Because, for your information, I'm not going into this as some rich girl hobby. For four years, after practice, I've slogged away at the *Daily Granthamite,* writing every kind of story under the sun." She referred to the student newspaper that came out five days a week. "I'm not using my contacts. I'm cleaning out my bank account and getting a one-way ticket to Lebanon, and from there I'll hunt down stories—stories about the real victims of this world."

"And what if you don't succeed? Then what?" he asked, his face getting closer to hers.

"Oh, I won't fail. And I won't give up," she said with conviction. "Because to me, it's worth whatever I have to do to expose the reality behind oppression, racism and especially wars. Wars aren't just about soldiers. It affects the lives of everyday civilians—families, women and children. And if I run out of money because I can't get someone to pick up my work, then I'll simply keep writing until they do. I'm willing to take that chance because sometimes you just can't take things slowly—moving only after you've weighed the pluses and minuses."

Vic opened his eyes wide. "You're crazy, you know that?"

Mimi laughed. "I may be crazy, but no one will be able to look back on what I've done twenty years from now and say, 'Well, she might have made a good war correspondent—even a great one—but she spent too much time worrying about health insurance premiums.'" Then she stuck her finger out toward him. "And what will they be able to say about you? 'When he was cut from training camp, he didn't bother trying to get picked up by another team. He weighed the pros and cons and became an accountant instead.'"

Mimi glared at Vic, expecting him to argue, to say she didn't know what she was talking about. But he was deathly quiet, menacingly silent. She back-pedaled a few feet, and stumbled against the low wall surrounding the reflecting pool. Spray from the fountain spattered over her head, beading on her ponytail and shoulders.

She saw him narrow his eyes and stare at her without blinking. Had she gone too far? she wondered. "Listen, maybe I shouldn't have carried on like that, you know." She tried to sound nonchalant.

He fisted his hands and took a step toward her.

Mimi stuck her tongue against the inside of her cheek. "You know, me and my big mouth. Sometimes

I can't stop myself—like pouring the water over your head." She looked over her shoulder, then back at him. "So tell me," she said brazenly, her chin high. "Should I feel worried here. Because, you know, I realize that aggression is an inherent element of your sport, especially for a linebacker. You're a linebacker, right?" Mimi guessed, having never been to a football game in her four years at Grantham—a heresy, she knew, but it had been another way to avoid her father who never missed a home game.

"Right tackle," he corrected, looming a little larger still.

She gulped. "I'm sure there's a big difference. But the important point I'm trying to make is that *off* the field, physical violence never solved anything."

"Maybe where you come from. But in my old neighborhood, it sure came into play." He tossed his jacket to the ground and took another step, moving his massive body deep into her personal space. "Why is it, that as infuriating, as irritating, as arrogant as you are—you also sometimes make sense? I just hate that."

Mimi frowned. She didn't know whether to feel complimented or wary. "Are you admitting that I'm right?"

Vic moved until there wasn't a millimeter of space between them.

She could feel his chest rise and fall, feel the heat generating from his skin and the cold wetness of his shirt. Immediately her nipples responded to the contrast, tightening into sensitive beads.

"The only thing I'm admitting is that there are times when you get under my skin," Vic went on. "You don't know me at all, yet you understand me in ways that even I sometimes don't. How do you do that?"

"Innate brilliance? Extraordinary insight?"

He stared at her, turning his head this way and that, as if trying to analyze every curve of her face. "No, you're smart, but I'm pretty sure I'm smarter. No offense."

"I'm not so sure about that." Actually, she was pretty sure, but she wasn't going to admit it. She was no dope. She may have been a legacy admission—her family had been Grantham graduates and generous donors for generations—but she had been at the top of her class at prep school and had aced the college entrance exams. True, her grades in college weren't exactly great, but then she had chosen to spend her time on sports, the newspaper and her social life.

Whereas Vic Golinski, despite devoting countless hours to football and the Big Brother program—she had listened to his introduction, as well—was graduating Phi Beta Kappa. In their junior year he had won the prize for the highest cumulative GPA for a student in the social sciences. Even if the guy spent every night in the library, he had to be extra smart to beat out all the other smart people at Grantham.

He pointed his finger at her, then at himself. "No,

I think it's because there's something between you and me—something despite the fact that we are polar opposites."

"Maybe we're actually attuned to each other in ways unimaginable?"

"Oh, I can imagine all right," he said teasingly. They continued to shift and sway, their faces so close to contact, but not quite.

Mimi felt giddy, felt herself tremble. "You know what they say? Opposites attract." She grabbed his finger when he pointed it at her. She felt possessive.

He looked at her hand on his. "Why'd you do that?"

Because she wanted him. "Because you shouldn't point at people," she answered instead.

"You're teaching me manners now?" He angled his head one more time and brought his lips near hers.

She angled her head the other way, but kept their mouths close. "So, is this where you assert your manliness and kiss me?"

He put his hands on her waist. Drew her hips to his.

She was sure she could feel evidence of his arousal. She put her hands on his shoulders and went up on her toes. She held her breath, closed her eyes. Felt his hands squeeze her waist, felt him lift her effortlessly off the ground. Felt him hesitate then…

Then toss her into the water.

Splash!

Mimi landed on her bottom in the shallow pool. She opened her eyes and coughed to clear her airway. Water streaked down her face and soaked her clothes.

She flailed, reaching out on either side to gain her balance. She tried to push herself up, wobbled and fell back on her rump again. Water weighed down her clothes, soaked her shoes. Overhead, the fountain showered her hair and face. "Argh," she growled.

Vic was doubled over—laughing uproariously. "How come if we're so attuned to each other, you didn't see that coming, huh?" he asked, grabbing his side.

He was right. She was sure he'd had something else in mind. But…but…whatever. She was madder at herself. And the jerk didn't know when to stop laughing. "So, you thought you'd get even, didn't you? Have a little go at me?"

"You call that little?" He wiped his hand across his mouth, trying to stop the laughter. There were even tears leaking from the corners of his eyes. "Maybe. Or maybe I just wanted to see what can happen to someone who insists on flying without a safety net."

She struggled to stand, the two feet of water making her clumsy. She whisked her wet ponytail back from her cheek and straightened her shoulders. "You think you're so clever to…"

She paused. And then she knew what she was going to do. Nobody made a fool out of Mimi Lodge—especially when she was sure she hadn't been mistaken about his arousal.

First, she wriggled out of her jacket. Then she kicked off one black flat. The other got dragged down with water, so she bent over, slipped it off and tossed it over her shoulder. Next she grabbed the hem of her black sleeveless shell and began peeling the wet material over her head.

"Whoa! What do you think you're doing?" He called out.

She freed her head from the top and threw the shirt over her shoulder. She saw him holding out an arm as if to stop her. "What does it look like I'm doing? I'm stripping down naked," she announced emphatically. "Now who didn't see that coming? So what are you going to do now, eh? You going to pretend you didn't have other things in mind? Oh, I know—you're too chicken to act. Or maybe you'd like to weigh the pros and cons?" she taunted him.

He looked around. "Hey, you can't do that. Someone might come by."

"I'll take that chance, especially since everybody and his little brother is down at the Reunions lunch eating and drinking to their heart's content." She undid the waistband of her pants and lowered the zipper. Then she stepped out of the legs, lifting one foot as she hopped in the water, and then the next.

She threw the trousers at him.

He caught them before they thwacked him in the face. "What about the cops?"

"What about the cops?" She stood there naked except for the wisps of nylon and silk that comprised her demi-cup bra and bikini underpants. The slippery, nude-colored underwear was wet and, she knew, just as transparent as his shirt. She reached behind for the clasp on her bra.

His jaw dropped open. "You could, you could be arrested." He gulped visibly.

She unhooked her bra and let it slide to the water below. The jets from the fountain hit the undersides of her small breasts. The chilly water made her nipples pucker tightly. She slipped one thumb in the side of her underpants. "You think I won't do it?"

"No, that's the problem. I think you just might."

"So you're attuned to me after all." This time Mimi threw back her head and laughed. Then she looked him straight in the eye, put her other thumb in the other side of her panties and did a little wiggle. "So what do you intend to do about it, Mr. Look-But-Don't-Leap?"

She wiggled some more as she worked the elastic waistband down her thighs.

"Well, I'm certainly done looking." He came in after her.

"My, my, you didn't even take off your shoes. Now that's impulsive." She held open her arms.

He slogged through the water to reach her.

And that's when the police sirens came wailing down the street.

CHAPTER ONE

A LOUD WAIL INTERRUPTED Mimi's whimpering. The mechanical, incessant noise went on…and on. Mimi pressed her forehead down. She wanted to cover her ears, and even though logically she knew that movement was impossible, she reflexively went to raise her arms.

She expected to feel the binding restraints and the shooting pain. Miraculously, there was none. Just the incessant ringing and ringing…

Then the noise stopped.

Mimi rolled over and opened her eyes. And realized she was lying on her own queen-size bed in her own apartment on the Upper East Side in Manhattan and not…not captive in that hellhole in Chechnya—blindfolded, beaten, alternating between bouts of despondency and glimmers of hope.

She turned her head on the downy pillow and gazed out the window toward the light—something she'd been deprived of for months, something that was now so precious. It didn't disappoint.

It was one of those rare winter mornings in Manhattan when the gray clouds of January had decided to take a holiday. The sun streamed in through the glass like some visionary painting.

It should have warmed her. It didn't.

Mimi still hadn't gained any weight back after she'd been kidnapped while on assignment in Chechnya, a forced confinement that had lasted almost six months. Two months had passed since her television news network had secured her release, but she still suffered an almost bone-numbing coldness.

She wriggled deeper under the white duvet cover. The feel of the expensive Egyptian cotton material reassured her without fully erasing the nightmare.

Mimi had never been introspective for a variety of reasons. She freely admitted the obvious one that she simply never had the luxury of time to stop and think. The other reasons she kept private, even from her best friend from college, Lilah Evans. But since… since the kidnapping—there, she'd said it—she was beginning to appreciate just how bizarre time and memory were.

For instance, off the top of her head, she had virtually no idea what she'd done all day yesterday. Yet the exact events of the day she was abducted remained crystalline clear. Not surprising, really, since every night when she sought comfort in sleep, she instead kept reliving that day over and over, each detail more vivid, each smell more penetrating, each sound more ominous, the pain…

She forced herself to focus on the cream-colored walls of her room. They were bare except for a few framed photos of colleagues and friends. Several showed her family: her mother blowing out candles on a birthday cake; her half-brother, Press, who'd graduated from Grantham University last year and was now in Australia; and her little half-sister, Brigid, a bundle of energy who was eight going on sixteen. There were none of her father. The photos showed people laughing, happy. She was in a few, too—laughing, happy. She sniffed, trying to recall the feeling. She couldn't. That was the thing about memory. It was selective, even when you didn't want it to be.

Mimi shifted back to the bank of metal-framed windows that looked out from her twelfth-floor apartment on East Seventieth, off Lexington. After years of renting various places around the City, she'd finally bought the condo when the real estate market hit a low a few years ago. And for the Upper East Side, it had been a bargain, all because her building was one of those white brick high rises built with good intentions but a total disregard of aesthetic appeal. Ugly didn't come close, and no self-respecting equities analyst or art gallery owner wanted to be caught dead in something so gauche. One day, though, she figured, white brick would be the new Art Deco, and she'd be laughing all the way to the bank.

The loud wail of the cell phone started up again.

She rubbed her eyes and turned to find her Black-Berry on the nightstand. Its slim black case jiggled across the glass surface. Mimi peered closely, not at the phone number displayed on the screen but at the table, checking for dust. It was spotless. The cleaning lady she'd hired since returning home came in twice a week. She was considering having her come in three times, but even she admitted that was absurd. This obsession she'd developed to maintain spotless control would pass. Still…

The phone rang on.

Mimi sighed and finally reached over. "Yes?" she said without much interest.

"Is that any way to answer the telephone, Mary Louise?" It was her father, Conrad Lodge III. Only he would use her given names instead of her nickname. "I suppose I should thank the heavens that you even picked up—as opposed to my many emails that you've ignored completely." His upper class, lockjaw manner of speaking sounded even more pronounced over the phone.

Mimi inhaled. "I didn't answer your emails because I haven't had time to open them." It was a lie, but then her family was good at lying. She hadn't actually bothered about the messages at all.

She shifted her position under the covers and stared at the wall with the photos again, zeroing in on the black-and-white shot of her mother wearing a silly party hat and holding forth a birthday cake adorned with lit candles. It had been Mimi's ninth birthday. She'd been in third grade at Grantham Country Day School.

Mimi recalled that birthday vividly. More than anything she had wanted to get her ears pierced. Her father had refused. "Who do you think you are? An immigrant child?" he'd asked scornfully. Her mother, only recently a naturalized citizen, had bowed her head and looked away.

As she lay in bed now, Mimi felt the hole in one of her earlobes. Conrad had won the battle that birthday, but as soon as she'd left home for boarding school Mimi had made a beeline for the nearest Piercing Pagoda. Maybe one of these days she'd actually get around to wearing earrings again.

From the other end of the telephone line her father cleared his throat. "I'm delighted you're keeping so busy during your time off from work."

Cutting sarcasm had always been one of his strengths, Mimi thought.

"Therefore, rather than wait for you to find the time, I decided to call *you* instead."

"Before you begin the lecture, I know I should come down to see the family," Mimi cut in, anticipating his demands. Grantham, New Jersey, Mimi's family's hometown, was an hour's train ride south of New York City. It was the epitome of a picture-postcard college town—Gothic university buildings and historic colonial houses. Its quaint main street—named Main Street, no less—boasted high-end jewelry shops, stock brokerages and coffee shops that catered to black-clad intellectuals and young moms with yoga mats tucked in the back of expensive jogging strollers.

"So, I promise to visit soon," she continued, only half meaning it.

"That would be most welcome," her father replied. "But actually, I am inquiring about something else. I'm on the organizing committee for Reunions this year. Quite an honor, really." Reunions at Grantham were a giant excuse for alumni from all the previous graduating classes to gather for a long weekend at their old stomping grounds, reminisce about the good old days and make fools of themselves by wearing silly class outfits and drinking excessive amounts of alcohol.

"Reunions? But they're not until June. If it's about giving Noreen plenty of notice that I'll be staying at the house, you don't have to worry." Noreen was her father's third wife. Mimi's natural predilection was to despise her stepmothers, but even she had to admit Noreen was pretty decent.

"I'm sure Noreen will appreciate hearing from you, but I repeat, that's not why I called. Really, Mary Louise. If you'd let me get a word in edgewise, you'd realize that fact."

Chastised but not humbled, Mimi bit her tongue.

A self-satisfied silence permeated the line. "I wanted to speak to you in regards to my position on the Reunions committee. I'm in charge of organizing the panel discussions."

Despite his chastisement, Mimi couldn't help but jump in with a comment. "I thought I made it clear to you and everyone else that I don't want to talk about what happened in Chechnya." She hated the fact that her voice trembled.

"Yes, you made that loud and clear when you took an extended leave from the network—though I still believe you should talk to the psychiatrist that Noreen found for you, the specialist in matters...in matters related to your particular circumstance." Conrad cleared his throat uneasily. "What I had in mind was more directly relevant to the Grantham student experience. Intercollegiate athletics, to be precise."

"What are you talking about? I haven't participated in any competitive sports since my senior year." Mimi was baffled.

"Which was the year you served on a panel at Reunions addressing Title IX and its impact on Grantham's varsity teams. As I recall, your comments were particularly offensive to certain male members of the audience when you advocated the demotion of the wrestling team to a club sport," Conrad noted.

"That's because there was no female equivalent," Mimi pointed out, the arguments still fresh in her mind. That whole memory trick again. "Anyway, *I* recall that the university administration agreed with me."

"And I have no doubt you'd be more than willing to defend the same position what...ten or so years after the fact?"

"Twelve, as I'm sure you know perfectly well." Her father might be an arrogant twit, but as a founding partner and long-standing chairman of a successful private equity firm, one thing Conrad Lodge III knew—and remembered—was numbers, any and all numbers. *Except for the date of my birthday,* she qualified silently.

But instead of enjoying her self-righteous sulk, Mimi suddenly experienced one of those lightbulb moments. "Wait a minute. You didn't call to merely reminisce about one of my more dramatic episodes, did you?"

"Since when have I been inclined to reminisce about you?"

At least he was honest. *This time,* she amended.

"No, I was thinking about reconvening the same panel of administrators, coaches and students from before. A do-over confab, you might say."

Mimi pinched the skin at her throat. "Well, I suppose the topic might be of general interest—might. As you're no doubt aware, there's been a number of recent headlines about colleges manipulating their athletic reporting to fulfill their Title IX obligations. But even if you buy into that premise, from the practical perspective, half the people who were on that panel must be dead."

"There you go again—jumping to conclusions. As it turns out, only one person has passed away—the former athletic director.

"I remember him," Mimi grumbled. The moron had refused equal locker room space to the women's water polo team until their demonstration senior year. She smiled, remembering the photo in the *New York*

Times of her leading her teammates into his office to use it as their changing room. Boy, did they get permission to share the men's locker rooms adjacent to the pool, but fast.

"But the rest are still active at Grantham or other universities," Conrad went on. "I even tracked down one of the coaches who's currently with a professional basketball team in Italy."

"And you honestly think you can get him and everyone else to come back for a rerun?"

"I already have. Everyone but you and one other person have been confirmed. Not many people say no to me." He stated it as a simple matter of fact. "Besides, they're doing it for Grantham."

"And *I'm* such a loyal alum—not," Mimi said. "But who knows, one of these days I might actually donate some money."

"And give generously. All Lodges are loyal alums." Her father's words had a certain déjà vu ring to them.

She'd been ten, and it was right after her parents' divorce. "All Lodge men go to Grantham," she remembered him telling her. They'd been on a sailboat in Seal Harbor, Maine. Mimi had had two options— stay in a sweltering apartment in Easton, a far less socially acceptable town just north of Grantham where her mother had moved, or two, enjoy coastal Maine's balmy breezes and wild blueberries—not to mention an unlimited family tab at the Bar Harbor Club in between tennis lessons. She'd chosen Maine.

Two weeks later, her mother had chosen an overdose of sleeping pills.

Her father cleared his throat, bringing her back to the present. "So do I have your agreement?" he asked.

Mimi recalled her first experience on the panel. "You know, I'm not sure I'm your safest bet. Not only did I tee off some people in the audience, I didn't exactly see eye to eye with some other members of the panel."

"One in particular, I believe—the captain of the football team. How could I forget the way you dumped a pitcher of water over his head." Conrad chuckled.

Actually, Mimi's mind had raced ahead to her stripping off her clothes in the Allie Hammie fountain.

"If memory serves me correctly, he rose above your antics with great equanimity. A true Grantham man."

She remembered something else rising. She smiled—at that and the picture of the cops arriving at the fountain. Equanimity had been in short supply. "You know, Father, I'm not all that convinced that a replay would provide the results you're looking for."

And that's when Mimi experienced a second light-bulb moment. Two in one conversation! Which could only mean… "Wait a minute. Don't tell me you're trying to create some drama?" She hated the fact that her father had so easily manipulated her—for his own purposes, no less.

"These alumni panels can sometimes be rather dry, much too intellectual. Do we really need to be lectured on our overdependence on oil or the future of the space program? Far more entertaining to watch sparks fly, don't you agree?"

Vic Golinski. Mimi hadn't thought about him since graduation. What she did remember was they were more than polar opposites. They were matter and antimatter. Wile E. Coyote and Road Runner. Get them together, and it was total combustion—as that one time had proved.

Not that he'd even remember her, she immediately dismissed. It wasn't like they'd ever hung around together in college. And hadn't he gone on to some pro football career? He probably had groupies at his beck and call.

"So what do you think?" her father prompted her.

Mimi wasn't ready to commit. "Did you say one other person hasn't gotten back?"

"That's right."

Mimi heard a shuffling of papers.

"Yes, it's the other undergraduate member of the panel…that former football captain…named…let's see…yes, here it is. Golinski. Witek Golinski. Quite a mouthful." He chuckled in a condescending way.

What a narrow-minded snob, Mimi thought with irritation. "Vic. He went by Vic," she corrected him. And impulsively, to thwart his smugness, Mimi blurted out, "Okay. I'll do it."

"I knew I could count on you." Again, that conceit.

You want drama? I'll give you drama, Mimi thought. She could be just as manipulative as her father—for her own ends. "Yes, I'll participate on the panel—on one condition, no, two actually. First, I'll do it, but only if Vic Golinski does, too."

"I'll call him as soon as I hang up," her father answered. "And the second proviso?"

"I want you to notify the fire department."

"The fire department? I don't understand?"

Mimi smiled for the first time in months. "Forget sparks. I predict a fire of major proportions."

CHAPTER TWO

"HERE'S YOUR ORDER, THEN—Ubatuba." Vic Golinski pointed to two enormous slabs of polished granite. They were stacked vertically in a wooden pallet in the brightly lit warehouse the size of a giant airplane hangar. Several 747s could have fit in the space with no problem. Rows and rows of identical pallets held enormous rectangles of different stone, all finished on one flat surface, rough and scored on the reverse. The high-tech space was filled with the mechanical whirring and beeping of a crane maneuvering a slab of pink-flecked granite to a flatbed truck stationed by the open garage doorway.

"Ubatuba is our largest seller and a fairly uniform stone," Vic explained. His voice was calm, solicitous, betraying none of the awareness that myriad tasks awaited him with a timeline of "yesterday."

He waved the young couple next to him to come closer. "Have a good look here. See how the flecks are regular and there's no discernible veining? That's typical of Ubatuba granite—not a lot of variation from one shipment to the next." He ran his hand up and down the polished side of the stone. "Still, I'm delighted you came in to check out your order. I always tell customers that it's best to come to the warehouse to see what they are getting, rather than take the salesman's word back at the store. It's your money and your kitchen, after all, and you want what's best."

The woman, her hand resting protectively on her rounded baby bump, stood with her mouth open. "It's beautiful," she said in awe, reaching out to touch the polished black surface for herself.

Her husband leaned in to get a better look before stepping back to take in the inventory that surrounded him. "Wow. It's like a museum in here," he exclaimed. "I had no idea there were so many types of granite."

"Not just granite. We've got *all* kinds of natural stone—marble, limestone, travertine, onyx, slate—"

"Vic. Vic Golinski." A loud announcement carried over the speaker system. "You're wanted on line one."

Vic looked apologetically at the couple. His football days were long past, but his large shoulders and massive build tended to dwarf those who stood next to him. "I'm sorry, but it seems I'm needed elsewhere. I tell you what. I've got your order information here—" he held up the clipboard "—but feel free to go ahead and take a look around. If you see something else you like, we can always change it. And when you've made your decision, just check back at the reception desk. That way we can finalize all the delivery arrangements."

He shook hands and nodded goodbye before heading to the door. As he moved along the cement floor, he winced. His lower back was reminding him of last night's pick-up game of basketball at Baldwin Gym, the basketball arena at Grantham University. It had been a mistake to play given his knees, but he hadn't been able to resist.

He pushed open a heavy door and entered the front office space. To the left, behind a decorative wall of marble stone with a cascading fountain, were the showrooms. Mosaic patterns, multi-patterned stone floors and walls displayed a seemingly endless variety of inventory. To the right, on the other side of the long reception desk, was a warren of cubicles and some larger offices along the front wall of the building.

Two women, both talking into headsets, were stationed to greet customers. One, Abby—a middle-aged woman with raven-black hair that Clairol needed to retool—looked up when Vic passed by. As she provided directions over the phone for the warehouse's location on Route One in central New Jersey, she raised her penciled eyebrows and made a circular motion by the side of her head, indicating that the person on the other end of the line was loco. Abby didn't believe in subtlety when dramatization was so much more satisfying. True to form, she snapped her fingers and pointed with her manicured acrylic nails— snowflakes adorned each tip—in the direction of his office. *Pronto,* she mouthed emphatically.

Vic nodded but only marginally picked up his pace. He'd long ago learned that whenever anyone wanted him, somehow it was ostensibly *always* a crisis. That seemed to be the best job description for his posi-

tion. In his opinion, there simply weren't that many
crises in the world, let alone at Golinski Stone International. And if it were a real crisis—a cave-in at a
mineshaft or flames engulfing an apartment building—the chances that a washed-up football player
who was now a natural stone distributor was the man
for the job were slim to none.

So with his usual display of understated calm he
headed for his office prepared to deal with whomever
was having an anxiety attack.

No doubt it would be his brother, Joe—or maybe
his father. Though Pop rarely showed at the office
these days. Ever since his sister, Basia, had started
divorce proceedings against "The Lousy Scumbag"
and moved in with Vic's parents, his mother and father had been drafted for babysitting duty for Basia's
three-year-old Tommy. That way, Basia could juggle
waitressing at a diner in Grantham with going back
to finish up her degree in accounting. Vic was convinced though that the real reason their parents—
more specifically, their mother—had jumped at the
idea was because she wanted to keep an eagle eye on
her only grandson.

Anyway, his kid sister had had to abandon college
when she'd gotten married and had a baby, which was
a real shame in Vic's opinion. Not that he didn't think
his nephew was aces. It's just that of all Golinski sib-
lings, Vic had always thought Basia was the one most
deserving of an Ivy League education. She was scary

bright, and he'd never understood why she refused to take advanced placement courses in high school.

"I want to be in classes with my friends," she'd say with a yawn. "Don't bug me. I'm not you."

"No, you're smarter than me," he'd reply. Fat lot of good it did him. Only thing she didn't fight him about was the violin lessons. He even paid for them to make sure she kept at it. Instead, it was his mother who hadn't seen the point.

"The violin? How's that going to put food on the table or help her find a husband?" his mother had repeated whenever anyone was in earshot.

"Mom, she's got a gift. Leave her alone," he'd responded.

His mother had just shaken her head. "I could understand if it was an instrument that she could play in the band at high school football games."

Vic would let the matter drop.

When Basia had graduated high school, Vic had taken comfort that she'd enrolled at Rutgers, the state university in New Brunswick. Then she promptly dropped out when she got pregnant, and then got married. Vic had had the decency not to point out to his mother that, see, Basia found a husband anyway—for all the good it did her.

But before Vic could get to his office, his brother accosted him outside his own, one door down from Vic's. "Vic, some guy from a private equity firm in Manhattan has been trying to get you for the past half hour. He said it was urgent," Jozef or "Joe" announced, practically treading up the back of Vic's brown Rockport shoes.

Vic didn't respond and instead headed through the open glass door to his own modest office. The wall facing the hallway was also glass, but blinds provided partial privacy. He maneuvered past a coat stand with his blue blazer and North Face jacket and headed around to his plain wooden desk. Then he squatted down in the back corner to greet the one member of his family who never failed to live up to expectations. "Hey, beautiful girl, Roxie. How ya doin'? How's the ear feel, huh?"

Two of the saddest brown eyes in the world looked up at him. A thick white bandage stuck out from one ear. A large white cone circumscribed her head, and in silent protest Roxie lifted her head and banged the hard plastic against his knee. But even that seemed to require too much energy, and she ended up dropping her head to her pillow.

Vic patted the long flank of the eight-year-old white golden retriever. "You're a good dog, Roxie, and I promise you I'll get that collar off your neck as soon as the vet gives his okay."

"Geez, you're more attached to that dog than any human being," Joe complained.

Vic looked over his shoulder. "That's because she's a better listener and certainly more loyal than just about anybody out there." He turned back to the dog. "Aren't ya, sweetheart."

Joe rolled his eyes. "Please, you're making me ill.

Just because you were taken to the cleaners by Shauna in the divorce is no reason to go all gaga over a dumb dog."

"My ex was welcome to anything she could get her hands on—anything except you, Roxie, right?" He scratched behind the dog's good ear. "That's why you've got to look after yourself."

Joe circled the desk to get closer to his big brother. Roxie immediately inched away on her belly. "Geez, you'd think after all these years she'd be used to me."

Vic went on petting the dog. "She can't help it. She had a hard life as a puppy, kicking around all those shelters. You've got to give her some slack."

"So what did the vet say?" Joe asked, making an effort to show some concern.

Vic rested his hand on Roxie's flank. "He said that the kind of tumor she had is ninety percent cancerous and spreads through the bloodstream. That's why he also took a large part of her ear in case it had already gone beyond the lump. But we won't know for sure until he gets the results of the biopsy in a couple of days."

"Well, until then, you could get Mom to pray for her. Light a candle, do the whole bit. You never know."

"Mom has her ways of dealing with problems, and I've got mine. I keep my nose to the grindstone and just do my job. Whatever happens with Roxie, happens. In the meantime, I've got the family to think about—and the hundreds of employees who depend on this company running smoothly."

"And don't think we're not all eternally grateful. It certainly saves me from having to be the responsible son." Joe commandeered Vic's desk chair and swiveled it around to face his brother. Then he crossed his legs, the tassels on his Gucci loafers jiggling as he lazily rocked his foot.

Vic gave Roxie a final pat and stood. The dog wearily thumped her tail on the ground. "Do you mind?" Vic indicated his chair.

"Be my guest." Joe rose and crossed the gray carpeting to the small leather sofa opposite the desk. He plopped down at one end and rapped his knuckles on the wooden arm. "But tell me, oh, wise and great brother, if you're so responsible, why haven't you answered your phone for the past half hour?"

Vic settled into his desk chair, slipped off his shoes and let his feet rest atop the carpet. "In answer to your question, I was showing a couple a slab of Ubatuba for their kitchen countertops."

"One slab? Of Ubatuba? What are they doing? Upgrading their galley kitchen in some track house in Levittown? Excuse me, but what are you—the CEO of the company—doing showing small-time customers their order?" Joe glanced dismissively around the office. "You know, I think it's about time you upgraded your décor, starting with the carpeting. What is it? Indoor-outdoor from some box store?"

"I like the carpeting." Indeed, Vic would never tell his family, but at times he really could do without padding around barefoot on cold marble floors. "And Roxie likes it, too."

"That dog of yours sheds all over this stuff."

Vic was unfazed. "If it bothers you so much, there's a vacuum cleaner in the janitor's closet."

Joe held up his hands. "No, thanks. Besides, Pop banned me from manual labor around the place after that incident with the forklift."

How could Vic forget? Forty thousand dollars worth of travertine down the drain. Joe wasn't much better when it came to driving that ridiculous Porsche 911 of his. At least whenever he wrapped that around a pole it was his insurance, not the company's.

Vic bit back a sigh. Why was he always the responsible sibling? True, as the oldest, he bore the burden of carrying on the family business and keeping his brother and sister out of harm's way. But deep down, he was afraid that he was just born old.

He continued in his usual mature, patient fashion. "No one else appeared to be free, and I don't like customers standing around waiting. As I've said before, a CEO wears many hats and pitches in wherever needed, even on the floor dealing with first-time customers. And two, more importantly for this company, that couple placed their order through Home Warehouse, whose contract with us—as you undoubtedly know since you're senior vice president in charge of sales—is up for renegotiation in the spring. *And,* seeing as they're the largest home improvement company in America, we need to continue to be their sole supplier of natural stone. So, if we satisfy their customers with top service, word will get back—trust me—and that will place us in a much better bargaining position."

Joe rolled his eyes. "Thanks for the lecture, Mr. Miyagi, my personal *sensei*."

"Anytime. My 'Wax On, Wax Off' lecture is scheduled for tomorrow." Vic rested his elbows on his blotter. "Now, who's so anxious to talk to me—" he shuffled through the pink paper slips "—that he keeps calling…what…three…no, four times?"

"The head honcho at Pilgrim Investors. I checked around, and they've got their own building on Park Avenue, besides offices in London, Tokyo and Shanghai. Rumor has it that they're planning a new office in Australia—the economy's booming there what with their large supply of raw materials going directly to China. They're players, big time—trust *me*." He shot back Vic's own words.

Vic could do without players. But business was business. "So, if there's a possibility of new construction, why didn't they contact you?"

Joe shook his head. "I tried pointing that out to him over the phone, but got nowhere. He's one of those blue-blood types who only talks to the top dog. If it gets down to the nitty-gritty, then his lackeys will step in and deal with me."

Vic rubbed his bottom lip thoughtfully. "All right, let's see what the big man has to say. Little does he know I was born in Trenton and grew up in a row house."

"Ah, but you're still the one with the Grantham degree," Joe needled him.

"See, if only you had stuck with football," Vic replied, and he could have said, "studied a bit harder," but he didn't. Why rub it in? Instead, Vic picked up one of the message slips and started to punch in the number.

Suddenly, Abby stuck her head in the open door. "Hey, boss, thought I'd let you know. That young couple you helped in the warehouse?" She worked the chewing gum in her mouth. Abby was a smoker, and since there was no smoking in the building, she was a constant gum chewer in between cigarette breaks in the parking lot. "Well, they ended up going with the Verde Typhoon granite from our Platinum Collection, and are now thinking about the Yellow Bamboo stone for the vanity top in the master bath. I told them no problem—we'd hold a slab, and they could just call in the dimensions. If we don't hear back in a day or two, I'll follow up."

Pleased, Vic nodded. "Good work, Abby. We just quadrupled the price of the sale. You could teach my younger brother here a thing or two."

Abby eyed Joe and laughed knowingly. "That's not what I heard. Word is he's the one who likes to play teacher."

Joe tugged at a starched cuff of his white dress

shirt. His onyx cufflink winked. "Hey, anytime you want to be a pupil I'd be delighted."

Abby threw back her head and erupted in a gagging smoker's cough. "Please, not only am I old enough to be your mother, I have three sons of my own. No one can spot bull faster than a mother of sons." Long divorced, Abby had grown up in the same Polish neighborhood of Trenton as Vic's parents, and it had been his father's idea that she work for the company.

"You two can go at it all day if you want, but some of us have work to do." Vic picked up his phone and started to dial again.

Abby saluted and scampered off.

For a fiftysomething mom she still looked pretty good in a tight black skirt, Vic thought. He leaned on his elbow and waited, listening to the phone connection.

"Mr. Lodge's office," a male voice answered at the other end.

Vic shifted the phone to the right hand so he could write with his left on a legal pad. "This is Vic Golinski from GSI, Golinski Stone International. I'm returning—" he looked at the slip again since names were not his strength "—Mr. Lodge's calls."

"If you'll hold, I'll see if Mr. Lodge is available."

"No problem." Vic began doodling a grid pattern on the legal pad. He covered the mouthpiece and spoke to Joe. "I'm on hold for the great man."

Then he leaned back in his chair and winked at Roxie. She blinked, her thick white lashes fluttering, but her brow remained furrowed. Roxie was one of those dogs that seemed to carry the weight of the world on her shoulders. Just look at her cross-eyed and she was convinced she had cancer. Maybe this time she was right.

"Mr. Golinski." A gravelly male voice drawled out Vic's name. The aristocratic overbite extended the last syllable into almost two. "Conrad Lodge III here. You're a hard man to track down, Mr. Golinski."

"Vic, please, and I'm sorry for the delay. Things have been slightly hectic this morning, but now I'm all yours. What can I do for you, Mr. Lodge?"

No first-name familiarity was reciprocated, not that Vic had expected anything else. But then he had a thought. *Conrad Lodge?* "I don't mean to be presumptuous, but your name is very familiar."

"Perhaps because you've seen me mentioned in the *Wall Street Journal* or the *Financial Times.*"

"No, that's not it."

"Yes, I suppose for someone in your line of work— stone and all—that wouldn't be your usual reading matter."

Vic didn't feel the need to convince him otherwise. What point was there in informing him that he had an MBA from Stanford and that GSI was now the leading distributor of natural stone in North America.

No, he wasn't about to set the record straight because he knew all about people like Conrad Lodge III. They liked to look down at people in "the stone business"—good honest people like his father, who worked with their hands and believed that if you worked hard enough, anything was possible—especially for your children.

No, he wouldn't give Conrad Lodge III the satisfaction of knowing he'd pissed him off. "I suppose you're right. I don't usually get beyond the sports pages—being an ex-jock and all," Vic responded. He leaned back in his chair and rested his stocking feet on the lip of the trash can next to Roxie's pillow.

The dog stirred and knocked the plastic cone around her head against the black container. Clearly, it annoyed her. If Vic knew that Roxie wouldn't bother the bandaged ear, he'd take the thing off.

Conrad chortled as if he were actually sharing the joke. "Of course. Which is exactly why I called."

"Not many people have any interest in my short-lived football career." Vic wasn't being modest, merely stating a fact. But he also knew that prospective customers, once they found out about his former sports career, liked to dish the dirt. Everyone was an expert or a fan, it seemed. Then after that ritual dance, they usually got down to business. "How can I help you?" He continued to draw on the pad, adding vertical lines to the grid pattern.

"You may recall that I've sent you several emails regarding Grantham University, in particular Reunions in June."

Vic had a vague recollection of deleting some emails with a Grantham email address. He figured it was yet another solicitation for the alumni fund or the latest capital campaign. Not that he didn't value his education and the opportunities it had opened up for him, but that didn't mean he was about to fork over more than his two hundred dollars a year that he obligingly offered. Let the Conrad Lodge the Third's of the world dip into their ample trust funds.... With a few quick jabs, he drew some arching lines, fanning outward.

Wait a minute... Conrad Lodge III?

Vic abruptly lifted his foot off the garbage can and planted both feet firmly on the floor. "Hold it. Now I remember why I know your name." He lay the pen on the pad. "You wouldn't happen to be Mimi Lodge's father?"

"Why, yes, Mary Louise is my daughter."

Vic looked down at his pad and frowned. He'd unconsciously drawn what looked unmistakably like the fountain in the courtyard of Allie Hammie. He ripped the paper from the pad and scrunched it up.

And that's when he hung up—without another word.

CHAPTER THREE

"Hey!" Joe jumped to his feet. "What the hell just happened?"

Vic rubbed his forehead, then held up his hand. "Not to worry." He hit redial.

Conrad picked up immediately.

"It seems we were cut off. My apologies."

Conrad didn't bother with any more preliminary chitchat. "You may know that my firm is considering opening another office in the Antipodes."

Vic rolled his eyes at the pretentious language. "Yes, I believe my brother, Joe, to whom you talked briefly, mentioned something about it." He nodded to Joe, who raised his chin.

"Yes, well…I know our design and construction team are in the process of sending out for bids."

"That's good to know. GSI has handled several projects in Australia and New Zealand, and we've had very positive reviews."

"I'll pass that information along. But that's not entirely why I called."

Why wasn't Vic surprised? When did a CEO get involved with building projects besides signing off on the design and then cutting the ribbon at the end?

"As I explained in my emails, I'm on the organizing committee for Reunions coming up this June."

"Congratulations, but I must confess I haven't attended Reunions since my senior year when I served on a panel discussion," Vic said. It was an experience he'd managed to put far, far away.

"Yes, that was a memorable occasion."

"Your daughter, I believe, made it particularly memorable." Vic tried to keep his tone even.

"Yes, Mimi is definitely opinionated, but I've never seen her so…shall we say…demonstrative?"

She may have been "demonstrative," but somehow it had been Vic who had been hauled off to the police station. Mimi had merely waved goodbye wrapped in a towel provided by the cops. "I guess that's what you could call it." His tone wasn't quite so even.

"Yes, well, the past is something we can't change, even if we'd like to."

That surprised Vic. Conrad didn't strike him as someone who was particularly introspective, let alone regretful. He wondered if Mimi's father was referring to something in particular.

He didn't know much about the family except what he'd heard as an undergraduate. You couldn't live in Grantham without realizing that the Lodges were very Very Important People. And as for Mimi, she'd run with a different crowd—the preppy jocks who knew all about lacrosse, and what brand of gin was best for martinis.

He knew she had become a hotshot war correspondent on the nightly news—her dream fulfilled, if he remembered correctly—who'd been kidnapped while on assignment in some ex-Soviet region and finally released. He wondered if the family had maneuvered that one the way they used to have the Grantham police in the palm of their hands. They obviously had connections everywhere. Whatever, he really didn't care. If a family member of his had been kidnapped, he would have used every possible means to free them also.

"On the other hand," Conrad went on, "perhaps what I am proposing is a way to redress past wrongs. You see, as it turns out, I am the chair of panel discussions for the Reunions in June."

"Tell me you're not proposing what I think you're proposing?"

"I think the possibility to revisit problems of equality in college sports is as timely now as ever. And since all the panelists have agreed to participate again, it will be interesting to see if any of their perspectives have changed."

"All the panelists?" Forget the others. Vic was only interested in one.

Lodge cleared his throat. "Yes, though, it is true that my daughter agreed to participate only if you served on the panel, as well."

Vic tipped his chair back again. "She did? I'm surprised she even remembered me."

"Interesting, she said the same thing about you." Lodge didn't elaborate. "In any case, I think the audience would be fascinated by your perspective as a former professional athlete. And no doubt more than a few of them will recall your courage all those years ago to take what might have been considered a refreshingly candid, though politically incorrect stance."

"If I didn't know better, I would say you're itching for a replay. Is your daughter still so easily riled?"

"That remains to be seen. Even if there are no fireworks, the anticipation that something might happen would be worth the price of admission alone, don't you think?"

Vic didn't know what to think. He glanced down at Roxie, who sighed a dog sigh. He hadn't wanted to wait until after the weekend, and the vet's office closed early on Fridays, so he'd had no choice but to collect her first thing in the morning. Now, he just wanted to get her home and comfortable. And wait for the prognosis.

Yet the businessman in him also wouldn't let go. Besides, the economy in Australia might be booming, but big commercial jobs in general were still few and far between. "At the same time you'd keep GSI in mind in regards to the construction of your Australian offices?" he asked.

"As two seasoned men of the world, I think we both understand the certain quid pro quo that is a part of doing business," Conrad replied. "You have my word that we will view your company's participation in a very favorable light."

Mimi Lodge. Just the thought of her was like a craw

in his side—an irritating feeling that just wouldn't go away. Like nothing and no one else he'd ever come in contact with. What was it Machiavelli had said? Keep your friends close but your enemies closer?

Well, Mimi Lodge wasn't so much an enemy as a troublemaker with a capital *"T."* All the Lodges were, he reminded himself, even the man on the other end of the phone line.

But Mimi Lodge was also the only woman who had ever aroused his passions so fully, so surprisingly. She'd blindsided him, that's what she'd done.

And now he wondered what would happen if they met again.

"So do I have your agreement, then?" Conrad prodded him. "It would mean a great deal to me."

If Lodge were at all the type of person to be sincere, Vic would have assumed that the older man genuinely meant it. He watched as Roxie licked the top of a front paw, sure evidence that she was in pain. Nope, he couldn't hang around the office any longer. "Just send me the details, and I'll be there," he said decisively.

They exchanged a few more cursory comments, Vic wrote down the information, and then the call ended. He swiveled around and faced Joe.

"So, did we get it?" Joe sprung from the couch.

Vic ripped off a sheet of paper and rose. He circled his desk and handed it to Joe. Then he stepped over to the coat rack and shrugged on his blazer. The action rekindled memories of the exact opposite where Mimi Lodge was concerned.

Joe frowned at the paper. "If I can navigate your handwriting, this is a contact at Pilgrim?"

Vic reached for the top button of his jacket, then decided to leave it open. Easier for driving. "It's the person you can contact in regards to our bid for their new building."

Joe whistled. "So how did you do it? I gather there's a Grantham connection?"

"Yes, it seems that my agreement to serve on an alumni panel at Reunions this coming June sealed the deal—or at least the bid." He reached for his winter jacket and turned back to his brother.

Joe looked incredulous. "Wait a minute. That hothead? The one who dumped water on you your senior year? Wasn't her name Lodge, too?"

Vic pulled out Roxie's lead from the pocket of his coat. "Mimi Lodge. His daughter. Conrad seemed particularly interested that we recreate our little tango."

Joe shook his head. "I don't get it. It sounds suspiciously like the old man is pimping for his daughter. Which is pretty creepy, even for someone like me."

"I don't think your sensibilities had anything to do with the offer, and I'm not convinced it really has anything to do with me, either." Vic walked over to Roxie and kneeled down to hook the lead to her collar. Then he stood up and Roxie awkwardly fol-

lowed suit. "If I didn't know better, I'd say the moti-
vating factor was guilt." *The question is whose?* Vic
silently ruminated.

CHAPTER FOUR

June, the Wednesday before Grantham University Reunions...

"YOU DIDN'T NEED TO PICK me up, you know. I could have taken the Link into town and then walked," Mimi announced. The Link was the single-car commuter train that connected Grantham to the mainline at Grantham Junction. That's where she was now—standing, on the southbound platform at Grantham Junction, having just disembarked from the express train from New York. It had been standing room only when she'd gotten on at Penn Station, and she'd only managed to secure a seat when she outmaneuvered a teenager with two Bergdorf Goodman bags and a Louis Vuitton purse. What was the world coming to anyway?

Her half-brother, Press, took her rolling suitcase from her without bothering to ask. "I'd already emailed you that I'd be back for Reunions, and the timing worked out. Besides, admit it—you would have given me grief if I hadn't made the effort." A year after graduating from Grantham, Press was living in Melbourne, Australia, where he was getting a master's degree in paleontology. He'd traveled halfway around the world to work with a scientist who was on the forefront of 3-D imaging of bone specimens.

Mimi looked him over. He seemed the same—maybe skinnier and now sporting a fashionably scraggly beard that was a darker blond than his short curls. He wore jeans and a T-shirt—a Hoagie Palace T-shirt. The T-shirt had her thinking. "How about we stop off for some hoagies—my treat. Unless you have other plans, of course?"

Someone bumped Mimi from the back. She tensed. *Damn.* She'd been doing better these past two months. She willed herself to breathe out slowly and recognize the bump as just a commuter in a rush. Much as she didn't go in for the touchy-feely stuff, seeing the psychologist recommended by Noreen had helped. Treatment for Post Traumatic Stress Disorder had greatly improved over the years. For Mimi, the sessions had helped her identify frightening memories and replace them with more manageable thoughts. That still didn't mean she was "cured."

Again, she felt pressure on her upper arm, and while she steeled herself, at least she didn't flinch. She glanced to see what it was and saw it was Press touching the sleeve of her leather jacket.

"Sorry, I guess I'm jumpy. Must be the excitement of returning to the old stomping grounds," she joked lamely. She peered into her brother's eyes to see if he'd discerned something more, but his gray-blue eyes looked more bloodshot than anything, and his face didn't show a reaction one way or the other. But then Press had always been good at appearing unemotional under the best of circumstances—or the worst. That was his way of coping, she realized. Hers was to rant and rave and run away.

"So food?" she asked again. Today she wasn't planning on running—at least, not yet.

"I'm always up for Hoagie Palace. Besides I need to stop in to say hi to Angie and Sal. If they knew I was in town and hadn't seen them, I'd be in a lot of trouble." Angie and Sal were the owners of the popular Grantham establishment and had probably been more involved with raising Press than his own parents had been.

He pointed out his car in the parking lot, and they marched down the platform to the stairs. Instead of bouncing her suitcase down the cement risers, he simply picked it up by the handle and carried it down.

"So, how are things in Australia?"

Press fished the car keys out of his pocket and beeped open the doors to the aging BMW. "Good, I guess. I mean, the work is great and my advisor is, too. Now that we've got the bugs worked out of the new 3-D equipment—it cost a bomb, I'll tell you— the measurements I'm getting on the specimens are amazing. Which is a good thing, because I just heard that my proposal for a talk at the big paleontology meeting in September was accepted."

"That's fantastic. But what about outside of work? Don't you like Australia?" Mimi had gone scuba diving in the Barrier Reef after successfully completing a story. And she'd downed more than a few beers with a crew from the Australian Broadcasting Corporation in the Rocks section of Sydney. Beyond that, the vast Red Continent was a mystery to her—one of those places she was always telling herself that she needed to explore. The thing was, she never seemed to have time for a vacation.

Press hoisted her suitcase into the trunk and came around to open the passenger door. "No, Australia's great. Just more different than I anticipated. I don't know why. Maybe because we speak the same language—or kind of the same language—I expected things to function the same way as in the U.S. My mistake." He held open the door.

Mimi hesitated. *You're thinking of being pushed into the car in Grozny, but this is your brother and Grantham,* she reminded herself. She willed herself to get in and fasten her seat belt. But she kept a death grip on the door handle. Then she forced herself to talk. "It's not easy, I know, to uproot yourself and live in another country. Everyone thinks it's so glamorous and exciting, but sometimes it's just plain lonely. I remember my mother complaining about it." She looked out the window as they negotiated the traffic out of the crowded parking lot.

"You know, that may be the first time you've ever mentioned your mother to me." Press tapped his thumbs impatiently on the steering wheel.

"I guess that's true. It just kind of came up." Mimi

looked out the window. The maple and ash trees were thick with leaves. Every time she came back to this part of central New Jersey, she was struck by how green it was, especially in June. "So do you have any roommates?" She turned back, changing the subject.

Press inched the car forward. "Nah, I decided to live alone after years of having roommates at boarding school and college."

"Maybe that's one reason why you're lonely? That can't be good if you're trying to fit in."

"Who said I was lonely? Anyway, you live alone."

"That's no recommendation." Mimi bit her tongue. She hadn't seen her brother since his graduation last year, and she didn't want to fight. "So what brings you back to our fair shores now? Don't think I'm buying your explanation about the siren call of Reunions. You were always as blasé as I was about the whole rah-rah thing."

He breathed in noisily.

Mimi recognized New Jersey allergies.

"I don't know," Press said nonchalantly. "It's been a year. I figured it was time to take a break. See some people."

"People?"

"Sure, there's Matt Brown. We met a ways back when we both worked at Apple Farm Country Club. You remember him, right? He graduated from Yale this year and is home in Grantham for a while."

Mimi nodded. "I remember him—the kid who

interned for Lilah with her organization in Congo. What's he up to?" Lilah Evans was her old roommate.

"I'm not totally sure. From his Facebook page it looks like he's going into the Peace Corps, then grad school. I thought I'd get more details, just hang out, you know?"

"Anyone else you just hanging out with?" Matt Brown was a decent enough kid, but Mimi thought there had to be a bigger draw to travel this far.

Press turned on the car radio. Katy Perry music suddenly blasted at megawatt force. "Crap. Someone's been fooling around with the stations while I was away. I told Noreen she should drive the car to keep the battery from going flat, but she must have let Brigid play with the dials." Brigid was their eight-year-old half-sister. "I mean, you don't see me going into her room and mixing up her Barbies."

Mimi smiled at his frowning face. She remembered the spats she had with him when she'd come home from boarding school and found he had swiped some of her Beanie Babies. Not that as a teenager she still played with them. It was just the principle of the thing.

He continued to fiddle with the buttons, neatly avoiding any further conversation. That was okay with Mimi. They rounded the steep curve by the gardening store, crossed the canal and entered Grantham proper, passing some modest clapboard houses from the early nineteenth century, then the university golf course on the left and some office buildings on the right. They even made the light behind the university theater where Press deftly avoided a throng of students crossing against the light. They must have stuck around after exams to work at Reunions. The hours might be long, but the money was good and the beer was free.

No matter how long she was away, Mimi was always struck by how Grantham never seemed to change. Oh, the sign at the convenience store on the corner might be painted a different color and one stock brokerage firm might be replaced by another, but basically Grantham remained the same picturesque enclave with Colonial roots that was everyone's ideal of a bucolic college town. Everyone's but Mimi's, that is.

She had always found the reverence for history and tradition stifling. Her quest growing up had been to fly away as far and as often as possible. But now two things were certain: Grantham was quiet, and it was safe. Right now, that was about as good as it got for her.

Press hung a right on Main Street and maneuvered around the cars turning left and those double-parked on the right. It was a slalom course for high-end European cars and the occasional Toyota. After they made the light at Adams Road, with the movie theater on the left and the university library on the right, Press pushed past the Catholic church and the flower stores before turning right into the parking lot opposite Hoagie Palace. They headed for the mecca of good, cheap greasy food that never, ever disappointed. It might be a weekday evening, but the line of customers was backed out the door.

Still, it moved quickly, and Mimi and Press were soon in the door, ready to lean over the high glass counter and give their orders to one of the cooks wearing the ubiquitous Hoagie Palace T-shirt.

"I've got this," Mimi reminded her brother as they inched toward the cash register after placing their orders.

"I'm going to get an Arnold Palmer, as well." Press elbowed his way to the cooler of soft drinks and bottled water on the side wall.

"Press, *caro.*" The woman behind the cash register lifted the counter and came to the other side. She embraced him and kissed him on the cheek. "Trying to sneak by without giving me a proper hello?"

"Just testing your reflexes, Angie," Press teased. Mimi was amazed to see that her brother—normally so reserved—returned the hug without hesitation.

"Carlos, take over the register, okay?" she called out. "Sal will be upset that he missed you. He's just gone to the barbershop. I was complaining that he was starting to look shaggy." Then she held Press at arm's length, her gold bracelets jangling, and eyed him up and down. "Speaking of shaggy, I like the beard. It's very sophisticated." She rubbed it lovingly. "So when did you come in?"

"About two hours ago," Press answered. "And I had to go pick up my sister Mimi. You remember her?" He nodded back to Mimi in the line.

Angie gave a hello nod. Mimi waved.

"Tell Sal not to worry. I promise I'll stop by the house tonight."

"Only if you're not too tired. I know you, Press. You never get enough sleep," she clucked over him.

"You only just got in?" Mimi tried to get his attention, but Press took no notice.

Angie held Press's face in her hands. "I can't tell you how upset I was to find out that Australia doesn't allow any food—even in containers—to be shipped to the country. I worried that you would lose weight. And you did."

Mimi shook her head. There was no point in trying to get his attention. He'd just gotten in after what? A twenty-hour trip? No wonder the kid looked exhausted.

The line moved along and she reached the cash register. "An Arnold Palmer to drink, and a chicken cheese steak hoagie and a meatball hoagie with two sides of fries," she announced. Then she stretched her neck over the countertop and addressed the chef working on her hoagie. "And could you put some extra hot sauce on the meatball?" A meatball hoagie with sauce was straight out of her college days.

"For once we agree on something," a male voice to her right declared.

Mimi turned. Blinked once. And didn't blink again.

"That's right." Vic Golinski saluted her with one finger to his brow. "Only, this time, I'm the one with the container of water." He showed her the large bottle he was carrying and unscrewed the top. "An open container of water."

He raised his arm.

CHAPTER FIVE

VIC TOOK A LARGE GULP, lowered the bottle and wiped his mouth with the back of his hand. "Vic. Vic Golinski, in case you didn't remember."

Mimi raised her head, then raised it more. "Of course. You're hard to miss." She'd forgotten just how big, how imposing he was. Maybe he was a little fuller around the jaw line and not quite so pneumatically blown up in the shoulder area, but she was pretty sure he could still bench press everyone behind the counter, and maybe the counter, as well. She stared at his chest—the top button of his blue Oxford shirt undone, the striped tie loosened and casually tossed over his shoulder—and wondered what else he could press....

"That's fourteen ninety-nine," Carlos announced. "Fourteen ninety-nine," he repeated.

Mimi shook her head and held up her hand. "Sorry, that'll be me." Flustered, she reached for her shoulder bag—and didn't feel it. She patted along her hip. Nothing. She looked down. "Oh, cripes." She peered over her shoulder, seeking out her brother. "Press, hey, Press," she called out.

He glanced over his shoulder at the sound of his name.

"Listen, it looks like I left my purse in the car." She

pointed outside. "I can run back and get it if you give me your keys. Or can you cover it, and I'll pay you back?"

Press pushed toward her, shaking his head wearily. "I don't have any cash, but I suppose I could use my debit card."

"That's all right, Press," Angie said reassuringly as she reached his side. She motioned for Carlos to vacate his post at the register. "I know you're good for it. You can pay me some other time." She waited as her assistant raised the flap in the counter for her to come across.

"Please, allow me." Vic pulled out two twenties. "Just add it to my bill. A meatball hoagie with hot sauce, side of fries and—" he raised his eyebrows at Mimi "—and one bottle of water—large and extremely wet."

"Don't be ridiculous. I'll just run back to the car. It's only across the street," Mimi insisted. She waved away his hand.

He squeezed closer to the cash register. "She'd give you the shirt off her back—and trust me, I've seen her do it. But it's probably faster if I take care of this." He kept his arm outstretched with the bills.

Mimi nudged him away with her elbow. "I'm sure I don't know what you're talking about." She turned to Angie. "I'll be right back, I promise."

"Will someone make up their mind?" Press asked behind them.

Mimi and Vic turned their heads, she clockwise, he

counterclockwise. Mimi raised her eyes. Vic lowered his. His nose almost grazed her forehead.

The cash register drawer opened with a loud ding.

Mimi and Vic turned back, she—lowering her head slightly, he—pulling back ever so much.

Angie reached out for Vic's twenties and deposited the correct change in his hand at the same time. "Okay, big boy, let's keep the line moving. We'll call you when your orders are ready," she said smartly, all five foot two of her substantial body imposing itself. One did not argue with Angie.

Needless to say, Mimi and Vic shuffled to the side and hovered as inconspicuously as possible against the side wall. Mimi pretended to look at the snapshots of patrons wearing Hoagie Palace T-shirts in places like Machu Picchu and the Parthenon in Greece. Out of the corner of her eye she could see Vic pocket his wallet and fold his arms across his chest.

Press sidled over and popped his can of Palmer iced tea. He eyed Vic skeptically. "Hey, do I know you?"

Vic uncrossed his arms. "Vic. Vic Golinski. I was a classmate of Mimi's at the university." He held out his hand to shake Press's.

Mimi glanced over. "Oh, sorry. Vic, this is my half-brother, Press Lodge. He's a Grantham grad, too," Mimi said. Press might be almost as tall as Vic, but Vic had about sixty more pounds of muscle on him.

"Hi, there." Press went through the handshake motions, then scratched his head. "Wait a minute. You used to play pro football, right?"

"Briefly."

"I remember seeing you play at the Meadowlands."

Mimi looked at Press. "You went to a game? With Dad?"

"No, of course not with Dad. It was a birthday party or something, and someone else's parents took me." He narrowed his eyes and considered Vic. "Yeah, I'm sure of it. It was a game against the Giants. There was this head-butting incident. And you were involved in it. Am I right?"

He shrugged. "That's so long ago, it's ancient history."

"No, no." Mimi shook her head. "Even I recall something about it. I mean, I was in Kuwait at the time, and the Armed Forces Radio was going bananas over this flagrant foul." She looked at Vic. "I remember it being totally out of the blue. And it sounded absolutely malicious. Were you badly hurt?"

"Oh, darling sister of mine—" Press chimed in, sounding pretty pleased with himself "—before you offer any after-the-fact consoling, I do believe your buddy here was doing the butting, not the player on the receiving end."

She opened her mouth. "Oh."

"Oh, is right," Press said with enthusiasm. "What a hit! And what a fine. If I remember correctly, it was a League-leading record at that time." He seemed very ebullient, practically bouncing on the white soles of his beat-up boat shoes.

"Not one of my finer hours. How about we just drop it?" Vic said, his voice eerily soft.

Press closed his mouth and opened his eyes wide. "Sure, no problem."

"A chicken cheesesteak, meatball with hot sauce, Arnold Palmer, another meatball with hot sauce and water," Carlos shouted out.

"I'll meet you guys outside with the orders," Press offered. He clearly knew a way out when he saw one and lunged back to the counter.

"Shall we?" Vic offered, holding his hand out for her to lead the way.

She nodded, and she could sense the crowd part not so much for her as for the large set of shoulders sheltering her to one side.

They stepped out of the door. Mimi stretched out a tight-lipped smile. Vic made a similar face. She looked down where the sidewalk was heaving from the encroachment of a large tree root.

"So do you come back often?" "You live around here?" they asked at the same time.

"You first." She nodded.

"No, you." He held out his hand.

She smiled nervously. "No, I don't get back much. But when I do it's always great to get a hoagie first thing back. Kind of like Grantham's version of *madeleines,* don't you think?" She sounded pretentious, even to her ears, but here among the throng of people on the street she wasn't relaxed. Not fearful, as she would have expected, but nervous—giddy nervous. Which was…well…unexpected.

Vic frowned.

"You know, Proust? How he smelled *madeleines*—the little French butter cookies—which evoked all the memories of his past?" She stared up at Vic. Why the hell was she talking about some nineteenth-century author, who truthfully, she'd never read more than a few pages of, when what she really wanted to ask him was, "So you do remember me? In a really bad way? Or maybe just a bad way?" *Or maybe not at all.*

Press forced himself through the doorway, leading with two large bags. "Here you go." He peered in the bags and handed one to Vic. "Yours, I believe." Then he slipped out a waxed paper covered hoagie for Mimi and a paper pouch of fries. "If you want ketchup for the French fries, I can muscle my way back in. Sorry, I forgot, but I'm happy to…" He cocked his head over his shoulder.

"No, I'm fine," Vic said.

"Me, too. I don't want anything to get in the way of the mounds of salt."

Press stuffed the bag with his food under his arm. "Listen, you guys, I just got this text about meeting some friends. They're free shortly. So, I don't want to cut your personal reunion short, but I'd like to get a move on if possible." He motioned with his car keys to where they'd parked across the street.

Mimi stood there, hugging her hoagie to her side. "I'll need to get my wallet out to pay Vic."

"No, don't bother. It'll be my treat," Vic offered. "Anyway, I don't want to hold you up," he said to Press.

"Don't worry about me, Press. I'll find my own way home," Mimi blurted out. "Whenever you get a chance, just leave my suitcase and stuff in the foyer. It's not like there's anything I need right away."

"If you're sure?" Press asked.

Mimi wasn't sure of anything—especially where Vic Golinski was concerned. Why had she told her brother to take off without her? More to the point, why wasn't she quite ready to say goodbye to Vic? Was it guilt for what she'd done the last time they'd crossed paths? Or maybe her hormones were sputtering to the fore after a long, bleak period? Or maybe she just needed to set the record straight before their next public showdown. Yes…that was it. She just needed to set the record straight—not that she intended to back down from her principles, but just to let him know that she wasn't looking for a fight.

"Okay, then," Press said breezily, seemingly unaware for the mental gymnastics Mimi was going through. "And nice meeting you," he said as a farewell to Vic before stepping off the curb, his head already half-buried in a bag of fries. A Land Rover made a quick stop, missing him by a few inches. But Press munched away.

"Were we ever that oblivious?" Mimi asked in relief.

"I thought you people were born that way," Vic replied.

"What?" Mimi turned back to him.

"Oblivious to others. Using words like *foyer.*"

"Foyer?" She was completely lost now.

"Yeah, you told your brother to leave your suitcase in the foyer of the house. Who uses words like that? Who even has a house with a foyer?"

"What's wrong with *foyer?* You want me to say *entryway* instead?" She shook her head. "Listen, I didn't stick around to argue. I wanted to make sure that since we're going to be sitting on that panel again that we should bury the hatchet." She set her jaw.

"You think I need to bury the hatchet? I could point out that you were the one who spilled the water."

"Which you just did. And I could point out that you were the one with the flagrant head-butting violation."

"That was different. That was a onetime occasion," he argued.

"And you think I just go around dousing people with water whenever it strikes my fancy?" She stared at him.

Vic seemed about to speak, then looked away. After a moment, he turned back. "Shall we agree to try to be civil? Or at least put up the front of being civil?"

Mimi peered around and saw that several people were slanting them nervous looks. She stood up straighter. "I don't see why not. Besides, it's not as if we really know each other to get all riled up anyway. And I'm sure that since I last saw you you've changed and…developed in many ways. I mean, you look…"

Her voice trailed off. Yes, she had already noticed just how physically developed he'd become.

"Older?" he suggested.

"Settled," she said instead.

"You make that sound like a criticism."

Mimi shook her head. "On the contrary, over the years I've grown to appreciate stability. It's like something isn't missing in your life."

He studied her face. "You think you know me?"

She touched the top of her hoagie bag. The burst of energy she had felt when first seeing him was slowly seeping away. And she could almost feel her eyes darting back and forth, studying the people passing by on the sidewalk or going in and out of Hoagie Palace.

Stop it! she reprimanded herself. *This is bloody Grantham, after all!* The biggest criminal threats were bored teenagers shoplifting from the drug store.

She squared her shoulders and fixed a smile on her face. "Let's start again. So, are you living nearby or did you just come in early for Reunions?" The Reunions festivities didn't begin until Friday evening, so there were a few days to go.

He studied her some more, then visibly eased off. "I live in town now. Actually, my whole family does. In a small town house development behind the shopping center."

Mimi nodded. "I think I know the one you mean. Brick? Kind of a Georgetown re-dux? Very exclusive. I bet you even have an aesthetically minded owners association."

"So you heard about the no clothesline rule, then?"
"You're joking?"

"Could I make something like that up?" he asked. A smile twitched the corner of his mouth.

"No, I guess not." She chuckled then gazed into his face. "So you think we'll be able to be civil to each other?" She cocked her head.

"Only with immense amounts of restraint." He shifted his bag of food to the other arm and cradled it like a football.

How fitting, thought Mimi. She was actually starting to relax again. Weird, the one person in Grantham who had vexed her the most now seemed capable of putting her best at ease. "If you want, we could eat our hoagies together?" She held up her paper bag.

"I was going to take it home." He hesitated. "Of course, you're welcome to come."

Why did she feel he was just being polite? And anyway, even though he had bought food for only himself, who was to say he wasn't meeting someone? For some reason, the prospect of having to make polite conversation with Vic Golinski's current squeeze was more than she could bear at the moment.

So, instead, she glanced down at her oversize wristwatch—not the sturdy Rolex from her mother, that one was gone forever—and started to back away down the sidewalk. "Thanks for the offer, but on second thought, I should probably head home." She held up her wrist and tapped the crystal of her black Swatch. "My family's probably wondering what's happened to me." Like that was really going to happen, Mimi thought. Whatever, it was as good an excuse as any.

"So, I'll be off, then." She pointed vaguely toward the center of town. Her family's house was located on the west side about a half-mile past the commercial stretch, in the Old Money residential section. Even the rhododendrons on that side of town could boast aristocratic lineages.

"I can give you a lift if you're in a hurry."

She shook her head. "Not to worry, I'm fine. Besides, I wouldn't want to take you out of your way." The ride in from the train station with Press had not totally been knuckle biting, but it had probably been enough to tax her stamina for one day. "It's not personal. I prefer to walk." Now *that* was the truth.

"Don't worry. I don't take it personally."

From the scowl on his face, she wasn't so sure.

"On the other hand, I'm parked in a spot down a ways—right in the direction you're headed. If you don't mind, I'll just tag along that far. That way you'll get the chance to meet my girl. She's waiting in the car." He seemed very chipper all of a sudden. "She's the hot sauce fanatic actually."

Was it too late to run?

CHAPTER SIX

CONRAD LODGE SAT in his usual leather armchair in the study of the Lodge mansion on Singleton Road, the thoroughfare that led into the "right" side of town. One-hundred-year-old sycamores shaded the sidewalks. Tall brick and stone walls and wrought-iron fences with security boxes guarded the magisterial homes, including the residence of New Jersey's governor.

"So how does she look?" Conrad asked. He cupped a cut-crystal tumbler with the finest single malt whisky, resting on a coaster featuring the Grantham University crest. In his other hand, he held a newly lit cigar. A red circle of flame shone around the gray ash center.

"How does she look?" Press repeated wearily. *How about how do I look?* This was the first he had laid eyes on his father since coming back to Grantham. His flight had gotten in around three in the afternoon. And by the time he had caught the train down and gotten a taxi home, it was after five. After five—but still several hours before Conrad's train was due in from Manhattan.

He had no sooner gotten home than he'd received

a message from his father's assistant to pick up Mimi at Grantham Junction station.

So, there Press stood, zonked out from jetlag and the crazy fourteen-hour time difference between the U.S. and Australia, enduring a cross-examination from his father. Did the old man think to ask how *his* flight was? If *his* planes had been crowded? On time? Let alone how his work was going in Melbourne?

Of course not.

His father had never asked him about anything that Press cared about. Business and Grantham—that's all he could talk about. "Why don't you go out for football at Grantham, the way I did?" his father had instead asked critically. "Why don't you talk to my friend at such-and-such investment firm about a summer internship? Do something real with your life."

All his life, Press figured he'd been a failure to his father's way of thinking. No, it was worse than that. It was more like his father didn't think of him at all.

Though Press had never gotten the impression that Dear Old Dad cared one whit for Mimi, either. Still, it had been on his father's marching orders that Press had returned for Reunions and to come and visit his sister. Truth be told, he would have returned anyway, but he wasn't about to admit that to his father. One, because Press didn't like to give him any satisfaction that they might be thinking along the same lines. *God forbid!* And two, this way his father had paid for the flight. Considering the cost of living in Australia, not to mention the sky-high price of the airfare, Press would have had to forego food in order to pay for the trip.

So he just rubbed his bloodshot eyes and mumbled, "She looks like you'd expect." Press might not be a "real Lodge man," but he had learned over the years that mouthing off provided only temporary satisfaction at best.

"Speak up, Prescott," Conrad ordered.

Press looked up. "She's kind of jumpy, but otherwise not too bad."

Conrad rested his cigar in a green Venetian glass ashtray. "No outbursts of anger?"

Press shrugged. "No more than usual. Mimi's never been exactly nonconfrontational."

"She didn't mention difficulties sleeping, eating, show difficulties concentrating, did she?"

"If I had known that my job involved making clinical observations, I would have taken notes."

"There's no need for insolence. You don't seem to grasp the severity of the traumatic situation your sister's been through."

"I know she had it pretty rough. I'm not totally insensitive, you know." He dug his hands in his jeans pockets. He felt his phone, a reminder that he was already late to meet Amara and Matt.

Anyway, like he'd ever admit to his father how he'd scoured the internet during his half-sister's captivity. He'd even joined chat groups with Eastern European members with the hopes of obtaining some inside information that didn't make it to the regular news media. That involvement, though, had scared him more than anything.

Just before his graduation last year, Mimi had told him that she was setting up an interview with some Chechen rebel. He'd known it was important to her—even more important than the other stories she'd covered. This one had been personal. Family. Her mother's family.

Then he had waited—for her to return from her interview. Only, she hadn't. He'd been worried sick for her. But he'd also felt sorry for himself. He knew it was selfish, but he couldn't help it. Because he realized—if he lost Mimi, he'd lose the only touchstone he had to a real sense of family.

Now, standing in his father's dark paneled study, he caught his father gazing off into space. If he didn't know better he'd say the man appeared consumed by his own demons. Though the more likely explanation was indigestion or alcoholic haze.

Whichever, he wasn't about to stick around. "So, if there's nothing else? I came home to grab a shower before I meet up with some friends." Press fisted his hands.

Conrad took a healthy swallow from his drink and returned his gaze to his son. "God forbid we get in the way of your social life. So, if I may be so bold as to ask—where is your sister?"

"We stopped off at Hoagie Palace because Mimi wanted to, and she ran into someone she knew from college who lives in town."

"Not Lilah Evans? Noreen told me this morning that she and Lilah were involved in some kind of Board meeting today for Sisters for Sisters, their nonprofit organization, and then a dinner afterward. That's why I have made arrangements to eat at the Grantham Club this evening." He hesitated. "Though perhaps Noreen got her dates confused, in which case I wonder where she might be." He nervously turned his cigar in the glass tray, knocking off the burnt ash.

If Press didn't know better, he'd think his father sounded worried. "I don't know anything about meetings or dinners. And it wasn't Lilah. It was some guy."

"Some guy?" His father drew out the second word. "Does this guy have a name?"

"Vic. Vic Golinski—the ex-football player."

His father arched one brow and smiled. He savored a sip of whiskey and followed it with a few puffs of his cigar. The smoke curled upward from the tip.

Then, after a long moment, he glanced dismissively at his son. "You may leave then to do whatever it is you're so *hot* on doing." He made it sound dirty.

Press's lip curled. Just being in the same room as his father made him feel dirty. He didn't waste any time crossing the carpet to the door. He reached for the brass door handle, then stopped and glanced back over his shoulder. "Oh, sir." He couldn't resist.

His father looked up.

"Don't bother to thank me for coming."

CHAPTER SEVEN

"SHE'S NORMALLY VERY SHY with people she doesn't know. So don't take offence if she tries to hide," Vic explained protectively. They crossed the street at the Indian restaurant that always seemed to be under new management. He pointed. "I'm just parked ahead in front of the dry cleaners. Her name's Roxie, by the way."

"You sure it's okay for me to meet her, then?" Mimi asked. She was looking at him like he was crazy.

Well, maybe he was. First off, he could have pretended not to recognize her in The Palace. *But, no.* Then he could have butted in line and paid his bill and hightailed it out of there. *But, no, again.* Then he could have easily waved goodbye and sauntered back into the rest of his life, with only a minor blip on the radar screen when they both served on the Reunions panel.

But, no.

Because he couldn't. All for reasons too complicated and yet too simple to explain. He was still ticked off. He was curious. He wanted to see if she'd remembered the guy she'd humiliated in front of hundreds of people, not to mention his father at the police station. He wanted to see if she would squirm. Act remorseful. Penitent. He was running out of adjectives.

Hell, he'd just wanted to see her.

Not that he'd had any problem recognizing her instantly, and not from seeing her on TV. As far as he knew, she hadn't been on air in months, maybe longer. No, despite the span of more than ten years, and that she now wore her hair much shorter than in college, he'd known her immediately. It wasn't as much as her voice, or her stance or even her face, it was something about the way the air seemed charged around her.

She was like some skittish colt. With the same long, lean body that he remembered so well. Which he could recall with infinitesimal detail from the one time her body had been plastered up against him. With the same proud set to her shoulders and arching posture—a testament to good breeding as much as good genes. Still skinny, though—too little meat on her bones to be vibrantly healthy like some well-tuned athlete—the way she had been in college. And too jumpy, like she always had an eye out for someone to pounce on her when she wasn't looking. So she looked.

And kept looking—surreptitiously—as they headed into town and past his car. He had thought he'd wanted to see her squirm with remorse, not…not anxiety. Oh, she tried to cover it up, acting as if she were simply curious about her surroundings. But come off it, how exciting was a closed bicycle shop, a religious bookstore and a phone company repair office?

He should have let her leave with her brother, or since she seemed set on walking, pretended his car was parked in the other direction. But that seemed pretty wimpy, even to his reluctant self.

Anyway, he'd been the one to insist she meet Roxie. And that one was a lot harder to explain. Oh, well. He'd make the best of it, and then move on.

"She's a bit conscious of her ear, too," he warned her.

"Her ear?" Mimi patted hers as if to mimic the question.

"That's right. She had surgery during the winter to remove a tumor that luckily proved to be benign."

"You both must have been so relieved." She pushed the French fries in the top of the bag with her hoagie and rearranged it more comfortably under her arm.

"The doctor said that plastic surgery was an option, but I thought why put her through any more pain and suffering just for cosmetic reasons. Don't you agree?" Why was he even bringing this all up? As if Mimi Lodge's opinion on how Roxie looked mattered one way or another.

"As long as it isn't disfiguring, I see no reason to bother. The world is overly obsessed with superficial beauty in my opinion."

She actually sounded reasonable. And if the fine vertical line between her eyebrows was any indication, she practiced what she preached. Not that he thought the wrinkle was ugly. Far from it. It made her look more thoughtful than the know-it-all he'd remembered.

Then he spied his car up ahead. "That's me. The gray Volvo station wagon." He saw Roxie sit up at the sound of his voice. From the looks of it, she'd been snoozing in the trunk. She quickly hopped over to the backseat and squeezed her head through the opening in the lowered window. Her tail fanned enthusiastically back and forth.

"Why didn't you tell me Roxie was a dog? I was all prepared for…I'm not sure what I was prepared for. I haven't quite gotten my head around you." Mimi picked up her pace and leaned down to the window.

"I wouldn't just bend over the window like that." Vic rushed up to her side. "It's not like Roxie'd bite or anything, but she's not entirely comfortable with new people…"

Too late.

Mimi already held her hand to the window, palm-side up, and was letting the dog get a good sniff. "Not bad, huh? Eau de Hoagie Palace. Tell you what. I'll give you a small taste, but just this once." She undid the paper around the hoagie and tore off an end.

Roxie lunged for the roll and gobbled it down. Then she sniffed around Mimi's hands and began licking her fingertips. Then Roxie put her front paws up on the armrest on the door and forced herself farther out the window. Her tongue came in contact with Mimi's nose.

Vic was stunned.

Mimi started laughing and threw back her head. This time Roxie's kisses landed on her chin. Mimi squinted, still laughing. "I don't know why you say she's shy. She's incredibly affectionate, aren't you, girl?"

Mimi pulled her face away and gave Roxie a good rub around the back of her ears. Then she let her fingertips slowly travel the smooth length of her floppy ears, massaging them gently.

Roxie, to Vic's surprise, didn't budge, didn't pull away from contact, convinced that she was about to die. Instead, she closed her eyes, her white-blond eyelashes fluttering, and purred. Yes, the same dog who was usually afraid of her own shadow was purring.

"Don't even consider plastic surgery. Your ear looks very distinguished. It gives you character," Mimi addressed the dog directly. "Right, Roxie?"

The dog licked her lips contentedly and rested her head in Mimi's hand.

If Vic didn't know better he'd say she'd fallen asleep.

Mimi turned to him, smiling. "I think your fears were unfounded, don't you?"

He opened his mouth. Nothing came out.

She didn't bother for a reply. "What kind of a name is Roxie? Wait, don't tell me." She stopped him.

He wasn't about to say anything.

"Short for Roxanna—Alexander the Great's wife. The History Channel. It's a guy thing." She seemed very pleased with herself.

"Actually, it's Edmond Rostand's Roxane. His play *Cyrano de Bergerac?*"

Mimi frowned. "The beautiful woman who recognizes the love of the ugly but gifted poet Cyrano instead of the handsome other dude—I can't remember his name."

"Christian," Vic supplied.

"Right, Christian. Of course you'd remember the details. As I recall, you were good with the facts." Mimi shifted her bag of food again and went back to scratching Roxie's wrinkled brow. "You know, Vic Golinski, from that story, people might get the impression that you are a romantic."

He blushed. *Dammit, blushing?* "It's more a case that I was feeling sorry for myself. I'd just been cut from my team and my future in football looked over. I needed someone or something to love me. And there's nothing less complicated than a dog's affection."

"Affection's never uncomplicated," Mimi responded absentmindedly.

The dog leaned her head to one side, indicating she wanted more scratching in a particular place.

Mimi obliged, and Vic noticed that she'd cocked her head in the same way as the dog. She'd even closed her eyes, her own deep black-brown lashes resting on her high cheekbones. For the first time, she didn't look brittle, like she'd crack if you touched her in just the wrong way. She looked…looked happy, secure. Loved. Pure and simple. Uncomplicated.

And then it hit Vic—why he'd insisted on Mimi

meeting his dog. Unconsciously, he'd wanted to see Roxie's reaction. To validate his own emotions.

Only, it hadn't worked out the way he had planned at all.

Or had it? Because now more than ever, he wanted Mimi Lodge bad.

CHAPTER EIGHT

"HEY, PRESS, IT'S SO GOOD to see you." Amara Rheinhardt jumped up from the steps in front of her dorm and rushed to envelop him in her arms. "I can't believe how long it's been since I've seen you. I've had a great Freshman year—except for organic chemistry. Not all of us were meant to be science gurus like some people I could mention. Anyway, chalk it up as a painful learning experience and definitely cross off med school as one of my career options."

"I didn't know it was one?"

She shook her head, her chin rubbing back and forth against his shoulder. "Well, maybe. But this course in Roman poets I took? What can I say? Ovid is my personal god—I don't care what they say about Horace. I'm already determined to work on him for my J.P." She referred to her Junior Paper, which was still a long ways off.

Press grinned at her bubbly enthusiasm.

"And working for Penelope—like you said, unbelievable. I mean, even though she was gone on sabbatical a lot the first semester, she still taught me so much about manuscripts and how to put together exhibits."

"Yeah, Penelope's great," Press agreed, closing

his eyes as Amara continued to hug him. Penelope Bigelow was the curator of the Rare Book Library at Grantham and Press had worked for her when he was an undergraduate. A lot of people might have found Penelope…well…odd. Her awkwardness in social situations and her tendency to spout highly erudite information had a way of making listeners head for the hills. But not Press.

He raised his arms and finally went to hug Amara back. Too late.

She broke her embrace and stood back to gaze at him.

Press felt a momentary loss. Which was silly, really. After all, it wasn't like they were boyfriend and girlfriend or anything like that. They'd merely met, by accident as it turned out, at Reunions last year. And they'd had a bunch in common. She'd been finishing up prep school and coming to Grantham in the Fall. He'd been just about to graduate. She hadn't been getting along with her father. He thought his was a jerk—and still did. They'd hung out. No big deal, even if she'd pushed for something more. There was no chance—he was going away, she was a kid. Then he'd introduced her to his friend Matt, and they'd gotten on fine—more than fine. No big deal.

So now, one year later, Press stuffed his hands in his jeans pockets and acted like…like he wasn't practically jumping out of his skin.

She gave him a glance up and down. "You look different. I thought you'd be all tan and stuff—spending all that time surfing or whatever you do in Australia."

"I've been in the lab every day. It's hard to get a tan that way. And it's actually wintertime there, not summer."

Amara banged herself playfully on the forehead with the heel of one hand. "Duh! What a dummy I am." She laughed at herself.

She looked great laughing, Press thought. All giddy, and her cheeks turned kind of pinky.

"Well, if you'd ever Skype me like you said you would, then I'd know that, wouldn't I?" she went on.

"Yeah, well, I'm pretty bad at that," he stammered. What was he supposed to say anyway? That he liked his work but was lonely. That he missed her? That he wondered if she had met anyone special?

"Aren't you going to say how good I look?" Amara asked him. She did a pirouette on the toe of her ballet flat—just like the ones Penelope wore, Press noticed. "Sophisticated?" she asked, and circled around in a silly dance.

Press bit back a smile. "Yeah, real sophisticated—especially The Simpsons Band-Aid." He pointed to the bandage on her hand between her thumb and index finger.

She held it up and inspected it briefly. "They were the only ones I could find at the convenience store this morning. I'm learning how to drive one of the golf carts for Reunions so that I can take around one of the old alums, and, would you believe it, I got a blister from shifting gears." She laughed at herself some more.

"Knowing you, I can believe it," Press teased her. He waved a hand in her general direction. "I like your hair that way, too."

She swung her head back and forth, her thick chestnut hair skimming her shoulders. "Yeah, it's easier with it shorter, plus I can still tie it up when I'm studying and stuff. Otherwise I end up looking for split ends the whole time."

"That's why I cut my hair shorter, too," Press joked.

Amara pushed him with her shoulder. She wore a tank top and a faded jeans skirt that cupped her bottom. The bare skin of her tanned arm brushed up against his T-shirt.

Press almost groaned. Actually, Amara *had* grown up a lot in one year. And he wasn't just saying that because of what she was wearing—though things had changed there, as well. No, she looked more confident, more cheerful. Gone were any remnants of her Goth days—the dyed black hair, the oversize black clothes dragging on the ground. Though he was glad to see she still had multiple silver hoop earrings in each ear and purply-black polish on her nails.

"I can't believe I'm seeing you, though. I mean, I didn't even know you were planning on coming to Reunions."

"I wasn't."

Amara looked perplexed. "You suddenly got nostalgic? I can't believe that. You were so hot to get out and see the world. I'd never thought you'd return to Grantham."

"It's kind of complicated. Part of it has to do with my half-sister Mimi." He wasn't about to talk about the other part—seeing her.

"Oh, gosh, yes. Her kidnapping was just awful. You must have been out of your mind with worry."

Worry didn't begin to describe the agony he had suffered through.

Amara breathed in deeply. "I made my dad promise he would never go to Chechnya for one of his shows." Amara's dad was Nick Rheinhardt, a celebrity chef and travel writer who had a show on cable television. After last year's Reunions, he was also Penelope's fiancé. "But she's okay now, right?" Amara rattled on at lightning speed.

"I guess. I don't really know. She just dumped me earlier at Hoagie Palace for some dude from her class at the university, so she can't be feeling all that bad."

"Oh, good. Hearing what happened to her made me jumpy about all the time Matt was in Congo. At least he's going to Sierra Leone for his Peace Corps stint. He claims that's safer, but still… He's so dedicated, determined to make a difference in the world. You know what I mean?"

"We can't all be saints," Press commented. Matt might be the closest thing he had to a friend in the world, but somehow he'd be just as happy if he didn't show up tonight. He looked around. "So where is the Albert Schweitzer of our generation anyway?"

He scanned the quadrangle. Bluestone paths dissected the grass and dogwoods sheltered against the gray stone walls of the Gothic buildings. The area was empty except for the students sticking around to work for Reunions. Black-and-orange banners with the years of various graduating classes hung from the second-floor crenellated balconies. Come this weekend, every room would be filled with returning alums.

"I thought I was the one running late," Press added.

"Didn't you get his text about having dinner with the Board of Sisters to Sisters?"

"No, I guess I missed that one." How come Matt had texted Amara and not him?

"He promised to be here as soon as he could get away. But if I know Matt, he'll stay until the last morsel, especially since Babička insisted on wining and dining everyone at her house." Babička, the Slovak term for grandmother, referred to Matt's stepmother's grandmother. It was kind of complicated, but seemed to work for him.

"Babička's an amazing cook. We'll be lucky to see him at all."

Amara laughed. "I know."

"You know?"

"Yeah. When Matt was home for spring break, he invited me to eat with the whole family at her house. It was amazing. I still remember the plum cake. Oh, my God." She gripped her stomach. "I think I gained ten pounds I ate so much. I remember I was on the treadmill like crazy the next week."

Whereas Press remembered Matt telling him about the significance of plum cake in Slovakian celebrations—and how it played a part in getting his dad and Katarina, Matt's stepmom, together—or so Babička had claimed.

She grabbed him by the arm. "Speaking of plum cake, I forgot to tell you. After I told my dad all about the meal she made, he decided to film an episode of his TV show in Slovakia. In fact, he invited me to come along as an intern on the show. Honestly, I'm not really interested in production and everything, but Penelope's going to come along, too—apparently the library in Bratislava has this amazing collection of Islamic manuscripts that of course she knows everything about. So I figured why not? Then afterward we'll all go down to Penelope's house in Calabria where I've got my fingers crossed that maybe she will agree to marry my father sometime soon. He is *so* desperate to slip a ring on her finger before someone else steals her away."

Press liked the idea of Amara getting out of town. "It sounds like you'll have a pretty cool summer, then. Only I guess since you won't be working on campus this summer, you won't be able to see Matt before he takes off." He tried to sound sincere.

"Actually, that's the really cool part. Dad talked Babička into coming along, too—as an interpreter and to kind of provide a personal storyline. You know, having her go back to her ancestral roots and seeing what had changed and what hasn't."

A black squirrel—a species found only in Grantham—scampered across the stone molding over the archway, its nails skittering across the rough limestone. Press glanced up and watched it dive onto a nearby tree. The magnolia branch swayed precariously under the weight, but the squirrel somehow safely navigated its way down the trunk and bounded off across the grass.

Press looked back at Amara. "Good for her. But you know, all this talk about food is making me hungry. I thought we were going to Burt's Sweets for a strawberry blend-in." The combination of French vanilla ice cream mixed up with fresh strawberries had been attracting local residents for two generations.

"Sure, but I still haven't told you the best part. Babička said she'd be happy to do it, but she insisted that Matt come along, as well—she thought the whole multigenerational aspect would enrich the story. For one episode, she's even going to cook for all of us in the kitchen of an old friend. Isn't that the greatest?"

As long as it's not plum cake for you and Matt, Press couldn't help thinking.

CHAPTER NINE

THE NEXT MORNING, now already Thursday, Mimi wandered down the grand staircase of the Lodge manse, past the wall of family portraits and photos, stopping on the landing to feel the warmth of the sunlight streaming through the Palladian window. She rubbed her arms through the sweatshirt she'd worn to bed, and noticed for the first time that the window seat was crowded with needlepoint pillows. William Morris-like animals scampered joyously through stylized acanthus and lettuce leaves.

The sound of voices filtered up from downstairs, and she continued on her bare feet down the carpeted runner to the ground floor. The noise was coming from the kitchen, and she circled around to the back of the house. There was no mistaking the source— the high-pitched wailing of her kid sister, Brigid, followed by the patient lilt of her stepmother, Noreen. The woman combined the fashion sense of a Vogue editor and the maternal instinct of Mother Theresa. One day she'd win a Nobel Peace Prize and accept the award wearing Dolce and Gabbana.

Mimi cut the corner of the formal dining room and pushed open the swinging door to the butler's pantry.

Sterling silver serving dishes filled the glass-fronted cabinets. Jars of granola, organic sesame seed crackers and various legumes of high nitrogen content and unknown origin were neatly lined up on the open shelves. Mimi pushed open a matching door on the opposite wall and entered the kitchen.

That's when she saw Brigid sitting on a stool, sprawled from the waist up over the central island. She lay facedown, her forehead resting on her upper arm. Her other arm was outstretched across a sea of dark granite, the fingers of her open hand grasping in the air.

"Is everything all right?" Mimi rushed in concerned.

Noreen turned around from the stainless-steel espresso coffee machine—imported Italian ceramic mug in hand—and sighed. "It seems Brigid is despondent because Cook made her cupcakes—all organic flour and agave sweetener, according to my instructions. And they have the lightest pink frosting decorated with rosebuds. Sounds like every young girl's dream, don't you think?"

Mimi nodded. She knew a cue when she saw one.

Noreen took a sip of coffee. "Unfortunately, Brigid had her heart set on daisies. Ah, the injustice of it all."

"Well, if you don't want the cupcakes, I'm happy to eat them instead. I can't think of anything nicer than rosebuds." Mimi stepped up next to her half-sister and rested her palms on the edge of the island.

Brigid shot upright. "No, they're mine."

"Brigid, there are more than enough to share."

Brigid screwed up her face. A sprinkling of freckles scattered across the bridge of her nose. "Okay, but only one." And just to make sure she got her fair share, the eight-year-old scooped one off the plate and placed it in a small Tupperware container. She snapped the lid shut and carefully loaded it into her Hello Kitty lunchbox.

"That's very generous," Mimi noted. "But, you know, I think I'll save mine until lunch. In the meantime, how about a hello kiss? I bet one from you is even sweeter than a cupcake." Mimi bent down and offered her cheek.

Brigid wrapped her thin arms around Mimi's waist then stretched her neck to plant a kiss on her cheek. "You smell yucky."

"Brigid, your manners. That's no way to greet your big sister." Noreen put her mug down on the countertop and readjusted the scrunchie holding back her ponytail. Dressed in form-hugging black yoga pants and a tight sleeveless shirt with a crisscross back, she looked ready for the gym.

Mimi lifted the arm of her sweatshirt close to her nose and detected the lingering odor of meatballs and hot sauce. Then she looked down at the front. There was a stain just below the "n" in Grantham—remnants of the hoagie she'd finished off while checking her email. Brigid might deem her ready for the trash heap, but Mimi actually took heart. After months of obsessive-compulsive behavior, she took it as a sign that she was finally beginning to chill out.

"I am so not yucky," she rebutted Brigid's comment. "That's the telltale aroma of the food of the gods. And if you're a good girl today, after school, I will spirit you away from this world of low-fat-low-carb-absolutely-nothing-artificial and introduce you to *real* world cuisine."

Brigid looked at her with horror. "Will it make me look like you?"

For the second time in less than twenty-four hours, Mimi found herself smiling. Her facial muscles strained from the unfamiliar effort.

Noreen shook her head. "As a devoted believer in good nutrition and the benefits of honest local fruits and vegetables, I could plead with you not to interfere with my methods. But I must confess, there's something about Hoagie Palace's French fries that could make the most devoted health food nut question her beliefs."

Mimi leaned toward Noreen and whispered loudly, "Tell you what. I'll get a large order and bring them back. That way it won't be as if you were really indulging—just making sure I don't overdo it."

"I'm so glad that I'll be able to save you from yourself." Noreen smiled and clapped her hands. "All right now, my sweet lassie. Time to get going. Otherwise you'll miss the school bus. My Pilates class starts promptly at eight, so I don't have time to drive you.

And your father is already on the train into the City, so you can't look to him, either."

Brigid hopped off her stool and wrapped her arms around Mimi's legs. "You could drive me, though, couldn't you?"

Mimi was about to say yes—who could resist a kid with red hair and missing teeth, who also thought you were the greatest person in the world after her mother and father, and even maybe her big brother, Press?

"No, she couldn't," Noreen answered for her. She picked up her daughter's lunch box and L.L. Bean knapsack and held them out. "Mimi is tired after her trip coming down here. You'll have plenty of time to see her when you get home."

Mimi got the message. There would be no spoiling her half-sister. At least, not at the moment. "Anyway, it's a lot cooler to take the bus to school with all the big kids," she informed Brigid.

Seemingly easily appeased, Brigid stepped back and slipped the straps of her backpack over her tiny shoulders—the navy blue coordinated with her striped blue-and-white shirt and blue cropped pants that were flared at the bottom. She stopped to kiss her mother, and then one more hug for Mimi, before she skipped to the mudroom and toward the back door. The final bang of the screen door followed as Brigid raced out.

Suddenly it was quiet.

And just as suddenly, an unexpected pang of anxiety gripped Mimi. She felt her heart race, her upper lip become moist. "Don't you...don't you worry that something might happen—her just taking off on her own?" Mimi turned to Noreen.

Noreen stepped over to the bank of windows on the side of the kitchen, and through the sparkling panes Mimi realized she could see Brigid skipping down the long red stone driveway. As soon as the girl was out of sight, Noreen walked swiftly to the front of the house.

Mimi followed and watched Noreen as she peered surreptitiously through the gauze curtains covering the sidelights on either side of the front door. Brigid followed the curve of the drive that led to the entrance where a hedge of hollies converged on two giant brick pillars topped by hand-blown electric lanterns. Wrought-iron gates, attached to the pillars, were open inward. A coded entry box was embedded into the side of one pillar, and it matched the control panel by the front door.

Noreen gazed at her daughter eager to start her day at school. Her eyes never left the window.

Mimi looked out the matching sidelight on the other side of the massive front door. She saw Brigid standing on the sidewalk, swaying her hips. She appeared to be singing her own personal background music. Then the noise of a school bus grew louder until it stopped and opened its door. Brigid swirled around and waved goodbye before dancing up the stairs. The doors fanned shut and the bus departed.

Noreen turned away. "It's our little game. I pretend I don't watch her go, and she plays along until the last minute as if to tell me she really knew all along. In any case, we're talking about broad day-light in Grantham, New Jersey—not exactly a high-crime area."

Mimi still couldn't help feeling uneasy. "I know you're right. It's that…"

Noreen stepped toward her. "I understand. And if it makes you feel more at ease while you are here, I can wait with her for the bus. Or better yet, why don't you?" She didn't bother to elaborate.

Mimi was grateful for her sensitivity. "Okay, I'd like that. I could say that I wanted to have some sister time together."

"I think that would be splendid. Now, if you don't mind, I really should be off. I try to squeeze in exercise whenever I can. Age has not been particularly kind to my hips. I can feel exactly where all the rich food from the Board dinner last night has settled." She patted her thighs.

Mimi couldn't detect any evidence of middle-age spread, but Noreen, as she'd come to realize, was something of a perfectionist.

"Would you like to come along, too? I'm allowed a certain number of guest passes at the gym," Noreen offered.

"No thanks. I think I'll do my usual workout at Delaney Pool on campus. I used to resent all the hard work at the beginning of water polo season, but now I find the swimming immensely therapeutic. Nothing clears the mind like the intense monotony."

"If you say so. Frankly, without the commitment

of a regular class, I'd probably never do anything. And speaking of commitments—" Noreen whisked her purple Prada bag off the narrow table in the foyer "—I'm sorry I wasn't here to greet you when you came in yesterday. I know your father and I are looking forward to getting together while you're in town."

Yeah, like her father was turning handstands in anticipation. "I wouldn't want to inconvenience you," Mimi said politely. "After my workout, I promised Lilah I'd get together with her, and I'm not quite sure what my plans will be after that."

"Oh, you'll get to see Sam," Noreen gushed about Lilah's one-year-old baby named for her father, Walter Samuel Evans, who had died unexpectedly just before the baby was born. "There's something so innocent about babies. I remember your father cooing over Brigid when she was born."

"Now that I find hard to believe."

"You'd be surprised. Your father can be quite attached to you children, the way all proper fathers should be. In fact, we had a conversation about that not long ago."

"More power to you if you managed to get him to admit that," Mimi said incredulously. "But I guess better late than never—especially for Brigid. It's important that she has a loving father."

"For you, too, don't you think?"

"I think it's too late for that."

"It's never too late." Noreen wrestled her keys from

deep within her bag. "Do you need a car, then? Conrad's Mercedes is in the garage."

"No, thanks, I'd thought I'd bike. Get some fresh air—as opposed to the stuff I breathe in the City."

If Noreen suspected Mimi's reluctance to get in a car, she didn't comment. "Well, make sure you grab a jacket. I know it doesn't look like it now, but the forecast is for rain. And don't forget—if you are free tonight, we'd be delighted to get together. Press, too. I know he's always up for a home-cooked meal. I can't promise anything fancy since Cook is off this long weekend, but I'm sure we'll make do. *Slán,* then." And she headed to the back of the house and out to the garage.

And like that, Mimi was alone. Oh, Press was probably sleeping off the jetlag in his bedroom, but for all intents and purposes she was alone. Ever since her mother's death she'd been alone.

Noreen said she could use a father's love. "I don't think so," Mimi responded out loud. Then she felt her cheek. "What I could really use is a slobbery kiss from a certain sweet dog," she decided.

Then how come her thoughts immediately jumped to kisses from a certain dog's owner?

CHAPTER TEN

VIC WENT ROUND AND ROUND, swinging his three-year-old nephew, Tommy, in a wide circle. His sister had called him earlier.

"I've got to work breakfast at The Circus and Mom isn't back, and there's still an hour to go before nursery school. I just can't leave him," she said in desperation.

"Where's Dad?" Vic had asked as he finished packing his gym bag. Four days a week he hit the gym before heading off to work. It kept the weight off from his mother's cooking. And it was force of habit, a prudent measure to ensure a sound mind and a sound body.

"Where's Dad? Oh, come off it. It's Thursday. Where do you think he is?" Basia had asked impatiently.

"Right. Racquetball with the guys. God forbid anyone gets in the way of his Thursday and Friday racquetball."

"So, if you can just fill in until Mom gets back from church?" she pleaded.

"What about Joe? He lives in town. You could drop Tommy off on the way," Vic replied. He didn't mind helping out, but why was it that everyone always called him first in times of need?

"Are you kidding me? I don't even trust Joe to take care of himself. The guy shows about as much responsibility as a feral cat."

"You know, if you'd let me pay for your tuition, you wouldn't need to waitress and be stuck in a bind this way," he pointed out.

Basia sighed. "Listen, we've been through all this before. Mom and Pop already let me stay at the house for free. You pay for my violin lessons. The least I can do is pull my weight as far as getting my degree. Besides, I think it sets a good example for Tommy—showing him his mom isn't afraid of hard work. But, Vic, I really don't have time to argue."

Vic shook his head. "All right. Bring Tommy over and I'll watch him 'til Mom shows up. But I was really hoping to get to the gym before work."

"Thanks, Vic, you're the best. If you ever need anything from me." But she'd already hung up the phone, and a few minutes later, she knocked at his front door and swept in, Tommy and his lunch box in tow.

So there he was, swinging his nephew around on the sidewalk in front of his town house. Tommy's squeals of joy permeated the small street. His laughter mixed with the calls of sparrows and robins that squabbled in the trees and the scramble of squirrels chasing one another up and down the rough trunks. Their mating rituals had already begun. Roxie lay on the sidewalk soaking up the sun. She was oblivious to animal life unless it was cooked and came sliced from the deli counter.

"No more, no more," he called out to Tommy. "I'm getting dizzy here, buddy." He slowed his rotation but still clasped his nephew firmly by the wrists. His legs were starting to feel wobbly.

A neighbor drove by in her midnight-blue BMW and waved. A divorcee in her early forties, she worked for the university in their alumni office. She was an avid gardener and even enjoyed having Tommy tag along when she was planting bulbs or flowers in the strip of common property that ran along their private road. Vic had asked her out for dinner once. And while their conversation had been enjoyable, it was clear to both of them that there was no chemistry to go beyond that.

"Uncle Vic, Uncle Vic, more merry-go-round." Tommy tugged at him.

Vic looked down. Aside from his dark hair, the boy looked just like his younger sister, and he remembered twirling Basia around the same way when she was a kid. "Okay, Tommy, one more time. But if you barf up your Cheerios, you're going to be in big trouble. You will personally wash my clothes."

Tommy laughed. "Silly Uncle Vic. Mom washes clothes. Not me."

"I wouldn't tell that to your mom." Vic adjusted his grip around Tommy's thin wrists. "Away we go," he said and started to spin the boy around. Tommy closed his eyes and put his neck back, reveling in the speed.

A gray Camry bumped up over the edge of the curb into the next driveway. The driver's door swung open. "Witek, what do you think you are doing? You could kill the boy." His mother jumped out of the car and scurried across the small lawn. She was dressed in black knit pants with a black blazer over a white shell. A gold cross hung from a chain around her neck. Aside from the brown-and-beige Coach tote bag with its signature "C"s, she could have been dressed for mourning. Well, in a way, Vic realized, she was.

Roxie stirred from her slumber and retreated to Vic's front stoop. The dog was afraid of Vic's mother—understandably.

Vic slowed his swinging. "Don't worry, Mom. Dad used to do this to us kids all the time."

"Just my point," his mother shot back. She grabbed Tommy and inspected him closely. "Are your shoulders all right, your wrists? You could have easily broken something."

"I'm fine, fine, fine, Grandma," Tommy said in singsong fashion. "We were just playing."

"Fine, but no playing like that on my watch, young man. Here are the keys." She held up her key ring. "Go in the house and wash up in the front powder room. Who knows what kind of germs you got playing outdoors. Then come stand by the front door until I come in."

Tommy ran off to the front door of Vic's parents' house, right next door to Vic's own. He stopped with his hand on the doorknob. "Bye, Uncle Vic."

Vic waved. "Kids are supposed to play outdoors. They've got energy to burn."

"Like you're such an expert on kids? We should all be so lucky." She crossed her arms.

Vic rolled his eyes. Now was not the time for his mother to lecture him on how she wanted some more grandchildren to pass on the family name before she died. The way she talked, you'd think she was closer to eighty than sixty. "I'll be off, then." He turned to go back to his own house.

"Hold up. Where's Basia? Why wasn't she taking care of Tommy like a good mother?"

"Give Basia a break, Mom. It wasn't her fault she had to leave for work and you weren't home." He felt very protective where his sister was concerned.

"But you know I always go to seven a.m. mass at St. Urzula."

Vic glanced at his watch. "It must have been an extra-long service. Anyway, you know there's a perfectly decent Catholic church here in Grantham. There's no need for you to go all the way to Trenton every day."

"We've been through this before, Witek," she said. "St. Urzula's is the old neighborhood church."

"But your neighborhood—your house—for more than eight years is here," Vic argued. He didn't bother to add that it was a house that he had paid for.

"That doesn't mean I still don't have ties with my old friends. Besides, I feel comfortable there. And it's nice to hear the older generation still speaking Polish."

"Mom, you were born in this country." As the years went by, his mother seemed to become more and more attached to her Polish heritage, even going back with church groups to various religious sites. Vic didn't get it, but then there were a lot of things he didn't get about his mother. "Listen, I respect your choices, but if you're going to be held up in traffic, could you call me on your cell phone. You carry it, right?"

"Of course, how else would I show everyone the latest photos of Tomasz? In any case, it wasn't the traffic that held me up. I wanted to speak to Father Antonin about Basia."

"What about Basia? Is something wrong? I thought her last semester went fine. Better than fine—all As."

His mother turned her head to check if Tommy had returned to her front door. When he still hadn't, she leaned forward and whispered, "She has a husband."

Now Vic was going to lose it. "You mean that deadbeat with a gambling problem? Once the divorce is finalized she'll be rid of him for good."

"Witek, he's still the baby's father," his mother protested. "And more to the point, marriage is a holy sacrament."

Vic shook his head. "And if you're worried about Basia's soul, don't. When she's passed on to greater glory, she can spend her time with me and the rest of the sinners."

"Watch your tongue."

"Hi, Grandma. See, my hands are clean," Tommy

called out from the open door. He held up his hands. Water blotches dotted the front of his striped T-shirt.

Vic's mother waved. "I'll be right with you, sweetheart. We'll change that shirt before you catch a cold." She pushed her large bag up to her elbow. "I have to go. But before I do, a friend of mine from Zumba class mentioned to me that she saw you talking to a woman the other day on the street." She raised an eyebrow.

"Now it's a crime to talk to women?" Vic asked. He didn't really want to get into a long-winded discussion, but he knew his mother wouldn't let up until she got details. "It was Mimi Lodge. You know, the TV reporter? She's back in town for Reunions."

His mother narrowed her eyes. "Since when are you so buddy-buddy with this Lodge woman?"

"She's not 'this Lodge woman.'" He was starting to feel as protective of Mimi as his sister. "Mimi was a classmate of mine at Grantham."

His mother stared at him.

He knew she was itching to say something more. "What?" he asked.

"Don't mess with those Lodges," his mother warned.

"Why? They're good for business. Joe's working on a major contract with her father's company now. If that comes through, you'll be swimming in Coach bags." That wasn't particularly nice, but so what. He couldn't be nice all the time.

"Grandma-a," Tommy wailed. "Can I have some string cheese?"

"That boy. Snacking all the time. Whatever happened to three square meals a day?" she muttered. Then she raised her voice. "Don't eat anything until I get there." She started to cross the neatly clipped grass.

"Bye, Mom." Vic headed up his front path. Just another day with the family.

"Witek, they're not our kind." His mother's voice boomed.

Vic bent down to pat Roxie, then looked across the lawn. "Don't tell me you still buy into the class difference thing?" Pretty soon his mother's thinking would regress to Victorian times.

She walked back across the lawn to him and pointed an accusing finger. "Pooh, pooh all you want. It still exists. Besides, that girl's mother? The reporter's mother?" She lowered her head and looked over her very expensive, ultra-lightweight French glasses. Vic knew because he'd bought them for her.

"What about Mimi's mother?" he asked.

"She's dead."

"That's too bad. But a lot of people lose family members."

His mother emitted a shocked breath. "As I know only too well." She raised her chin like a warrior ready to do battle. "But her mother?"

Vic nodded.

She struck her blow. "They say the father killed her."

CHAPTER ELEVEN

CONRAD STOOD ON THE platform at Grantham Junction waiting for the 8:05 Amtrak. Gone were the days of the private bar car attached to the front of the train, and the assurance that you'd be traveling with a certain type of people—fellow investment bankers, partners in major law firms. Even the occasional advertising executive had been allowed into the mix just to keep things lively.

Of course, all that was history, dating to the time before women had been allowed to join the upper echelons of the workforce—not that Conrad would have ever voiced that sentiment out loud. Noreen would have forcefully taken him to task at even the faintest whiff of misogynist leanings. Still, Conrad was not one to believe in coincidences.

He flicked his left wrist up, and the sleeve of his Burberry raincoat slipped back. The starched cuffs of his monogrammed dress shirt stuck out the requisite half-inch from the sleeve of his pinstripe suit. He always wore French cuffs, and his gold cufflinks with the crest of Grantham University gleamed. Conrad enjoyed putting them on each morning. He found them reassuring, a symbol that certain traditions would never cease to exist despite the ever-changing world.

He checked his Rolex. The train was now three minutes late. He had a meeting at ten o'clock, but it wasn't as if he was worried about being late. After all, given his position in life people waited for him.

Frankly, if he still had a driver take him into the City as he'd done every morning during the years he was married to Press's mother, he wouldn't have been forced to wait around on a concrete platform, buffeted by flying grit every time the Acela train whisked through without stopping on its way to Washington, D.C.

Alas, the chauffeured car service had come to an end when he married Noreen. She had convinced him that it was every good citizen's duty to take public transportation whenever possible—good for the environment, she said. He hadn't needed much convincing. He would have even taken the bus for her. No… maybe not the bus.

So as he waited on the platform, Conrad eyed the young man standing next to him—tight jeans, black leather jacket, a tattoo crawling up the back of his neck. Conrad looked down. The man's black boots needed polishing. That may have offended him the most.

"The 8:05 Amtrak train will be arriving on the northbound track in one minute," a crackly voice announced over the loud speakers.

Conrad moved along the platform next to the third

billboard down from the stairway. When the train stopped, he would be directly in front of a door.

The train approached the station from Trenton and ground to a noisy halt. The metal doors slipped open. The leather jacket young man tried to nudge his way in first, but Conrad placed his polished brogue just so, blocking his path. In getting on the train, like all things, he liked to come in first.

Shifting today's copy of the *Wall Street Journal* to the same hand as his briefcase, he stepped inside and opened the inner door to the carriage on the right. Conrad always went to the right.

Then he found his favorite row—fifth on the left— and took the seat next to the window. Before sitting down, he unbuckled and unbuttoned his tan raincoat and the top button of his suit jacket, then slipped his BlackBerry out of his pocket. He placed his leather briefcase on his lap, the newspaper on top so as not to get ink on his clothes, and settled in for the hour ride.

He nodded curtly at another similarly dressed middle-aged man who sat next to him. Like Conrad, he immediately pulled out his phone, and the two sat in silence as the train pulled away from the station, speeding along until its next stop in New Brunswick. From there, it would travel express to Newark before terminating at Penn Station in Manhattan. On days when the weather was pleasant—like today— Conrad liked to walk across town to the office. He might be sixty-two, but he was a fit sixty-two, with his twice-weekly squash games at the Grantham Club of New York.

As the train jostled slightly on the tracks, Conrad scrolled through his messages. He liked to get an early start on things since the Asian markets had already opened, and he frequently had communications from Shanghai and Tokyo.

Otherwise, it was a good time to delete the flood of unsolicited résumés from job seekers or answer more personal items—updates from fellow members of the Reunions committee or invitations for lunch with friends and colleagues. His assistant Jeremy would follow up on the details of these meetings. Like all good assistants, Jeremy had an unerring ability to fob off people Conrad wasn't interested in seeing, or pin down those who he did.

Speaking of Jeremy, Conrad noted there was a message from him marked CONFIDENTIAL AND URGENT.

It wasn't like Jeremy to use capital letters—his solid education at St. Paul's and Haverford had instilled in him the gaucheness of overkill.

Conrad clicked on the email and the text popped open.

Mr. Lodge:
As you know, the decision to promote several members of the firm to partner has increased the fully vested members to a record number.

Which is precisely why Conrad had voiced his objections when the motion had come to a vote several weeks ago. But the resolution had passed anyway, much to Conrad's chagrin. He anticipated a splintering into factions, a development that he would have to crush sooner rather than later.

He read on:

In view of the unwieldy nature of this top-heavy structure, one which will undoubtedly make major decisions more difficult...

Didn't I say those exact same words at the meeting? Conrad thought with amusement. So now they were coming around to his way of thinking, after all.

As your former assistant, I have therefore been directed by the other partners of the firm to inform you that your position at Pilgrim Investors is no longer required.

Conrad stopped reading. He blinked, then reread what he'd just read.

This decision is effective immediately. Since you are no longer an employee of PI, you will need to report to Security upon entering the building. From there, you will be escorted directly to Human Resources, where you will find personal items from your former office.

"Former assistant? Former office?" Conrad said out loud, enraged. The man next to him slanted him a skeptical glance before going back to his own messages. Conrad had personally selected the wood paneling and eighteenth-century French antiques for that office.

Since you initially instituted the policy, you are no doubt aware that PI's protocol requires immediate lockdown of a former employee's computer and business items, thereby ensuring the propriety of the firm's business. Human Resources will also be happy to discuss with you the terms of your retirement and benefits package.

In closing, let me say how much I learned under your guidance and that I wish you well in your future endeavors.

It was signed by one of the new partners.

Conrad put his hand to his heart—or what eldest daughter, Mimi, always ready with the snide comment, called his "blood-pumping muscle." Indeed, he could feel it beating rapidly, painfully. He might not have a heart, but whatever it was, it was breaking.

He stared blindly out the grimy window at the passing blur of scenery. A coup. An office coup, clearly led by this…this snot-nosed partner who Conrad had personally mentored. A Harvard man. He should have known. Conrad rubbed his forehead. It was clammy.

Could this really have happened? To him? The

founder of the company? Surely he had enough support from the old guard on the board, Conrad reminded himself. Or did he? He *was* the only founding member still active, the others having retired to charitable work or a life divided between homes in Aspen and St. John. And the number of new partners could have formed a voting block by peeling off a few of the older ones who had been chafing at the bit to change the strategic direction of the company. *Yes,* he supposed, *it was possible.*

Conrad looked up and noticed that the train had stopped. New Brunswick, he realized. He saw the towers of Rutgers over the elevated train platform. People clambered on board. A conductor shouted. Then the train took off with a lurch.

Conrad lowered the phone to the newspaper on his lap. He looked down at the screen. It had already turned black. The front page of the Journal jiggled up and down with the swaying of the train, the words unreadable. He wondered…

Wondered how was he going to tell Noreen.

And then almost immediately, he wondered how he was going to face his fellow classmates at Reunions this coming weekend.

CHAPTER TWELVE

THE CHLORINATED WATER sluiced over her body as Mimi performed a perfect flip turn at Delaney Pool on the university campus. It was the homestretch of her 2500-yard workout, a modified version of the program from her water polo days. She wasn't back to the 5000-yard program, which would have taken roughly two hours, but she still did the mix of sprints, distance swimming and water polo-type strokes. The latter included heads-up freestyle without using the wall to turn around, backstroke with a breaststroke kick, as well as heads-up butterfly with a breaststroke kick. The combination was exhausting. The result was improved stamina, but also an inability to think of anything, which was better than just about any therapy that she'd tried.

There was something about water, she noted. She remembered the first time she'd jumped into the small, overly chlorinated pool in the sports club on the Upper East Side of Manhattan. It dulled the mind to the outside world, but heightened the senses, and not just the pain in her muscles and her lungs, but the sensations of touch and smell. If someone was wearing perfume or a strong deodorant, the odor penetrated. It was as if all her pores were open and inviting to the world around her—that she was one with her surroundings instead of feeling like a skittish outsider. In a word, it made her joyous.

Which was pretty ironic when you considered how many people, including Mimi in her youth, had found swimming laps tedious beyond despair. But now, with a final sprint to the wall, Mimi felt nothing but exhilaration—and complete exhaustion as she held on to the tiled gunwale and sucked air into her oxygen-deprived lungs.

She reached up and removed her swimmer's goggles and her red silicone swim cap, then peered at the large round clock mounted high on the wall. She was checking her time—fastest yet—a good sign, but also registering the time of day.

She didn't want to be late in meeting Lilah at Bean World, the local super-cool coffee shop on Whalen Avenue in town. Up until now she'd actually avoided her best friend. She hadn't seen the point in rehashing the events of the kidnapping, but mostly she didn't want to see the concerned look in her friend's eyes. Lilah was this superempathetic person—unlike her, Mimi readily admitted.

But now it occurred to her that she really *wanted* to meet with Lilah. Because she wanted to ask her about Vic. It was only fair. Hadn't Mimi peppered Lilah with questions two years ago during Reunions about her renewed acquaintance with their classmate Justin Bigelow, the onetime lady-killer and good-time boy?

During that weekend, lo and behold, superserious Lilah had been the one to finally tame the wild man. Soon afterward, the two married and their blissful union seemed to defy the gloomy divorce statistics.

Mimi wanted to ask more questions—but not about Lilah and Justin. Well, she would politely inquire about their work in Congo and how things were going in their new house, not to mention the baby. And then she'd get to what really mattered—what Lilah thought about Vic. There was something about him that appealed to her at this stage in her life. Or maybe it simply was Roxie. Okay, she was a sucker for his dog. And the man went with the dog, surely? But the truth of the matter was, there'd always been something about Vic Golinski.

God knows, it wasn't as if she was looking for love. As far as Mimi was concerned, love was a lot of fabricated hooey, with the exception of Lilah and Justin's relationship. But for her? No way.

What she wanted to discuss wasn't burgeoning love, therefore, but unanticipated glimmers of lust. And if she was going to get sage advice from the one person she truly trusted in the world, she would have to get a move on, especially because her mode of transportation was Press's Trek bike.

Mimi hoisted herself out of the pool and walked swiftly to the women's locker room down the hallway. Delaney Pool was a state-of-the-art racing facility—a welcome addition to the old dark and dingy gymnasium pool—and as an alum, she could still use the facilities for free. And, hugging her towel around her, she jogged in her flip-flops through the cavernous structure.

It took her less than five minutes to shower and slip on her clothes. She didn't bother with the hair dryer, and instead whipped a wide-toothed comb through her chin-length hair, pulling the dark strands straight back from her forehead.

She barely glanced at the mirror to check on how she looked. After all, there wasn't much to fuss about a pair of jeans and an oversize white shirt. Once upon a time the cotton blouse had been formfitting, but Mimi figured with the sleeves rolled up, it fit in with the "boyfriend" style that seemed so popular in New York these days. Actually, the jeans were new—two sizes smaller than what she used to wear. She hated wearing belts, and her old ones simply wouldn't stay up on their own.

She bent over to yank out the old canvas knapsack she'd found in her bedroom and stuffed her belongings inside the big compartment. Then she slipped on the old pair of boat shoes she'd found in the mudroom. They looked like they must have belonged to Press at one time. At least they fit her—more or less. Kind of like the black zip jacket she'd "borrowed", as well.

On the other hand, there was his bike. When had Press grown so much taller than she? Nothing like not being able to sit in the saddle the whole time. And when she had to stop for a traffic light, she'd had to balance her toes against the curb. There was no waiting flat-footed on the pavement with the crossbar so high.

After checking to see that she hadn't left anything, Mimi banged the metal door shut, swung the backpack over one shoulder and headed out of the locker room and up the stairs to the top entrance of the building. The bike racks were tucked to the side of the walkway that ran between a large parking lot and Baldwin Gymnasium, the university's multi-purpose sports complex. This section of the walkway—with the pool building on one side and the football workout facility on the other—was notorious for producing a wind tunnel effect that could almost blow you off your feet.

Mimi pushed open the wide glass door and in anticipation of a mighty gust of air, stopped under the concrete canopy to zip up and put up the hood of her jacket. Noreen had been right about the forecast—why wasn't Mimi surprised? It had started to rain—in this particular location, sideways.

Mimi hunched over and clutched the neckline of the jacket around her chin. The sides of the hood blocked all peripheral vision. She kept her head pointed to the ground, her focus a few paces in front of her, and walked briskly toward the bike rack. The wind picked up and belted her chest. "Crap," she muttered and bent farther forward, blind to anything more than an inch in front of her.

And smacked straight into a hard surface.

She yelped. Then looked up. Her hood fell back

from her head. Rain pelted her face. It stuck to her
eyelashes, and she brushed them off with the back
of her hand. She squinted. She hadn't bumped into
a pillar.

She'd made contact with Vic Golinski's back.

CHAPTER THIRTEEN

Vic BREATHED IN THROUGH his clenched jaw. The rain soaked through the shoulders of his blue blazer and darkened his khaki trousers. A puddle had formed around his dark loafers. He was running late for a meeting with the California plant manager and he could just imagine the snarl of traffic on Route One. On top of which, his dog—his supposedly loyal companion—had decided to take a walkabout on the other side of the Baldwin Gym.

And somehow, despite the fact that there was practically no one on this part of campus first thing in the morning, and that the walkway was wide enough to fit a battalion of infantrymen walking abreast, some idiot had managed to bump into him—right where his shoulder blades came together and where all the stress of life always seemed to congregate.

He rolled his shoulders backward—hearing the telltale crackling of incipient arthritis after too many hits on the football field—and slowly turned his neck—yet more crackling—to get a look.

Why wasn't he surprised? He hadn't seen the woman for almost twelve years, and here they'd run into each other—literally this time—twice in two days.

"Listen, I'm sorry I bumped into you like that," she apologized quickly. "The hood of my jacket was pulled so low, and I was staring at my feet just trying to make a beeline to the bike rack. I didn't even see you there. I didn't do any damage, did I?" She looked up.

"It was a low blow, but I think I'll survive," he replied, actually sounding charming—which despite his brother's evaluation of his interpersonal skills, he was capable of being.

He glanced briefly over his shoulder to check that Roxie was still poking around at the far end of the track before turning the full weight of his critical stare on her. He noticed Mimi's lower lip was blue and trembling. "You look freezing. Can I give you my jacket? It's a bit wet." He lifted it by the lapel.

"Don't be ridiculous." She waved him off, looking self-conscious. "It's just lack of body fat—it tends to make me chilly. But enough trips to Hoagie Palace and I'll be generating heat like a furnace."

He had to smile. Smile at her candor, her determination and her vulnerability all at the same time. He remembered his mother's words from earlier this morning to avoid the Lodges.

How could he?

Then he looked over his shoulder nervously again.

"Something out there?" Mimi glanced across the field.

Vic pointed to the far end. "Just trying to keep an eye on Roxie. After my workout, I decided to let her off the leash and stretch her legs. Normally, she sticks pretty close, but this time, I don't know. Maybe she's picked up the smell of deer coming through here." Roxie was wandering by one of the portals to the football stadium now, and Vic was in no mood to go after her. "If I start running after her, she'll just think it's some kind of game and take off."

Mimi stepped to his side. "Do you have any treats? Something to lure her back?"

Vic glanced her way. The rain was easing up, but he noticed that several drops had beaded on the ends of her dark, spiky eyelashes. They were so long, he noticed. So dark against her pale skin. He was momentarily spellbound.

"Treats?" she repeated. "Dog bones? Rawhide chews? Pastrami sandwiches?"

Vic smiled. "Unfortunately, my goodies are at home or at the office. I hadn't counted on her deciding to do a reconnoiter of the back forty." He tried calling out her name, but all that elicited was a gentle wag of the tip of Roxie's fanlike tail.

Vic sighed. "Obviously this would happen when I was in a hurry." He gave Mimi a look of exasperation.

"I don't know if this will help, but I guess it's worth a try." Mimi lifted her hand and, forming a circle with her middle finger and thumb, placed her fingers against her bottom teeth and whistled. It was the siren call to New York taxi drivers everywhere. And Roxie. The dog pricked up her ears, caught sight of Mimi and came running.

Vic stared, truly amazed. "You know, I've always wanted to be able to do that."

Mimi looked sideways. "What can I say? One summer at sailing camp and I learned how to handle a rudder, blow smoke rings and whistle. Oh, and French kiss." She seemed oblivious to Vic's open-mouthed reaction.

Mimi squatted down and let Roxie run into her open arms. Then she pulled back and ran a finger along the indentations of Roxie's furrowed forehead. "Hey, girl, why the concerned face?"

"Don't take Roxie's worrying personally," he responded to her conversation with the dog. "She frets about the state of the world—everything, really. In fact, if you touch her the wrong way, or get too interested in a particular spot on her body—say, when I'm checking for ticks—she's convinced she's going to die."

"Poor Roxie. No one should have to bear so heavy a burden—especially when so much is out of your control anyway."

He watched the wrinkles in Roxie's forehead relax as she lavished kisses on Mimi's face. "It's incredible the way she responds to you."

"It must be the smell of chlorine from all my time in the pool." Mimi let Roxie have her go, and then she gave a final pat and went to stand up.

Immediately, she grabbed the inside of her thigh. "Ooh. I can feel that. I thought I felt a tweak to my hamstring during the workout, but now it's for real. Must be the cold. It should be an interesting bike ride."

"Then let me give you a ride. I can fit the bike in the trunk of the car. It's a wagon, remember? Besides, Roxie will probably run off if she sees you leave without her."

"You could put her on a leash?" Mimi pointed to the plaid lead in his hand.

"She'll whine like crazy, trust me."

Mimi held up her hand, palm up. "Look, it's stopped raining."

"C'mon. You'll only be injuring your hamstring more. It may have stopped raining—" it was true, the sun was winning the battle and peeking out from behind the clouds "—but your body's still chilled."

She frowned. "I thought you said you were in a hurry for some meeting or other?"

"How far out of my way can it be? Grantham's not that big of a place," he argued. "C'mon. Where are you headed?"

"Bean World."

"Geez, Lodge," he exclaimed, using her last name—jock to jock. Somehow that made it easier, more natural. "That's only a few blocks out of my way."

She looked torn.

He frowned. "Listen, if I didn't know better, I'd say your refusal was personal. This makes twice in two days—not that I'm counting."

She rubbed her nose, sniffed, then sniffed again.

"It's not, really." She raised her head to look him in the eye. "I mean, it's personal, but not about you, that is…" She toyed with the strap on her backpack, searching for words.

Vic arched an eyebrow. "If it's not personal about me, are you saying it's personal—meaning *you?*" He pointed.

Roxie, sitting between them, gazed from one human to the other.

"Mimi?" Vic prodded her when she didn't reply.

Mimi shifted her gaze to the wide expanse of sky. "Hey, look. A double rainbow. I can't remember the last time I saw one. Maybe Mongolia when I was getting a demonstration on falcon hunting?"

"Mimi?"

"Or was it Reno?" She acted like she hadn't heard him. "I remember eating at this Italian restaurant—not bad, actually—and coming out and looking across the street at a pawnshop, and overhead were two rainbows."

"Mimi? Look at me."

Mimi eyed him nervously.

"It's not me. It's the car that's got you spooked, isn't it?"

She nodded—barely. "No one ever said you were dumb."

"I don't know—I believe you said as much twelve years ago."

"I said you were misguided, even pigheaded—but

that's definitely not the same thing as dumb—not by a long shot." She paused, the muscles in her neck taut. "You're right. Ever since I was kidnapped in Chechnya—I don't know if you heard about that?"

"It would have been hard not to," he conceded.

Mimi smacked her lips. "Yeah, I guess it got a lot of coverage. Anyway, I was abducted in a car, blindfolded and now I get kind of antsy—more than kind of, actually—about getting into one. I mean, I barely managed to let Press drive me from the Junction, and he's family…whatever that means."

"Look on the bright side. It must save a fortune in taxis in New York," Vic said positively.

The corners of her mouth turned up a little.

"Look, I promise you have nothing to worry about. Roxie will be there the whole time, and, trust me— she'd never let anything happen to you. Talk about loyalty at first sight—which has absolutely nothing to do with chlorine. And if Roxie can't convince you, I'll give you another good reason. My ex-wife—"

"Bringing up your ex-wife is supposed to help me get over my irrational fears?" She was teasing him.

Vic took that as a good sign, that she wasn't quite as tense. "Your fears aren't irrational. They sound pretty reasonable to me, considering what happened. If the same thing had happened to me, I'm sure I'd be holed up in my house, afraid to come out."

"Well, I'm not that far removed from that state." She studied his face with a lopsided smile. "You're a good guy, Vic Golinski, despite what I may have said about you. Okay, what I *did* say about you." She paused. "And I just wanted to let you know, I've never told anyone else about my car phobia."

Vic was touched, like something important had just happened. But he wasn't going to let it go to his head—at least, not in front of her. "So, are you going to let me finish or what?"

She crossed her arms. "Okay, tell me about your ex-wife."

"Granted, Shauna—"

At the mention of her name Roxie started whining.

Mimi looked down. "Is she trying to tell me something?"

Vic laughed softly. "Roxie was not a fan of my ex, and the feeling was mutual."

Mimi lifted her head. "I have a feeling I have nothing to fear, then."

Vic cleared his throat. "Anyway—" he glanced down at Roxie "—she who shall not be mentioned was, as she used to say, 'Committed to Feng Shui.' I don't remember much about it except that she was constantly changing around the furniture in our condo to create better peace and harmony."

"Did it work?" Mimi asked, her head cocked. Arms still crossed, she tapped her fingers on an elbow.

"Right up until the point my contract wasn't renewed. After that, the karma never seemed to align."

"And how is this supposed to give me the courage to get into your car?"

He held up his hand. "Let me just finish. Anyway, according to Sh—" he stopped himself in time "—according to you-know-who, a double rainbow is apparently a sign from the cosmic universe, indicating something wonderful is about to happen. Not only that, one good thing will lead to another—'cause there're two?" He made an arching shape with his index finger. "So, what do you say?"

Roxie was the one to react first. She rose and grabbed the leash dangled from Vic's hand. Then she batted her long lashes at Mimi and wagged her fanlike tail.

"See, how can you say no to that?" Vic looked from his dog to Mimi.

Mimi nodded. "Wow, I wouldn't want to disappoint Roxie. Besides, she can help in what psychiatrists call desensitization—helping me re-experience the scary thing thereby making it less scary. Basically, she just needs to sit close to me—real close."

"Honey, the dog would Velcro herself to you, if you let her."

Mimi laughed.

He took that as a yes. "Shall we?" he offered. "I'm just parked in the lot, one of the first rows. I'll wait while you get the bike."

She hitched up the backpack on her shoulder. "Okay."

He watched her walk gingerly to the bike rack—obviously her leg was hurting her more than she wanted to let on. Then she leaned over to undo the lock and unconsciously shook her head, like a dog drying out its fur after a quick dip in a stream. Vic noticed how the dark brown, almost black strands were sculpted back from her face and had taken on amber highlights. They haloed her pale skin, emphasizing her high cheekbones and long, attenuated nose.

And that's when he experienced one of those unexpected flashback moments. He was young and sitting in the old Polish church in Trenton. He saw the devotional paintings hanging on the walls of the side chapels in their gilt frames and the way the rows of votive candles in the tall metal holders cast a flickering, mysterious light on them. Going to church had never held any special religious significance for him, but the mystery, the exotic nature of the icons in the smoky light, had been fascinating for their magical beauty.

He stared, unable to take his eyes off her. She had that same mystery to her. Not that his reaction was devotional by any stretch of the imagination.

Mimi wheeled the bike next to him. She frowned, then looked around before focusing her lush mahogany-brown eyes back at him. "What?"

"Your hair." He blurted out the first thing—well, the first censored thing that came to him. "It dries quickly."

She ran a hand through the slicked-back strands, messing them. "Yeah, I know. It's serviceable, but that's about it. I just can't deal with the whole stylist-salon scene right now."

"Actually, I was going to say it was sexy."

He'd come a long way from church in Trenton.

CHAPTER FOURTEEN

THAT SAME MORNING, Press lay in his bed, trying to decide if it was worth getting up. He was supposed to get together with Penelope at the Rare Book Library, but that wasn't until after lunch. She had emailed him something about a Reunions show featuring manuscripts that dealt with time and memory.

"I look forward to hearing all about your studies," she had written. "I know you will be excited to see Woodrow Wilson's diaries that he kept while at Grantham University. Then there are some delightful folios from a volume of Diderot's *Encyclopédie* depicting time piece mechanisms. But the manuscript of St. Augustine is truly the piece de résistance. Do you think anyone will appreciate it except you, Amara and me? Only time will tell. That, by the way, was my attempt at a joke."

That was so Penelope. Some people never changed. As opposed to his good buddies—Matt who was a no-show, and Amara who seemed to do nothing but talk about Matt.

It was inevitable that they would grow apart, he supposed, with him being so far away and doing completely different stuff. Maybe he had only himself to blame for being the worst correspondent possible. Besides, it's not as if he had encouraged Amara to keep in touch, either. At Reunions last year, he had been the one to give her the cold shoulder when she practically threw herself at him.

But she had been a kid, just about to graduate from prep school, whereas he was four years older. Two different worlds, two different paths. Anyway, like he was boyfriend material? His idea of commitment was to watch a movie from start to finish. As for relationships? It wasn't his style. True, the hook-ups that were so common at college these days seemed pretty bloodless to him. But the alternative—pledging your trust and loyalty to one person—seemed destined for failure, especially if his family's history was anything to go by.

So, okay, she hadn't appeared to be pining after him. He could live with that. But did she have to latch onto Matt like he was the next Messiah? Hopefully, he and Matt would be able to get together soon before they both took off again, and then he'd find out what was really going on.

Speaking of Matt, Press glanced at his cell phone to see if he had texted him. Nothing, but then it was probably too early. He'd only woken up because he was totally screwed up with the time difference. Maybe if he was lucky, he could roll over and get some more sleep. He'd just get up to close the blinds and block out the sunlight. It was gray outside, but still light enough that it interfered with sleep.

He pushed back the quilt that he'd had since prep school and got up. His bedroom was pretty much untouched from when he was younger—the autographed baseball posters, the ship model and the Grantham University banner with his grandfather's class year tacked up over his dresser. On his desk sat an old computer that looked primeval, and he couldn't imagine what kind of software it ran. Needless to say, his laptop was on the floor by his bed, charging. He stepped over it and reached out for the cord by the window.

And that's when he heard the loud gagging noise. His first thought was Mimi. He forgot all about the window and went running out of his room and down the hall toward her bedroom in nothing but his boxers and the T-shirt he'd slept in. He flung open the door.

The room was empty.

"Mimi?" he called out and walked to the center of the room. The double bed was neatly made, a beige comforter pulled up tautly under a mound of pillows. He pivoted around. The armoire doors were shut, the dresser, covered in a white lace runner had a brush and comb placed just so, a bottle of perfume positioned directly to the side. He continued to survey the room—her suitcase open on the blanket chest, a pair of opened-toed flats lined up to the side.

"Mimi," he said out loud again and craned his neck to look in the bathroom that her room shared with Brigid's farther down the hall. But that was empty, too. Maybe he'd imagined it....

The noise started up again. Press backed out and

listened carefully. It was coming from the side wing of the house.

Confused, he walked gingerly toward his father and Noreen's bedroom around the corner. His fingertips traced along the country French toile wallpaper with farm animals and gamboling farm maidens. He hesitated.

And heard the retching noise again, this time louder.

Press picked up his pace, then stopped at the partially closed bedroom door. He knocked.

There was no answer.

Only another bout of gagging, louder.

He pushed the door wide open and strode into the room. "Hello? Is anyone there?" he asked. *Well, duh? There has to be somebody, but who?*

He crossed the carpeted floor, past the giant canopy bed with miles of gauze and mounds of embroidered pillows, the clothes tossed over delicate chairs, the bottles of lotions and perfumes. "Hello?" he inquired tentatively,

He stopped at the threshold to the en suite bathroom and stuck his head inside. He gasped. "Noreen?"

His stepmother was squatting next to the toilet, her head over the toilet bowl. She weakly lifted one hand and flushed. Then she wiped her mouth with the back of her hand and slowly looked over her shoulder. "Press? How long have you been standing there?"

He shook his head. "Not long, but long enough to see…that you're sick."

She slumped to a sitting position, bracing her back against an enormous claw-foot bathtub, and leaned her head back. She inhaled slowly through her mouth, her eyes shut.

"Is there anything I can do? Should I call Dad?"

She shook her head and opened her eyes, focusing on him. Her skin was pasty and moist. Her hair had half fallen out of her ponytail and a lock was plastered to her cheek. She unzipped her warm-up jacket and slowly stretched out her legs.

"There's no need to call your father. He should just be getting to the office now, and I don't want to bother him. I'll talk to him this evening when he comes home."

"And tell him what? What's wrong?" Press was scared. Noreen normally seemed so healthy, invulnerable.

"Nothing's wrong. Something's right, in fact. I'm pregnant." She blinked and stretched out a wan smile.

"You're what?"

"I'm going to have a baby. *We're* going to have a baby." She breathed more easily now.

"But…but…you're old." Press grabbed on to the doorjamb with one hand. "And Dad is…is…he's practically ready for retirement."

Noreen laughed. "I'm not that old, thank you, and I doubt if your father will ever retire. Oh, he's slowed down like I've asked him to, but he's much too vigorous to ever give it up totally."

Press was trying to wrap his head around the news.

He was going to have another sister—or maybe a brother this time. He actually found the thought appealing—especially the brother part. "Does Dad know?"

"No, you're the first to hear the news. I just got confirmation myself." She raised an arm and pointed to a pregnancy kit opened on the marble-topped vanity. "It's just like last time—getting sick right away, that is."

"But what about your job? Traveling to Congo? You can't exactly do all that if you're pregnant and…and throwing up all the time."

Noreen sighed. "If this pregnancy continues like the last one, I'll be over the nausea in a couple of months. So, of course there'll be adjustments, but there's no reason to think that I won't be able to continue working, even traveling up until a month or so before the baby's due. I'll find out more after I've seen my obstetrician. It's not as if this baby was planned, but a baby is always a blessing."

Press wasn't about to get into a discussion about birth control with his stepmother, but he couldn't help thinking. "You really think he'll be happy?" He couldn't imagine his father looking forward to the patter of small feet around the house. Though he did seem to dote on Brigid as much as his limited contact allowed.

There was the sound of marimbas playing. Noreen and Press looked up. It was Noreen's cell phone on the bathroom vanity.

Press stepped over and got it. "It's my father," he said, passing it to Noreen. "I'll just wait in the other room." Press pointed over his shoulder.

"Thank you." She looked up and smiled. "See, maybe he anticipated the good news? It must be fate."

CHAPTER FIFTEEN

"SEE, YOU DID IT," VIC ANNOUNCED as he pulled into an illegal parking space in front of the liquor store on Whalen Avenue. Bean World was across the street, and already the line was out the door.

Mimi unhooked her seat belt. "You're right. I didn't break out into one cold sweat the whole journey. Though I did have a white-knuckle grip on Roxie's collar." For the duration of the ride, Roxie had dutifully stood up in the backseat and rested her head against Mimi's headrest. Even with her seat belt on, Mimi had been able to twist around and caress the dog's fur.

"And thank you for all my kisses." Mimi gave the dog a kiss on the snout in return. Whenever they'd hit a red light, which in Grantham was about every two seconds—or it seemed like it—Roxie had used her doggie sixth sense and given Mimi quick "buck-up" licks on her cheek.

Now that they'd arrived, though, the kisses had come to an end. Mimi already missed them. She held on to the door handle, ready to get out, and hesitated for an awkward moment wondering whether she should lean over and give Vic a thank-you peck on the cheek. But she decided he might think that was just too forward. Besides, it didn't look like he was making any similar move, so she let it pass.

"Listen, thanks for the lift. I can't tell you how much it meant to me—really," she said. She gave him a quick nod of sincerity.

That didn't seem to allay the awkwardness at all. If anything, she only felt more nervous. Time to get out and get Lilah's advice—that was for sure. "So, if you could wait a sec, I'll just get my bike out of the trunk." She pressed down the handle and scooted out quickly, grabbing her backpack as she went.

"Here, I'll help you." He put the emergency flashers on and after carefully looking in the rearview mirror and then over his shoulder, opened his car door. He circled around and lifted the lid of the truck, then hauled out the bike with minimal effort. He set it down on the ground with the handlebars facing Mimi and looked at her. "I don't think you should downplay what you just did. I'm sure it wasn't easy. And I was happy to help. Really. Roxie, too."

"I think Roxie must be my good luck charm." She bent forward through the open trunk lid and ruffled the dog's snout. Then she straightened up, adjusted the knapsack and gave Vic a sideways glance. "And you were a big help, too."

"You're going to be all right with your leg? Getting home?"

She touched her thigh. "I'll just take it easy. It's just a strain. I can always walk from here." She grabbed the handlebars, debated saying more, decided not to, and was about to push off when... *Oh, why not?* "Listen, as thanks, why don't I take you out to dinner tonight?"

Vic waved off the suggestion. "That's not necessary. I always give lifts to good-looking women—even ones who have humiliated me in public."

"C'mon, that was over twelve years ago." She made a face. "You're going to make this hard, aren't you?"

"Frankly, I never thought that one day I'd be able to give you a ride without freaking out, too. It must be all Roxie's influence—on me."

Mimi smiled and shook her head. "Well, now that we've agreed that she's a powerful mitigating force, bring her along, too."

Vic crossed his arms and narrowed his eyes.

"Are you going to make me beg?" Mimi asked. Exasperation showed in her voice.

He shook his head. "No, as tempting as that might be."

"And here I thought you were such a nice guy."

He held up his hand. "Oh, but I am. I just said tempted. Anyway, I accept—with pleasure."

Mimi felt a pressing need to swallow. "I tell you what, why don't you stop by when you're done with work, and we'll take it from there."

"It could be close to seven. I've got a pretty full day, plus the commute."

"Don't worry. We'll dine fashionably late. You know the address?"

"I know it." He reached up and closed the trunk lid. "What can I bring?"

"Nothing. Just Roxie."

Vic laughed. "Why do I get the feeling that she might be the main attraction?" He didn't wait for her to reply, but walked back to the driver's side, looked around and got in.

Mimi moved to the sidewalk and waited for him to leave. And as he passed her, he gave a brief wave. Mimi held up her hand but didn't move it, watching as Roxie jumped into the trunk. Her large head grew smaller as the car drove off past the library before making a right turn at the light.

She stared until they were out of sight. And that's when she realized—Roxie might be her talisman, but Vic Golinski was...was... She dropped her hand and turned to cross the street.

Only then did she notice her friend Lilah waiting on the bench in front of Bean World, rocking a stroller back and forth. Her head was bent, there was a smile on her face and her lips were moving. She appeared to be deep in conversation with the baby. Mimi wondered how long she'd been sitting there, how much she'd seen. She called out.

Lilah looked up and waved enthusiastically. She angled around the stroller, bent down to get the baby's attention, then pointed in Mimi's direction.

Mimi crossed the street, wheeling the bike next to her. She had known all along that Lilah would make a great mom. With her thick hair pulled back in a

haphazard ponytail, her rumpled T-shirt and paint-
er's pants and Birkenstock sandals, she glowed with
the freshness of down-to-earth motherhood. She
might not have the whole situation under control, but
she would always come through with love and the
requisite touch of humor.

Mimi bumped the bike up the curb and leaned it
against her hip so she could embrace Lilah in a great
hug.

Lilah caught the embrace awkwardly around her
shoulders. "Wow. A public display of affection!
What's happened to the no-touch Mimi I've grown
to know and love?" She joked, though there was a
decided element of truth to her words.

Mimi released her friend and bent over to make a
kissy face at the baby. "I guess it's the sight of a re-
splendent Madonna and child that has me moving
out of my normal comfort zone. Hey, Sam. Who's
the cutest ever?" The baby had only wisps of pale
blond hair and a rash on his chin, but he was cute in
that imperfect, adorable doughboy way. In fact, the
imperfections only made him cuter.

Mimi picked up one of Sam's tiny hands and let
the delicate fingers curl around her index finger. "My
God, feel that grip. The kid is going to be so strong."
Mimi rubbed her cheek against Sam's velvety-soft
cheek. "So strong that you're going to be able to push
your Aunt Mimi's wheelchair around for her in her
old age."

Mimi glanced up at Lilah who was standing agog.

"What? You've got this look? Haven't you ever had people go goo-goo-ga-ga over your baby?"

"Yes, of course. Because I do have the most wonderful baby ever. But it's more than that. You seem more your old self again—more confident, more self-centered."

"Somehow that doesn't sound like a compliment." Mimi looked up from her crouching position.

"Oh, it is, it is. And don't get all uptight. I'm not going to make you tell me about your whole ordeal and the emotional turmoil afterward. I know from previous conversations and your—shall we say—blunt instructions, that the whole topic is off-limits."

"Good, so why don't we talk about something that is definitely *on*-limits. Mr. Wonderful here." Mimi squished up her nose for the baby, who giggled in return.

"I don't know. At two in the morning when he's inconsolable and wide awake, sometimes I don't find him Mr. Wonderful," Lilah lamented. "And you mentioned his strong hands? Ha, his nails are the things that are really deadly. Razor-sharp, all the better to scratch my boob with while he's nursing. You wouldn't think anything could be so painful."

"Naughty boy." Mimi pretended to wrestle with Sam, trying to pull her finger out of his death grip but letting him wag it back and forth all the same.

Sam was so proud of himself he erupted in a bout of hiccupping laughter.

Mimi patted one of Sam's chubby legs clad in a

stretchy green outfit and stood up straight. "Ooh, that hamstring is still a little tight." She pressed her hand to her inner thigh. Then she locked the bike to the bench and held out her hand. "Shall we go in? I can take the front of the stroller and you the back. Then when we're inside, I can give you, little man, your extra-special present from your favorite aunt Mimi." How strange that she had automatically adopted a familial relationship with Sam, even though she eschewed her own family.

"Good idea." Lilah waited for Mimi to circle in front and start up the short stairs to the entrance of the coffee shop. "I thought I saw you get out of a car when you arrived, but I didn't recognize the person driving," she asked innocently—a little too innocently.

Mimi shouldered open the heavy glass door and held it with her back until Lilah and the stroller were safely inside. "I was wondering how long it would take you to ask. It was Vic Golinski. From our class," she answered casually. She went and stood at the end of the line. "Why don't you look for a table and I'll get the order? What'll you have?"

"No way I'm walking away from that bomb. Did you just say Vic Golinski?"

Mimi peered into the glass display case. "Gee, those shortbread cookies look good. I can't remember the last time I ate something like that. It must be the workout this morning. Made me extra hungry. Can I get you one, too? That and a double shot latte?"

"Let's share. I'm still trying to take off baby

weight—hence the sacklike pants." She pointed to the overalls. "And a decaf latte—I'm nursing and I'd rather Sam didn't stay up all night with a caffeine high. But enough about the order." Lilah pushed the stroller up next to her despite the lack of room. "You were with Vic Golinski? The ex-football player?"

Mimi shrugged like it was no big deal. "We happened to run into each other when I got out of my swim at the pool, and he offered to give me a lift. No biggie."

"No biggie!" Lilah shrieked.

Sam looked up at her with a tight prunish face.

Mimi looked down. "Oh, see, you're scaring the baby. Don't worry, Sam, your doting auntie will soothe your troubled brow."

Lilah grabbed a ring of plastic keys from the webbed pocket of the stroller and jiggled them in front of her son.

Sam stuck out a starfish hand and grabbed the ring, stuffing one of the toy keys in his mouth and gumming it ferociously.

"Plastic keys can replace a doting auntie any day," Lilah cracked. Then *she* frowned. "But I remember you and Vic being like oil and water. Didn't you get him thrown into jail before graduation?"

"That story is so blown out of proportion. The police merely took him to the station, where they let him go. Besides, we're adults now. We're perfectly capable of carrying on a polite conversation despite our past differences."

Lilah raised a skeptical eyebrow. "Mimi, I know you may find this hard to believe, but I've never been naive." She inched forward in the line, pushing the stroller to part the waves of coffee drinkers. Then her phone started to ring. "Rats. Just when this conversation was getting interesting." Lilah checked the screen. "Let me just get this. It's Noreen. We're supposed to get together later this morning to discuss a new proposal to the Gates Foundation."

Mimi tried not to listen to Lilah's conversation and instead rocked the stroller back and forth to amuse Sam. It seemed to work, because he started drooling with a very happy expression on his face. Deep in the recesses of her memory, she recalled doing the same thing for Press when he was a baby. She remembered taking him for a walk around the neighborhood with the nanny—God, it had been a young Noreen!—and that he'd been more interested in leaning over to look at the stroller wheels go round and round instead of listening to the birds or watching the cars go by.

Lilah hung up and frowned. "Well, that was odd. Is something going on with your family that you're not telling me about?"

"Not that I know of. But then it's not like I ever could tell you what goes on under that roof. I can tell you all about Brigid's ballet classes and swim lessons—she loves to talk and talk on the phone about that stuff—but beyond that…" Mimi shrugged.

Lilah retook possession of the stroller and moved it along. There were only a few people from the front of the line. "Noreen says something's come up because she has to go into New York today. Something about your father and work—she wasn't exactly clear."

Mimi shook her head. "Like I said. I'm probably the last person to know what's going on. Probably my father needs his hand held at the tailor's."

"Good. That this gives me more time to get some juicy gossip. I mean, I'm just a boring new mom trying to run a nonprofit in Africa on no sleep. I can't even stay awake long enough at night to watch reruns of *The Big Bang Theory*. Please tell me there's something amazingly rapturous going on between you and Vic Golinski."

"Rapturous?" Mimi raised her eyebrows.

"Oh, you know what I mean. Vic Golinski." Lilah gazed off into space, then shook her head. "I was always too afraid to talk to him in college, frankly. He was so serious, even stern. He can't possibly put up with your usual snide remarks, can he? Let alone forget about the past contretemps, shall we say? And you can't possibly abide all that stick-in-the-mud demeanor. Geez, he made Mr. Rochester in *Jane Eyre* look like a party animal."

"Where do you get off using words like *rapturous* and *contretemps?* Anyway, you don't think he's man enough to let bygones be bygones?"

"I don't know him, but I do know you. The Mimi Lodge I know can't let bygones be bygones. What's going on with you two?"

"Your order?" the barista asked. A young woman

in her twenties, her hair was shaved into a Mohawk, with the center stripe a vivid green—which somehow or other worked with the tattoo of Bambi on her upper arm.

Mimi rattled off instructions and elbowed Lilah aside when her friend reached for her wallet. "It's my treat."

Before Lilah could protest Sam threw the keys. They landed on the small counter with the take-out lids, stirrers, sugars and shakers of cinnamon.

"Hey, great aim, Sam. Your grandfather would have been proud," Mimi congratulated him. Lilah's father had been a star baseball player in college and had even insisted on playing in a softball game at Reunions two years ago.

Lilah sighed wistfully. "Yeah, Dad probably would have outfitted him with a glove by now." She retrieved the keys and did a quick straightening of the counter.

Mimi pocketed her change and moved to the pickup area. "Which reminds me—first things first, Sam's present."

"Fine, but just remember, I'm your best friend. If you don't confide in me, who are you going to confide in?"

Out of the corner of her eye, Mimi saw some people get up from a front table. "Quick, cut off that student on crutches for the table by the window. A baby stroller trumps a leg injury any day."

"I'm prepared to head block an old lady *if* you agree to talk to me—dish the dirt. God knows, you made me tell all about Justin two years ago." She pushed the stroller like a steamroller to the small round table in the front.

When the order was ready, Mimi joined Lilah, taking in a bentwood seat opposite her.

Lilah unstrapped the baby and lifted him to her seat. He immediately started banging the table with his fists. "Keep that hot cup on your side and dish," she said to Mimi.

Mimi did as she was told, then ducked her head into the backpack and pulled out an oversize envelope. "Here."

Lilah took it. "What's this?"

"Open it and you'll find out."

Lilah undid the fastener at the back and slipped out some paper. She glanced at the cover letter, then flipped to the attached document. "What the…"

"It's four shares in the Trenton Lightning—that's the Triple-A baseball team in Trenton."

Lilah looked up. There were tears in her eyes.

"I figured that since Sam is named after your father, he would have liked it."

"I'm going to cry." Lilah sniffed loudly. "Quick, give me one of those paper napkins." She blew her nose. "You know, there are times you outdo yourself, Mimi Lodge."

"C'mon. It's no big deal."

"Yes, it is. It's wonderful and it's remarkably sensitive. But don't worry—I won't divulge your sentimental side."

"Good. Because I'd never hear the end of it." Mimi took the cups off the tray and passed Sam one of the little spoons. He immediately put it in his mouth. "Now, me and Vic," Mimi went on. "It's like this." She explained about running into him twice, how he was funny and charming and devoted to his dog. And how he'd managed to get her to ride in a car even though she was scared silly after the kidnapping.

Lilah sipped her drink. "So you're telling me…"

"That he's mellowed. No, more like aged well."

Lilah nodded. "Why is it that men only seem to grow up and get interesting when they're older?"

"Hold on a minute. You can't tell me that back in college—even though you were engaged to someone else—you didn't find Justin attractive?"

"Sure I did. Any woman with a pulse practically went gaga. But that's different."

Mimi frowned. "How's that?"

"That was a crush. What we have now is potentially the beginning of love."

"So you're saying that what's between Vic and me is love? I don't buy that." Mimi shook her head.

"What I'm saying is that it's worth considering." She let the statement hang in the air until she asked, "So, have you made any plans to meet him again? I mean, you *are* seeing him again, right? Even you can't be idiotic enough to let whatever it is just pass."

"No, I'm not completely hopeless." At least Mimi prayed that was the case. "I wanted to thank him… and kind of apologize for what happened all those years ago. So—" she leaned forward "—this is where I really need help. You see, I offered him dinner."

Lilah whipped her cell phone out of the front pocket of her overalls. "For this we need the big guns. My sister-in-law."

"Penelope? I thought she was a curator of Rare Books?"

"She is. But she's also a goddess of the Italian kitchen."

Mimi felt her own phone vibrate in her jeans' pocket. She slipped it out and saw the text message. "What do you know? Noreen." She turned the screen to Lilah. "It seems she needs to reschedule our dinner. She has to go into New York to meet my dad. He must really be throwing a hissy fit. I'll get back to her later." Mimi went to rest the phone on the table, but thought otherwise when she saw Sam's eyes light up. "You boys and your gadgets. Anyway, to get back to the subject of dinner—do you think Penelope could do Polish?"

CHAPTER SIXTEEN

JOE STUCK HIS HEAD in Vic's office doorway. "So, look what the cat finally dragged in. No offence."

"None taken." Vic shuffled through the pink message slips on his desk, and when he saw nothing that required an urgent response—or at least any more urgent than the usual—he placed them on his blotter and looked up.

"I was referring to Roxie." Joe glanced down at the dog curled up on her orthopedic foam bed.

"I was, too." Vic tapped the edge of his desk. "So I gather from the messages—" he pointed at the pile on the desk "—that our rep from the West Coast is late—fog at Newark with storms in the Midwest backing up the flights?"

"Yeah, lucky for you. Waltzing in—" Joe glanced at his gold Rolex, a ridiculous affectation, never mind the expense in Vic's opinion "—what, forty-five minutes late. That's not like you, Mr. Someone's-Got-To-Keep-the-Family-Business-Going Golinski. If I didn't know better, I'd say you had a big night last night. But then, I do know better. You probably were engrossed with something on the History Channel about King Tut's tomb." Joe smiled warmly.

"No, a minimarathon of old *Law and Order* episodes," Vic corrected. He noticed Joe's loosened tie. "And what time did you get in?"

Joe slumped into the couch. "About ten minutes ago. And let me tell you, I was up late last night, too, and it wasn't due to some TV marathon. More personal, if you get my drift."

Vic sat stone-faced. His brother liked to think of himself as the playboy of the Western World, or at least of central New Jersey. But Vic was pretty sure that it was more bluster than anything. Still, he didn't want to deflate his brother's fragile ego. His role was to be the responsible, grumpy older brother, looking disdainfully down at his ne'er-do-well brother. And in point of fact, that's what he was.

But sometimes... Like this morning, in the rain, in the sunlight afterward... The double rainbow... Even if you didn't believe in signs—and he didn't—it was an unexpected backdrop to a magical moment....

"Earth to Vic. Earth to Vic." Joe snapped his fingers.

Vic shook his head. "Sorry. My mind was wandering for a moment." He rested his elbows on the desk. "Now, do you really want me to ask for the gory details of your latest conquest, or can we get down to business?"

"Yeah, yeah, we'll get to all that." Joe studied him. "But first I want to know what's up. You're acting kind of bizarre this morning."

Vic cleared his throat. "I was thinking of Mimi

Lodge. I ran into her after my morning workout. Actually, she ran into me, if you must know." He scratched an eyebrow.

"Just like that?"

"Yes, just like that. These things happen, especially in a small town." He sat up straighter—any straighter and he'd need a chiropractor to unlock his spine.

Joe grinned but had the good sense not to push any further. "Well, all I can say is, keep up the good work. This project with Pilgrim could push our sales into a banner year, and in this economy, that's worth a lot." Then he rubbed his chin. "Still, you wonder—why the father tied the deal to you romancing her. Is there something wrong with her? She always looked pretty hot on camera, but then, you never know what a person is like in real life."

"Conrad Lodge did not ask me to 'romance' anyone—just to serve on a Reunions panel with his daughter. It was a perfectly reasonable quid pro quo—more than reasonable from the company's point of view, wouldn't you say? And frankly, I don't think it would even occur to him that a Lodge—any Lodge—would be interested in a Golinski."

"I see what you're saying." Joe rose from the couch and walked to the open door. Then stopped. "Still, if you need reinforcements, you know who to call. Me."

Vic picked up the pink slips again, looking for something to do with his hands. "Thank you for the offer, but I believe I can handle the situation. She's invited me to dinner." He looked up.

Joe smiled widely. "I knew it. So what do you intend to bring?"

"Bring?"

"To dinner, of course. Personally, I like to take some rich chocolate dessert. All women love chocolate, and if you bring along the whipped cream, too, you never know…"

Vic frowned. "I think a bottle of wine is a more prudent choice."

Joe tapped on the doorjamb. "To each his own. In any case, let me know if you hear anything about the deal with her father's firm. Things were moving quickly for a while, and now they've gone silent."

"That's not really unusual. There's a lot of complicated financing involved."

"I know, but still, I'm nervous. You haven't heard anything from the father, then…since the initial call?"

Vic scoffed. "Let me be the nervous member of the family. I'm good at that."

"Just don't blow it with the daughter, whatever you do," Joe warned him. "After all, aren't you always saying that a CEO has to pitch in wherever necessary?"

"I never thought I would say this. But there are times I wish you wouldn't listen to me," Vic muttered.

CHAPTER SEVENTEEN

PRESS GRABBED A SMALL table along the wall of the Circus Diner. The brown laminate surface had two paper placemats. Silverware was bundled up in a paper napkin on the left side of each mat.

A breakfast joint that offered bacon and eggs and waffles and all the usual morning fare at all time of the day and night, the Circus was another Grantham establishment—not so much for the university student crowd but for the townies. The Volunteer Fire Brigade always gathered there for breakfast on Tuesdays and Thursdays. Several local lawyers had their standing orders of two eggs scrambled with hash browns as they glanced over their briefs before heading into the office. And a core group of retirees gathered for oatmeal and stewed prunes and talked about property taxes and parking problems.

Nobody ever seemed to comment on the yellowing posters of Ringling Brothers Barnum and Bailey, or the cracked clown masks affixed to the paneled walls. The Circus would never be cool and have Cirque du Soleil paraphernalia or Big Apple programs. It was hopelessly dated—just the way everyone wanted.

Press pulled out his phone and glanced at the

time. Eleven-thirty. Matt had finally contacted him that morning, after that whole surprising thing with Noreen. Press still couldn't believe it. He wondered what Mimi would think, but she hadn't shown up before he had to leave for town.

Anyhow, after failing to show last night, Matt had suggested they get together for breakfast-lunch at the Circus. Amara wouldn't be able to make it because she had this babysitting thing for Lilah Evans.

Maybe it was better that it was just the two of them anyway, Press thought. That way he'd have a better chance of finding out what exactly was going on between Matt and Amara. Maybe he'd even ask him about getting a new baby brother or sister when you were old enough to have a baby yourself. Matt's dad and stepmom, Katarina, had had a baby boy when Matt was in college, after all.

"Coffee?"

Press looked up. A girl about his age, her blond hair pulled back in a loose braid, her face devoid of any makeup except for what looked like Vaseline on her lips, held up a glass coffee beaker.

"Coffee?" she repeated again.

"Sure," said Press. He watched as she hustled over to a nearby waitress station and filled a heavy white ceramic mug. Then she returned to the table with the mug and a small saucer with little packets of cream.

"Sugar and Sweet 'N Low are on the table. Menu?" She slipped a laminated menu out from under her arm.

Press took it. "I'm waiting for another person, but I'll look it over in the meantime."

"Sure, no problem. You can order whenever. The kitchen's kinda backed up right now anyway. The Rescue Squad is having their monthly meeting— they're always big on pancakes and fried eggs *and* hash browns *and* bacon. At least if someone goes into cardiac arrest, the others should know what to do."

Press laughed and watched as she sashayed her way to the large group in the center of the cavernous room. A bunch of them sported zip jackets with the same logo. The EMT guys, he figured.

Then he wondered why he'd never seen the waitress before, especially because she looked about his age. Not that he was a regular patron at the Circus. Come to think of it, he'd been there maybe all of two times. He definitely remembered once—when he was nine and the Grantham Youth Soccer League had held its end-of-season pancake celebration for the winning team. Press had always been on the winning team. That's what Lodges were supposed to do.

He picked up the mug and swallowed a mouthful of tepid, bitter coffee. Bean World it wasn't, but Press figured after four free refills, he'd have the caffeine equivalent for a third of the price. For someone on a budget, he'd learned to develop budget tastes. Basically, he'd become a vegetarian—not for philosophical reasons but because meat was so expensive.

Then he saw a familiar face pull open the door and trip over the rubber threshold. Yup, that was Matt.

"Hey there. You been waiting long?" Matt slid into the chair opposite him.

"Long enough," Press replied.

"Ouch, someone's grouchy this morning," Matt said.

Press glanced at his friend. Matt never seemed to change—tall, gangly, brown hair sticking out over one ear. Well, not quite. "You working out?" he asked.

Matt lifted his right arm and made a muscle. "Yeah, I started lifting weights this year—but I'm still pretty pathetic."

"You got that right. Though don't tell me you can actually grow a beard now?" He pointed to the scraggy shadow on Matt's cheeks.

Matt laughed silently, bobbing slightly in the chair. "Yeah, hope springs eternal, I guess. Now that graduation is over and I don't have to look beautiful for photos, I thought I'd give it a go. The mustache doesn't want to cooperate, though." He ran his index finger along his upper lip.

Press took another sip of coffee. It was really the pits, but the caffeine seemed to be doing the job. "What about Amara? She like it?" he asked casually.

"Amara? I'm not really sure." Matt appeared oblivious to the underlying inquiry.

"You guys hanging out a lot, then?" Press kept at it.

Matt straightened the container of jelly packets on the side of the table. "On and off. Too bad she's tied up today with babysitting and some kind of orientation for working at Reunions. It would have been great for the three of us to get together like old times. Though I guess we've still got the rest of the weekend."

Press gripped the edge of the plastic folder that held his menu. "You sure that's what Amara wants?"

"Why not? I mean—" Matt interrupted his reply when he saw the waitress approach the table.

She handed over a menu. "Can I get you coffee, too?"

"No, just milk.'

Press dropped his head and shook it. "No wonder you can't grow a mustache," he said.

Matt made a face. "Don't listen to him," he said to the waitress, and then he held up his hand. "Hey, didn't you go to Grantham High School? You look kind of familiar."

She rested her hand on her hip. "We live in town now, but back in high school we were still in Hamilton, so I went to school there."

"Hmm, maybe it's just seeing you on the street, then. I'm Matt by the way. And this is Press. We both grew up here."

"I'm Basia," she answered with a smile.

"Cool. Is that Russian? I always wanted to learn Russian," Matt said eagerly.

Press rolled his eyes. Matt was so pathetic.

"No, Polish. It's the nickname for Barbara, which always sounded like some old woman's name to me."

Matt laughed. "I definitely like Basia a lot better, too."

She smiled shyly, sinking her neck into her shoulders. "Thanks. I'll just get your milk, then, and when I come back you can give me your orders." She smiled again and went off.

"She's kind of cute, don't you think?" Matt watched her from behind.

Press raised an eyebrow. "Don't you think you've got enough on your plate?"

"What? You mean, with going away soon with the Peace Corps?"

And somehow the conversation got steered away onto other topics, like having to get all these shots for rural Sierra Leone, where Matt would be based. Or how his graduation went and what was going on with his family. And Matt's asking him all about Australia and trying to figure out if maybe Press could come visit him before he came back to the States when he finished his master's degree.

It was all well and good—more than good, Press realized. It was the kind of easy talk that he'd been lacking for almost a year. "You know, I hate to say this, but I actually missed you," he admitted. He pushed back his chair. "And, God, I feel sick now. I ate so much." They'd both ordered double French toast, and Press's stomach was pushing against the waistband of his khaki shorts.

"Talk about a wimp." Matt rose and stumbled around the leg of his chair. "It's good seeing you, too," he said as they walked to the cash register to pay. "I mean, I've got friends from college and everything, but there's something different about talking to somebody who knows you from way back when."

"If you're not careful, you'll start sounding like all those loyal alums who come back every year to their reunions and reminisce about the good old days."

"Well, Yale class reunions are only every five years, so maybe I'll grow out of all that."

"I sure hope so—otherwise this friendship is history." He leaned over the counter. "Could we get the check?" he asked Basia.

She was bent over, studying something spread out on the counter. She was tapping with her foot and moving her finger along as she read.

Matt arched his neck to see over the ledge. "Hey, is that a musical score?"

She looked up. "Oh, sorry. Sometimes I get distracted. Let me get your check." She flipped through the pages of her order pad and found theirs.

"So you're studying music?" Matt asked.

"Performance. Violin, actually. At Rutgers. But I'm also doing a degree in accounting. I mean, I'd love to be a professional musician, but what are the odds? So, I have something to fall back on, which is kind of necessary for someone like me."

Press assumed she meant someone who didn't have parents who'd support her once she was out of school.

Matt was off on a completely different subject. "Wow, what a coincidence. I played violin in the high school orchestra, and for one year in the Yale orchestra. When I stopped my sophomore year, my parents practically had a fit."

"I can't imagine stopping. To me, playing is essential—kind of like oxygen and strawberry blend-ins from Burt's."

"Aren't they the greatest?" Matt asked.

Press crossed his arms and just stood aside, a silent spectator.

"I understand what you mean about music," Matt went on. "I still love it, but I guess other things kind of took over. You know, I still haven't gotten the nerve to tell my old violin teacher. She was this amazing musician—went to Juilliard, got a Ph.D. and everything. She's crazy and was really tough, but she was fantastic."

"You don't mean Tina Chang, do you? She's my teacher—I mean, I still study with her." Basia held out the check.

Press took it unnoticed.

Matt started doing his quick hopping thing. "Wow, talk about a small world. You know, maybe that's why you look familiar. We must have crossed paths coming and going at her place. Did you have lessons on the weekend? Evenings?"

"Saturday, late afternoon."

Matt bobbed his head.

Press reached for his wallet and pulled out a twenty-dollar bill. It was time to get the show on the road. He supported his friend, he really did, and this Basia kid looked pretty and clearly was talented and all.

But how come Matt, with his lame conversation and dorky ways, was able to attract two cute girls, huh?

Do I have bad breath? Dandruff? Body odor? Am I just that unappealing to women? No, certain women, he modified. *Amara...* Not that he was interested in her. After all, in less than a week, he'd head back to Australia.

"Are you planning on coming to any of the Reunions activities?" he heard Matt ask. "Press, here, usually gets me in. I'm sure he can get you in, too, if you want."

For the first time in the conversation, Basia seemed to notice him standing there, too. "Oh, thanks," she said, taking the check and the money. She rang up the bill on the cash register. "I know my brother's on some panel on Saturday, so I suppose I'll try to go to that. He's a Grantham grad. I'll have to change my schedule around, though, which might not be that easy."

"Oh, you got to. What's he talking about? The energy crisis? Diplomatic relations with China?"

"No, actually it's some college sports thing, something about equal rights."

Press turned back. Something struck a cord. "Hey, your brother? He wouldn't be—"

"Vic Golinski." She handed Press the change.

"No. keep it." Press shook his head. "My sister's talking on the same panel—Mimi Lodge."

"Oh, my God. She's the one who…"

Press nodded knowingly. "Yeah, I see the story's famous in your family, too."

"What? What's so famous?" Matt asked.

Press turned to him. "It was before you moved to Grantham. I was maybe ten or eleven."

"Yeah, I was twelve, I think. I still remember this huge fiasco. If you've got a minute?" Basia asked.

Matt nodded.

She closed her score with a grand thump. The swoosh of air sent a photo flying out that had been tucked inside the cover.

Matt reached in the air to rescue it before it tumbled over the ledge. Naturally, being Matt, he made several futile attempts, which left Press to deftly catch it on the downswing. He passed over the three-by-five snapshot. "Hey, cute kid. Your nephew?" Press looked at the photo, tilted it so Matt could see, then handed back the photo.

"Actually, my son, Tommy." Basia admitted with a proud smile.

"You know, on second thought, I think I better get going," Matt announced.

And before Press could get him to pay his share of the bill, his good buddy was out the door and gone.

CHAPTER EIGHTEEN

THE WARM BREEZE BATHED her skin like a dry lotion. The buzzing of cicadas filled the air. And the newly mown lawn smelled with an "Our Town"-like sweetness. All was right in the world, especially judging from the sound of chomping.

"I'm so glad those dog treats were a big hit. The bag said it was wholesome chicken, whatever that means. So I figured I couldn't go wrong...even if it isn't strictly picnic fare." Mimi knew she was rambling, but she couldn't help it.

Vic lay sprawled on his side, propped up on his elbow, a glass of red wine in his hand. He was watching his dog seriously chewing away at one of Mimi's treats. "I think Roxie believes that chicken jerky is appropriate for any dining occasion," he answered, looking very content himself. "And you know, at this very moment, in this particular setting—" he spread his arm wide, wineglass in hand "—with this particular company, I might add—" he nodded at Mimi, who nodded back "—even I wouldn't turn down chicken jerky."

What more could she ask for?

Mimi had absconded with one of Noreen's ultrachic, ultra-expensive wicker picnic baskets. The kind that contained real silverware, cut crystal wineglasses and bone china, a monster candelabra and a wool tartan blanket no doubt handwoven by faithful serfs at some laird's castle.

After Lilah's phone call, Penelope had rushed to the rescue with some *arancine,* stuffed rice balls, that she just happened to have whipped up—as well as prosciutto from her local purveyor. Mimi didn't even know what a purveyor was. Oh, and would she ever forget Penelope's stuffed figs?

"They're the soul of simplicity but the epitome of sensuality—Dionysian, one might even say," Penelope had declared, using a classical illusion that seemed perfectly normal to her, albeit semi-unfathomable to the rest of the world.

Now, after stuffing herself silly—quite possibly in a Dionysian manner—Mimi sighed. She flopped on her back, her arms spread out to her sides. "God, I can't remember the last time I was here. Maybe in third grade when we studied New Jersey history."

She'd chosen the Grantham Battlefield Park on the western edge of town. The rolling lawn was bordered by thick copses of trees. An old farmhouse overlooked the site of a decisive victory for Washington and his troops during the Revolutionary War.

The sun was just setting, the streaks of pink low in the skyline. Now the glow of the candles became more prominent. So the wax *was* dripping on the blanket.

Mimi didn't care. Instead she gazed at the flickering light of fireflies dancing in the silky dusk.

"You know, whenever I see fireflies, I always think of being a kid in Grantham in the summer. A time of innocence," she declared. She glanced over and saw that one of the flying insects had landed on Roxie's nose.

The dog twitched and shook her head. The lightning bug took off and circled above, pulsing flashes of light. The dog stopped chewing long enough to watch its swirling path.

"See, even Roxie's entranced," Mimi noted.

"Nah, she's just wondering if she can eat it," Vic said.

Mimi turned her head his way. "And here I had declared you to be a romantic. How wrong could I be?"

"I'm merely a good judge of my dog. Besides, who said my romantic impulses weren't fully functioning?" Vic sat up, grabbed the bottle of red—he'd brought wine in the end, after all—and poured more into her glass. Then he set the bottle back on the sterling silver coaster and sidled up the blanket. He lay on his side closer to her.

Mimi was highly conscious of his presence…his warmth, his smell, his maleness. She gulped. If she were nervous before, she was doubly nervous now. But she wasn't going to run and hide like she'd been doing for so many months. Something inside her wouldn't allow it. He wouldn't allow it, she knew.

He sipped his wine. "The food was great, you know."

"I can't take any real credit for it. When I decided that a picnic was probably the best way to go—because, naturally, I wanted to include Roxie—"

"Naturally." He smiled.

At the sound of her name, Roxie stopped chewing on her chicken jerky and looked up. Vic rubbed her side with the soul of his shoe, and contented, she went back to concentrating on her treat.

"Anyway, I enlisted the help of my old college friend Lilah Evans? You remember her?"

Vic narrowed his eyes. "Our class at Grantham?"

Mimi nodded.

"To tell you the truth, not really. But I have heard about her organization that helps women in Africa. From your story on television, to be exact."

Mimi rubbed her ear somewhat self-consciously, thinking about him watching her when she didn't know it. "Yeah, Congo. Anyway, her sister-in-law, who's this total fruitcake in my opinion—nice but a fruitcake—is Penelope Bigelow."

"Now *her* I remember. A few classes ahead of us. Valedictorian. Bookworm. Thick glasses."

"No more glasses—laser surgery, gorgeous in this tumbling-hair-Mia-Farrow kind of way. But she *is* still a geek. Anyway, she also happens to be this amazing Italian cook—the type that makes her own sausages."

"That type exists?"

"Apparently. Anyway, she also always seems to have enough food on hand to feed an army of people."

"Or at least enough for a picnic for two," Vic put in.

"Exactly. So, after bringing over all this stuff to the house, she then gave me strict instructions about what kind of bread I was supposed to buy and where. Like she didn't trust me to not buy sliced white bread." Mimi held up her hand in disgust.

"But sliced white bread makes the best peanut butter and jelly sandwiches," Vic announced.

Mimi opened her eyes wide. "Doesn't it? And do you remember that Fluffer Nutter stuff? The fake sticky whipped cream?"

"The best, especially straight out of the jar."

"With your finger, not a knife?" Mimi leaned forward. "Do you know my current stepmother, Noreen—who in many ways is an outstanding person despite the fact that she's married to my father—doesn't let her daughter Brigid eat anything that isn't totally healthy? I had to sneak some into the house the last time so Brigid could get the full experience," she confided.

"Glad to see you're still a troublemaker," he joked.

"Does a leopard change its spots?" She lifted her head to drink some more wine, then rested back on her elbows. She gazed at the darkening sky and tried to pick out the three stars of the only constellation she knew.

"You know, I got to admit, of all the food tonight,

my favorite was the meatballs. They remind me of the Polish meatballs my mom makes."

"They were the only things I made. They're called *kurzunush*. It was my mother's recipe." She pointed into the sky. "There. I found it. Orion."

Vic slid on his back even closer to her. "Yup, and there's Cassiopeia." He pointed overhead and to the right.

"Where? I don't see it."

He took her hand in his and guided it to the spot. "There. Do you see the W?" He moved her hand from point to point.

"Yeah, that's amazing." Mimi wasn't sure she was talking about the stars or the feel of his fingers on hers.

"And over there in Ursa Major? That's the Big Dipper." Still holding her hand, he guided it almost directly overhead. "Can you see the handle bending down to the bowl?"

"I think so. It's really big. Like, duh? No wonder it's called the Big Dipper." She turned her head, her nose practically brushing his ear. She caught a faint whiff of his shampoo—minty. "This is the first time I've seen the Big Dipper. It must be all the wine. I haven't had anything to drink in I don't know how long, and I guess it's gone to my head."

Vic turned his face toward hers, positioned his nose next to hers and breathed silently for a second or two. Then he turned back to face the sky. "Hey, if you think that's cool, let me show you something *really* cool." He gently maneuvered her hand up and to the right. "There. You see it? That's the Little Dipper, which is kind of hard to see because most of its stars are faint except for two in the bowl." He outlined it as he spoke. "So, those two stars are called the Guardians of the Pole because they dance around Polaris— kind of like groupies."

"You'd know all about those," she said wryly.

"I refuse to be riled by that comment."

"Okay, I'll give you a break." She refocused on the heavens. "So which one's Polaris? That's the North Star, right?"

"Correct. Now pay attention."

"Like you'd let me do otherwise?" She felt a thrill tingling her toes.

"Don't be cheeky," he chastised good-naturedly. "So, extend the line between the Guardian stars in the bowl about six times the distance between them and you come to the North Star. See? It's at the end of the handle, and it's pretty clear because there aren't any other bright stars around it."

"Oh, my God. I see it."

"Now, Navigation 101. Extend your arm to the left and that's west." He brought her arm across his way. Her forearm brushed against the cotton of his shirt. "And to the right? That's east."

Their joined arms passed over her. But this time he stopped short of letting his upper arm rub against her sweater.

Mimi tried to concentrate on the star gazing lesson and not the rapid beating of her heart. "So how do you know all these things?"

"I was a Boy Scout. Eagle Scout, in fact."

"I should have known. I bet your whole family was there for the ceremony. Just like I bet you all still get together for dinner every Sunday."

"Midday meal, actually."

"See, I knew it. That's why you're such a straight arrow. You grew up with a lifestyle bathed in classic Americana."

He let their joined hands drop between them and shifted his head to look at her. "Whoa, there. You think that just because I come from an ethnic blue-collar background, my family life is all sunshine and lollipops? We may all live near each other—I bought my parents a town house next to mine, you see—but that doesn't make for total peace and harmony. I mean, my father and mother barely speak to each other except to say 'Pass the butter, please.' We're big on butter in my family. And my mother is convinced that everything we do is fraught with danger. She even bawled me out for horsing around with my three-year-old nephew this morning. You'd have thought I'd hung him over some windswept cliff.

"Then there's my brother. Well, let's just say commitment or a solid work ethic has never been a part of his vocabulary. And did I mention my kid sister?"

Mimi shook her head.

"She's a single parent *and* going to school, all the while thinking she ruined her life by marrying a compulsive gambler at the age of nineteen. What do you say to that?"

Mimi mulled over the information. "Wow. To think you're so…so normal."

"I'm not sure that's a compliment."

"I wasn't being snide. Okay, maybe a little, but there's no crime in being normal. It's just that it's not particularly—"

"Sexy?" he asked.

"On the contrary, you can't imagine how very sexy."

CHAPTER NINETEEN

SO WHY WAS VIC'S KIND of normal very sexy, indeed?

Mimi wiggled to scratch an itch—not really sure if it was more than skin deep. "I mean, for a straight-arrow guy who only appears to own one kind of clothing—blue button-down shirts and khaki pants, you must know you're a hunk?"

"You find me physically attractive despite my sartorial limitations?" Vic asked.

"You make it sound so superficial."

"Well?" He raised an eyebrow.

Mimi rolled her eyes. "Well, of course there is that. But if I merely thought that you were something pretty to look at, I wouldn't bother talking with you now."

"I'm so relieved," he said with mock approval.

"No, you know what I mean. There's a certain substance. But I can't quite put my finger on it. So, help me. Tell me about yourself. You were married?" Mimi pretended not to notice the sudden pang of jealousy.

"Briefly, while I was playing pro ball out in California. I wanted unqualified adoration. Shauna wanted a Lexus and a place with an uninterrupted ocean view."

"What happened?"

"I was cut from the team, and I found out her adoration was qualified."

"Ouch."

"It happens. She got the Lexus and the condo. I got Roxie."

"That sounds fair to me." Mimi nodded thoughtfully. "So, after you were cut, you didn't try to sign with another team? You gave up on your dream and opted for something more conventional, something with more promise of stability, less risk?"

"Yes, yes, I *am* really that stodgy. But—" he held up a finger "—if I may point out, twelve years ago a certain someone told me that my plan to play professional football wasn't risky at all." He lowered his chin and stared over his brows.

"You shouldn't believe everything people tell you, especially twenty-two-year-old know-it-alls with a high propensity for moral outrage."

He chuckled. "Glad to know that you can be somewhat self-critical."

"Were we talking about me? I wasn't aware of that," she mocked.

He shook his head. "Anyway, the team decided they no longer had any use for my services—this was after the whole head-butting incident that your brother so kindly brought up yesterday."

"Was it only yesterday? It seems like it was ages ago."

"Yes. I do have that stultifying effect on people."

"Quit it." Mimi boxed him on the shoulder.

"That's all right. Anyway, first they ordered me to see a shrink who diagnosed that I was suffering from unresolved anger issues from my childhood."

"Who isn't?" She didn't mean it as a joke, even though it came out that way.

"Then I got a whopping fine from the League, after which I was pretty much persona non grata. Which, truthfully, didn't completely bother me. I knew my playing days were numbered. I was never good enough to be a star, let alone a guaranteed starter. So I decided to get out with only one concussion and a few broken bones and strained ligaments."

"So what about now? I don't really know what you do."

"You really want to hear this?" He looked doubtful.

She nodded. Her head rubbed against the wool fibers of the blanket.

"My father, like his father who came from Poland, was a mason. He laid tile floor, stone walls, Carrera plazas like the one at Allie Hammy."

"Cool."

"But pretty backbreaking. I knew that after business school at Stanford my family expected me to come back East, preferably close by, preferably in the family business. But there was no way I was going to build stone walls for a living—as honorable as that is. Instead, I looked at the market and saw the incredible boom in natural stone finishes—all those granite kitchen countertops, marble bathrooms and restaurant floors, all those corporate buildings. Marble granite—they signify solidarity, timelessness, natural beauty—lasting wealth. And you gotta remember this was still when the economy was chugging along."

"So you grew the business?"

"Not just grew it. Shifted focus from fabrication to supply and distribution. Golinski Sons International, GSI, is now the leading distributor of natural stone in North America with ten distribution centers in the U.S. As our website states, we offer an extensive line of natural stone products quarried in thirty-five countries on four continents, and our purchasing agents are located in China, India, Brazil and Turkey. Sorry, this is all very boring."

"Not at all. I know nothing about stone. And all this expansion and stuff came under your leadership?"

"I suppose, but it's a family effort. My dad is pretty much out of the day-to-day operations, but you can't keep him out of the warehouse in New Jersey, and he personally supervises the showrooms, laying some of the stone himself."

"Ah, a perfectionist like his son."

Vic didn't deny or agree. "Then there's my younger brother, Joe. He's a senior VP and head of sales, though I'm not sure he's totally committed."

"Ah, not like his older brother."

"Well, we all have our strengths. Business is still good, not gangbusters anymore thanks to the dip in the economy. But God bless the women of America who all want granite countertops."

"You should see the acres of granite in my family's kitchen."

"What color?" he turned and asked.

He was serious, she realized. "Kind of streaky gold and red, maybe brown."

"Yellow Bamboo. It's from our Platinum collection. Top of the line."

"Nothing but the best for the Lodge family."

Vic rolled on his side and faced her. "Anyway, I'm sure that's as much as anyone wants to hear about stone."

She turned on her side, a mirror image of him. If they were any closer, they could kiss. Almost.

"It's really kind of fascinating. How many people are actually in the business of making things, as opposed to merely manipulating numbers on a computer screen. You can actually walk into somebody's house or some business and say, 'Hey, I helped do this.'"

"You make me sound so virtuous."

"That's not such a bad thing," she confided.

"But it's not exciting."

"Excitement isn't always what it's cracked up to be." She picked at a twig that had landed on the blanket.

"Excuse me, aren't you the one who covers wars and mass uprisings? That doesn't sound like you do a lot of sitting at a desk or going to lunch in fancy restaurants."

"True, but I haven't done all that for a while now."

She drew circles on the blanket with her finger. "Not since…ah…since…"

Vic reached out and laid his hand on Mimi's to still it. It was the gentlest of pressure, more warmth than force. "Listen. You don't have to talk about—the whole kidnapping thing. I understand. I'm the last person in the world to advocate baring your soul about something painful. And in your case, I can't even imagine how awful it was."

Mimi stared at his hand atop hers—the bond. Normally, she would have denied any need for a connection, for help. But now…here…with the candles sputtering their last gasp, Roxie's rattling breathing, the velvet-black of night—the motions of the heavens and the stirrings in her heart anchored by Polaris—she wanted that connection. Needed it. With this man, this normal, sexy soul lying next to her.

She inhaled deeply and took, what was for her, a leap of faith.

"I can't really talk about the time they held me. I was so scared. All those months—the fear, the mix of kindness and cruelty from my captors, the uncertainty. The uncertainty was almost worse than the physical and emotional pain. I wish I could be strong, not still have nightmares about it, and be able to put the whole thing behind me."

"It's not a competition. No one's judging whether you're strong or not. That's irrelevant. Bad things happened. It takes time to get over it. The important thing is you're home and you have time."

"I suppose you're right. I mean, I know you're right. But the way it ended was all kind of anticlimactic— so sometimes it's hard to grasp that it's really over. You see, there wasn't some dramatic raid to free me, and I certainly wasn't clever enough or brave enough to figure out how to escape."

"Please, if anyone could have escaped, it would have been you. I'm sure of it."

"Thanks." She fisted her hand and slipped it away from his. Then she stroked her throat slowly. "As I understand it, because really—I was totally outside the loop—the network's insurance company found a company that specializes in negotiations, you know, recovering family members who have been kidnapped by drug czars or oil company execs taken in some remote jungle by revolutionaries. Anyway, they used a consultant on the ground in Chechnya. He contacted a trusted local, who then handled the communications with the kidnappers."

"It must have taken forever."

"Yeah, I don't think these things are exactly speedy. More like the kidnappers proposed some ridiculously high figure—like twenty-five million plus the release of some rebels or criminals who were in jail. It was never totally clear if they were rebels or just lawless criminals or some combination. Then there was a counter offer of less money—which the kidnappers refused. Weeks went by. Agony for everybody, I'm sure. Then finally an agreement." Her voice shook.

"Whatever the TV network paid was, I'm sure, still enormous, and I can never repay them."

"I wouldn't worry about that. The network made a ton of money off your work."

"That's kind of you to say."

"It's not kind. Securing your return was a major story in and of itself. I'm sure they feel a moral obligation to protect their employees, but bottom line it's just good business."

"When you put it that way." Mimi chuckled philosophically.

He frowned. "What I don't get is why you went there in the first place. If the History Channel serves me right, the war in Chechnya has been over for a bunch of years now, and you're a *war* correspondent, right? I mean, I know the place is still dangerous, especially for correspondents—especially correspondents who try to talk to people who don't agree with the current government. But why go there now?"

Even in the darkness, Mimi could feel the intensity of his stare.

One more step. One more leap of faith with Polaris as her guide. "The truth? I went looking for my mother."

CHAPTER TWENTY

VIC WASN'T EXPECTING that one. "Your mother?"

Mimi sighed. "Actually, I went looking for her memory. She's dead."

"I'd heard. I'm sorry."

"Why do people always say that—that they're sorry? You didn't know her. You weren't responsible."

"But I can empathize with your loss."

"It was a long time ago. And in some ways, I almost think my mother was never here—I mean, here in Grantham. Not really. She was originally from Chechnya, you see."

Vic shook his head. "I never would have guessed. I always figured you for this Mayflower descendant."

"That would be the Lodges, my father's side of the family. The family that never knew what to make of my 'ethnic' mother—even though she came from a diplomatic background."

"But she was obviously a big force in your life. Otherwise you wouldn't have risked so much."

"To be more precise, she's like the ten-ton elephant in the room," Mimi admitted. "How can I explain?" She thought a moment.

"My mother, Raisa Tlisova Lodge, was this incredible, ethereal beauty—all high cheekbones and pale skin against dark hair." Mimi mimicked the description with her hands. "My mother's father had been a member of the Soviet diplomatic corps posted to Washington, D.C., during the Cold War. Then one day, he marched into the State Department and declared he could no longer support the Communist government. The story goes it was April First—you know, April Fool's Day?"

Vic nodded.

"Anyway, it took a while for the American officials to decide it wasn't a joke, but when they realized the intelligence value that he had as the military attaché, they whisked him, his wife and only child, Raisa, to a safe house. Chechnya, their homeland, became history since they could no longer travel back there. Not only that, they couldn't contact their Chechen family and friends. There was always the possibility of reprisal, and my mother used to tell me how her father trained her to look over her shoulder, memorize faces in a crowd, be alert for possible enemies."

"Sounds pretty paranoid," Vic commented.

"True, but you gotta remember the times. It was the height of the Cold War. Terrible things were going on. Anyway, while my grandfather may have been trying to protect my mother, his actions fostered this sense of isolation and fear in her. Her way of dealing with it, when I look back on my childhood, was to seek the approval of her adopted community and family—things like serving on school committees, joining the gardening club and baking pumpkin pies for Thanksgiving."

"They say converts are always the most devout."

"Yes and no." Mimi held up her finger. "You see, her wish to adopt a new lifestyle ran counter to her desire to memorialize, to romanticize the past that she'd lost. I remember her telling me bedtime stories about her remote mountaintop village or *aul*. How it was this magical place full of traditional music and colorful peasant dances, with spectacular gorges and dense forests. She was especially proud of the hospitality the people showed toward all visitors."

"It sounds like a fairy tale."

"Exactly. It wasn't real. So, not only couldn't she go home, she created a home that never existed. I mean, it was a doomed situation." She paused, then a slight smile covered her face. "But I don't mean to paint her as this dark, constantly depressed person. There were times when she was so much fun—the way she'd suddenly dance around the room to music or liked to jump in piles of leaves. Her laugh—it was contagious. And her sense of humor kind of snuck up on you—very subversive, really." She glanced over at Vic. "I think that got to my father more than almost anything. He had this sneaking feeling that deep down she was making fun of him—which, of course, she was. And his all-consuming ego could never take that." She set her mouth. "She was unique. Beautiful. But fragile. Terribly fragile." She breathed in slowly.

"So what happened in the end?" he asked softly.

"In the end?" she repeated. "In the end, she committed suicide. Right after my parents divorced. She was living alone in an apartment. I'd left with my father for Maine. I should have stayed, though. I knew she was going through a rough time."

"But how old were you at the time?"

"Ten."

"You were just a kid. You couldn't take care of someone with serious emotional issues."

"I know, I know. If anyone's to blame it's my father. The man dumped her for a younger woman. So, okay, they fought constantly, and my mother would go into these dark moods and refuse to come out of her room—but was that any reason just to end a marriage when there was already a kid?"

"Mental illness is difficult to deal with even under the best of circumstances." He saw Mimi start to bristle. "Whoa, I'm not trying to defend your father, merely point out the obvious."

"The obvious is that my father never had an empathetic bone in his body. There was no way he could not be the center of attention, let alone deal compassionately with someone less than stable."

Mimi raised herself to look at Vic, still lying next to her on the scratchy plaid blanket. "So you asked me why I went to Chechnya?" She didn't wait for him to answer. "I went because I wanted to get some understanding of just who my mother was—and to put her ghost to rest. Because this is the really astonishing part. As luck, or fate—my superstitious mother would have definitely said fate—would have it, the village deep in the mountains where the rebel was supposed to be hiding from the Russians? The one I was going to interview? That village? It was my mother's."

"All right, I can see why you wanted to go. So, tell me, did you find the colorful peasants and the deep gorges?"

She raised her eyebrows in disbelief. "What do you think? I mean, even if they existed at one time, after two wars for independence this particular village had become synonymous with bloodshed. But *I* had to see for myself. Make this connection, find something that helped explain my mother."

"So what did you find?"

She nervously drew a line with her finger on the blanket. Back and forth, back and forth. "I never got there. I was in Grozny, the capital, on my way to set up the meeting when I was kidnapped in broad daylight, hundreds of people looking on as they were rushing to work. After that, I was moved from one remote location to another, blindfolded the whole time and then kept in windowless rooms. I could have been in my mother's village at one time, but I'll never know. And as far as getting any insights into her psyche from a ruthless bunch of thugs? That would have been a stretch—not that I didn't have lots of time to think about it." She laughed bitterly.

"At least you had the courage to face your demons. How many people can say that? Most people run away or go into denial, compromise their lifestyle so as to keep those nagging, painful memories at bay."

Vic should know. He was a master of compartmentalizing, of keeping his life so orderly, so busy, that it was devoid of any emotional extreme. It left no window to deal with things beyond day-to-day issues. That was why pro football—with all its physical and emotional highs—would never have been a healthy long-term option.

The way he'd fashioned his structured, focused life kept the sadness in check, the guilt tucked away and the anger under control—all remnants from the events of his childhood that he kept buried, hidden from mind. Besides, it wasn't as if he lacked for simple pleasures. He read, he worked, he played with his dog. His emotional capital was tied up with keeping the whole Golinski boat afloat financially.

But this wasn't about him. It was good that Mimi had opened up, but her vulnerability was obvious. He had always pictured Mimi Lodge—and, believe you me, on more than one occasion during and after college—he had pictured her in various states of clothing and lack thereof. Anyway, he'd always envisioned her as one of the eternally lucky ones, a person whom the world blessed with a confident glow, someone who came from privilege and felt entitled to nothing less. To find out she was more—much more complex— shook his carefully ordered world, unmoored him from the steadiness of her internal North Star.

But he had no intention of giving her up. Not when

he was just beginning to scratch the surface. True, he might have gone into this whole Reunions deal with her father as a rational business decision, but Vic knew there was nothing rational about his dealings with Mimi and his yearning to see more of her. What this involvement would do to the even-keeled world he had created for himself was yet to be seen. Somehow, some way, it felt right.

"You know, this might seem trivial and all after what you've just been through——" He started slow.

She gave a sputtering laugh. "Please, I could use some triviality right now. I sound more morose than a Russian novel."

"In that case, a propos of nothing, I was just thinking how I really resented you after the whole panel water-dumping fiasco."

"As opposed to thinking what a nut I've become now?"

He waved his hand back and forth to deny her comment. "No, now you sound perfectly sane to me, a lot better than I'd be if I'd gone through what you'd experienced. No, back then—in college—it was your whole attitude. The whole certainty that you were right and that anyone who didn't agree with you was a dope of the first order. The fountain episode was just the icing on the cake." He was being truthful.

"I suppose that's true. Back then, I lacked, shall we say——"

"Tolerance?" he suggested.

"Okay, for lack of a better word—tolerance." She

didn't seem offended. "But as to the fountain thing, I've got to confess—I don't know what came over me back then. I mean, I remember having this over-whelming urge to rankle you. It was so easy, and I couldn't resist. And when I saw the fountain, I had this vision of *La Dolce Vita.* You know, the Fellini film? Anita Eckberg splashing away in the Trevi Fountain? I realize I'm no Anita Eckberg—even back then." She looked down at her boyish figure.

He stared off into space. "Actually, you really turned me on," he confessed. "Jumping in the foun-tain. Daring me to follow you."

"And you did, didn't you?" Mimi smiled.

"You bet. I was so mad and so horny all at the same time. And, boy, did I pay for it." He chuckled.

The Grantham cops had arrived and arrested him for criminal mischief and disorderly conduct. Yet somehow in the course of getting *his* particulars, they had merely handed Mimi a towel and clucked on about how they didn't want her to get a cold. Clearly, they'd recognized a member of the storied Lodge fam-ily, and were giving her special treatment.

"C'mon. You were only locked up for an hour or so, and all the charges were dropped," she protested.

"Please tell me I don't have your father to thank for that favor." Actually, with the mention of her fa-ther, he realized he was going to have to come clean about his business bargain. But not now, not when he had this feeling…this really good feeling.

After all, he was the king of denial.

Vic picked up Mimi's hand and entwined his fingers between hers. "You've got big hands," he observed. "Capable hands. No nail polish. I like that."

"How can you even tell when there's hardly any light left? But you're right. No polish, no fuss. Nothing to get in the way of a quick in-and-out assignment."

"But you're not on assignment." He turned their clasped hands upside down and kissed her palm.

"Ooh." She reacted like she'd been pinched. "And I'm quite happy about that right now."

He looked up. In the last remnants of candlelight he was sure he could see her pupils dilate, though perhaps that was his male ego making him imagine it.

Mimi tilted her head. "So, tell me. Now that we've bared our souls, I'm still not sure why I'm so attracted to you. We don't seem to have anything in common, except an unfortunate run-in in our past. You appear to live in starched shirts, whereas I don't even own an iron. I remember you arguing against equal opportunity for women athletes if it jeopardized men's programs. And while you may have changed your attitude, I somehow doubt it. And I hate to think what your political views are. And yet…" She eyed him.

"Maybe it's because I'm simply the most attractive man you've ever gone on a picnic with?" His voice was playful.

"That's true. But I haven't been on many picnics, period." She studied him some more. "I think it's because you have a dog with one big ear and one little ear."

Roxie snored contentedly from her spot on the end of the blanket.

"I think it's also because you care about your family even though they drive you crazy," Mimi went on. "And I think it's because you like to swing your nephew higher than is strictly necessary." She paused. "And quite possibly because you're the best-looking man I've ever been on a picnic with."

He reached up and cradled her cheek in one hand. "I like that."

"But by the same token, why are you attracted to me?"

He smiled, noting her insecurity. "Let's see. I'm attracted to you because my dog likes you, and she doesn't normally feel comfortable around just about anyone. I like that you make me forget I was ever a Boy Scout."

"Eagle Scout," she corrected.

"See? I'd already forgotten." He rubbed the tips of his fingers against her soft skin. "And then there's the matter of your meatballs. Don't tell my mother, but they're better than hers."

She leaned her chin into the heel of his palm. "Please, I don't want to get between you and your mother."

"No problem. But let's leave my mother out of the discussion."

"And we're agreed we're not going anywhere near politics, religion or the Equal Rights Amendment."

"Agreed," he affirmed.

She breathed in deeply. "So, you think something's going to happen between us?"

"Oh, yeah." He tilted his head and brought his lips close to hers.

"Me, too," she conceded. She arched her neck so that the distance between them was even smaller. "Tonight?"

"Quite possibly." Without warning, he grabbed her and rolled over onto his back, taking Mimi with him. For a tall woman, she was surprisingly light as she lay atop him. Her long, lanky body molded perfectly into his. She wiggled her hips. More than his interest sparked.

He looked up at the stars and inhaled the freshly mown grass, a sure sign of promise. Cars drove by on the two-lane road a couple hundred feet away. But somehow the engine noise seemed farther, the vestiges of modern time and a hectic world beyond reach. A split-rail fence surrounded an oak sapling—nurtured from an acorn from the original Grantham Battlefield oak that had witnessed Washington and his ragtag bunch of troops defeat the better-equipped British army. Here, in this historic place, time was expressed in the form of nature reviving and growing from old memories.

He reached up and cupped the delicate curve of Mimi's ear, then let his index finger trail down the line of her jaw, the rounded point of her chin. "You know, I'm glad you chose this place. It's magical."

She shivered when he slipped two fingers inside the turtleneck of her thin sweater and stopped on the center juncture of her collarbone. "Plus it's within walking distance from the family house. An added bonus."

"You got in my car once and survived." He splayed his hand on her breast. She pressed into it.

"Yeah, but I didn't want to risk being more nervous than I am already."

"You're nervous?" He moved closer to her as if to kiss her.

She readily responded, lowering her head to his. "You're not?" Her lips almost touched his.

"Well, it doesn't stop me from being a man of action." He closed the gap between them with a gentle kiss that immediately deepened into a slow exploration of taste and desire. They let their tongues dance, their lips search, their teeth nipping to taste here and then there.

When they finally broke apart, Mimi gulped for breath. "We won't disturb Roxie, will we?"

Vic glanced in the direction of the dog, sprawled out next to the picnic basket—no fool she. "In case you hadn't noticed, the dog has been asleep for quite a while."

Mimi turned her head and peered in Roxie's direction. A loud snore arose and mingled with the chirping of cicadas. "You're right. She's down for the count."

And Vic took full advantage of it, applying the full force of his concentration to something sensual instead of practical for a change. With his mouth and his hands he explored Mimi's face. He spanned his hands around her slim waist and through the fine wool of her sweater rubbed his thumbs along the undersides of her small breasts, gradually moving upward to tease the taut peaks of her nipples.

Mimi groaned and buried her head in the side of his neck. Her fingers frantically worked the buttons of his dress shirt, fumbling in the dark. "You've got too many tiny buttons," she complained, panting.

"I know exactly what you mean." He held her and hoisted them up together. She sat up on his lap, watching while he yanked the shirttails out of his trousers and worked to undo his shirt. Then she took her turn and yanked her sweater over her head, leaving only the wisp of a camisole covering her pale skin.

Vic moved like a man possessed, stripping his shirt off his chest and down his arms. His unbuttoned cuffs caught on his wrists. "Oh, the hell with it!" he exclaimed and forced them over his hands, the buttons popping off from the force.

Then he reached for Mimi and they went tumbling down on the blanket again. This time Vic was on top, his bare chest against her torso, with only the small bits of lace separating his skin from hers. He ran his hands up and down her sides. "You feel incredible. Amazing."

He felt her shiver. "You're not getting cold, are

you?" He'd noticed the way she seemed to bundle herself up in sweaters and turtlenecks on otherwise mild days.

Mimi shook her head. "Not if you keep rubbing me that way. And, please, don't stop." She grabbed the back of his head and without any grace whatsoever—but with a clear message—brought his lips down to hers. This time she was the aggressor, nipping and teasing his lower lip, darting her tongue in and out to mimic lovemaking.

Without breaking their kiss—and thanking the heavens above that his knees and back were cooperating—Vic reached down for his belt buckle and, one-handed, undid it. She was doing something with her tongue along the ridge of his top teeth that almost had him floating, but luckily he kept control of his coordination, not to mention his dignity. He closed his eyes, rocked slightly and concentrated on moving the zipper down one agonizing notch at a…

Which is when car lights—high beams, there was no mistaking the intensity—shined directly on them. A car door slammed.

Vic stilled his hand. Lifted his head.

Then another car door slammed.

Mimi turned her head sharply.

The sound of footsteps could be heard on the gravel by the shoulder of the road.

Vic swore and quickly zipped up his pants. He searched around for his shirt, but found Mimi's turtleneck sweater first. He passed it to her.

She wiggled it on, still on her back.

Aroused from her sleep, Roxie started to bark.

"Quiet, girl," Vic commanded. All he needed was to have her bite a cop. He was sure they were violating local ordinances by being in a park after dark. Quickly, he located the end of the dog leash before she could take off.

Roxie strained at the end and barked protectively, with totally false bravado.

Vic got to his knees and waited for the inevitable. "Mimi Lodge," he muttered with a philosophical harrumph, "getting close to you for any period of time is nothing but trouble with a capital *T*."

CHAPTER TWENTY-ONE

"HEY, MAN, DON'T TELL ME the cops have police dogs now?" It was a young male, late teens. He stopped near the road's edge, the car headlights exposing his silhouette. His features may have been obscured, but the outlines of a six-pack of beer were easy to discern.

Roxie, straining on the leash, barked protectively.

Mimi scrambled to her feet and put her hands on her hips. "What the..."

"Roxie, quiet," Vic ordered, then directed his attention to the two figures frozen by their car. "Sorry, boys, the dog's loud but perfectly harmless."

"How come if he's perfectly harmless I can see his teeth from here?" The driver of the car moved cautiously sideways. He carried a beer bottle in one hand.

"It's a she, and maybe she just wanted to let me know that you've committed two criminal offenses—driving with an open container and underage drinking."

"What are you? A lawyer?" The passenger asked brazenly. The six-pack swayed toward them.

Roxie growled again.

The kid stepped back.

Vic shushed her. "Listen, guys, what you do is your

business, but it's only fair to warn you that the lady here—" he indicated Mimi "—is a cop magnet."

"Thanks for the ringing endorsement," she murmured under her breath.

"If you want to avoid a hassle," Vic went on calmly, "let alone the grief you're going to get from your parents when they have to come bail you out, you'll dump your beer in the nearest trash can, go home and play Skyrim." He made no threats, but the ring of authority in his voice was clear.

"Sky what?" Mimi asked, stepping closer to Vic.

As if on cue, the wail of sirens penetrated the night air. Now that the sun had fully set, a chill had truly begun to set in.

The sirens grew louder, more insistent. The two kids whirled around. "Geez, he wasn't kidding. We're outta here, man." They scrambled back to the car.

"The beer?" Vic reminded them.

"Oh, yeah." They raced to a nearby rubbish bin and dumped their stash before hightailing it back to their car. It peeled away from the shoulder, the spinning tires sending a shower of pebbles across the grass.

Mimi watched the escape and shook her head. "Talk about a mood breaker." She turned to Vic. "Somehow I have this feeling we're not going to have a night of passionate sex, let alone reach first base."

"Not if those sirens are any indicator." He looked at her sideways. "And, just to refresh your memory, we had already reached first and were on the way to second."

"Oh, right, I seem to recall that." Her throat tightened. All too clearly she remembered it.

"It doesn't sound like I was having much impact on you."

Mimi shook her head. "*Au contraire*. It was more a question of being overwhelmed."

"Nice try."

"Besides, the night is young. Who says it has to end here?"

"As far as the park is concerned, I think that's pretty well no longer an option. On the other hand, I do live alone. We could take this stuff back to your family's place, get my car and explore each other's bodies on my king-size bed, not to mention the other six rooms of my town house—if you don't count the two and a half baths. On the other hand, why neglect them?"

"Now, that's my idea of decisive leadership. Tell me, did you ever think of applying those skills to revolutionize the stone business?" she teased.

"Hah, hah. Now stand to the side, and I'll fold up the blanket," he ordered, waving her away. "Roxie, you, too." The dog had plopped herself right in the middle of the plaid.

It was quick work, with Vic grabbing the last meatball. She held on to Roxie's leash with one hand and slipped the other in his as they left the park for the surrounding neighborhood of large old Colonial-style houses, half-timber Tudor estates and the occasional award-winning modern dwelling. The glow of tasteful streetlamps supplemented the state-of-the-art security systems. Grantham was a remarkably safe town, and most residents didn't even lock their homes or doors. But not in this neck of the woods, where the preponderance of priceless art collections and lavish sets of jewelry were frequently featured in magazines and newspapers.

Relaxed, Mimi was in no rush as she let Roxie stop and sniff practically every blade of grass. "I can't believe I'm actually enjoying myself in Grantham," she announced, waiting while Roxie examined a branch of a giant holly bush with infinite fascination.

"I can't believe I'm holding hands with Mimi Lodge," Vic said.

Mimi gave him a sideways glance. "You make me sound like the fatted calf."

"I wouldn't use that metaphor exactly. But back in college, I remember watching you and some of the other members of the Women's Water Polo team walking together to go to your Social Club. You all glowed with this supreme confidence of good schools and money. You seemed untouchable."

"Hardly. I think we were a very down-to-earth lot. But I guess you're right. We used to hang out a lot together because we were all members of Lion Inn."

Roxie had had her fill of holly and jingled her collar that she was ready to move on.

"What club did you belong to?" Mimi asked.

"I didn't. I was an independent." The term referred to someone who didn't join a Social Club, Grantham

University's version of coed fraternities, which were the hub of social life on campus.

"I'm surprised. All the clubs must have been eager to get you. Didn't football players always join Colony?" she asked, mentioning another club across the street from Lion. The clubs were located on Edinburgh Street on the edge of campus, their architecture ranging from brick Southern Plantation to Gothic Revival.

"Maybe. In any case, I didn't join because, number one, I didn't have the money for the fees, and number two, I didn't want having too much of a good time to get in the way of my studying or football."

"You really were a Boy Scout, weren't you?"

"I was practically born that way," he admitted. They stopped at a traffic light.

Normally, Mimi would have barged ahead since there were no cars, but with Vic she didn't feel that compulsion to push forward. Instead, she reflected on what he'd just admitted. "You know, I hope you've gotten over thinking of me as untouchable."

He squeezed her hand. "I think I've already demonstrated that fact." He paused. "And before you say anything, this…this is not about fulfilling some kind of post-adolescent fantasy. That's not the kind of person I am."

"I believe you because unlike me, you clearly do not bear grudges—well, maybe reasonable ones, but I don't think you'd ever manipulate someone for your own gains."

He suddenly shifted his focus on a distant car, the headlights streaming on the paved road.

"You know, if we're being entirely truthful about our college days, I have a confession to make, too," she said, trying to regain his attention.

It worked. He turned back. The light changed and they crossed the street.

"Back in college? Back when you probably thought I never noticed someone like you?"

"Don't tell me you secretly stayed awake at night wondering just how exciting it would be to do assignments in differential calculus together?"

"Please. Unlike my scientific little half-brother, my brush with mathematics was brief and far from illustrious. No, what I'm talking about is this one lecture course in Civil War history. Maybe you remember? It was scheduled at some ungodly early hour, but it was really popular because the professor was so good. And it needed to be held in the big lecture hall, the one that slanted down toward the front where the professor stood." She raised their joined hands and swooped them down in a sloping fashion. "You always sat in the front row."

He cocked his head. "Yup. Four seats in from the left aisle seat. Always the same seat. I'm left-handed and with those swivel-up desks, I always had to sit on the left so that I could still see the professor while I took notes."

"I never noticed that, but it makes perfect sense." She swallowed. "Anyhow, it got so I always checked that you were there. I found it...reassuring, especially since I usually crept in late, way in the back. I'd do that and first thing, seek you out, check that you were there. And of course you were—"

"I took attendance seriously."

"As I would have expected. Anyway, I remember you always sitting in profile, your jaw jutting forward, tight curls covering your head..."

"My hair was longer then."

"You're right. But shorter hair suits you now—more mature."

Vic groaned.

"No, no, that's good. But let me finish. The thing was, I'm sure the lecture was fantastic, but more often than not, I'd find myself staring at you sitting all stoic and rapt up in the class. I thought you were the best thing to wake up to."

"So you're telling me that this is just a chance to live out *your* post-adolescent fantasy?"

She shook her head. "In some ways yes. But I'm not that sleepy-eyed girl any longer. I mean, that was just a fantasy. I never actually approached you." He'd adjusted his stride to her shorter legs, Mimi realized. So they moved in perfect synchronization. A unit, with Roxie leading the way.

"I probably would have thought you were crazy."

"And I probably would have considered you a stick in the mud, but still... Maybe that's why I reacted the way I did that day of the panel. I was finally working off all that unrequited fantasy."

"Is that what you'd call it?"

"Whatever. It was in the past. I'm not interested in reliving history. I look to the future now." She squeezed his hand. "Definitely forward looking."

He bent down and kissed the top of her head.

She sighed.

The flashing lights and wailing siren of an ambulance whizzed by.

Mimi tensed.

He drew her closer, shifting to wrap his arm around her shoulders. He leaned down and rubbed his cheek against the side of her head.

Mimi breathed a little easier—just. "There must be some terrible traffic accident judging from the commotion. I hope those two kids didn't get in a pile-up." They stopped and waited for another traffic light to change. Roxie obediently sat. Mimi's family's house was in the next block, four houses down from the corner.

"I'm pretty sure those kids aren't involved," Vic assured her. "The police sirens started while they were still messing around at the battlefield."

The light changed, Mimi jiggled Roxie's leash, and they all crossed. "You're right. I'd forgotten." They passed a gray clapboard house on the corner half-hidden by a tall hedge of hemlocks. Then came a Victorian folly painted the ubiquitous Grantham yellow. Its turrets and cupolas reached above the tops of the ancient sycamores.

Mimi pointed. "You know, I always thought that

place looked like something out of Mary Popp—"
She stopped.

Roxie didn't anticipate the suddenness and jerked
on the leash.

"What?" Vic asked.

Mimi pressed her lips together. "My family's place?
Just up above. The flashing lights? They look like
they're there."

Indeed, the sky above the six-foot-high wall of
holly bushes was blazing bright. Mimi wiggled out
of Vic's embrace and took off. Roxie, given the chance
to run, seized the opportunity and pulled out in front,
the leash taut under the force of her pulling.

Vic caught up with them within a couple of sprint-
ing strides. "Hold up. You don't know what's going
on."

Mimi didn't stop. She sped through the open gate
at the entrance to the house. Two police cars parked
head-on at the columned portico. An ambulance, its
back doors open, blocked them from the rear. The
house itself was ablaze with light. The front double
doors stood wide open.

Mimi could feel her heart rate rocket upward, her
throat tighten. She weaved through the parked vehicles, her chest pounding ready to burst. All sorts
of thoughts flashed through her mind—her mother's
suicide, her kidnapping, fear that something had happened to Brigid or maybe Press.

She heard the crunch of gravel next to her. Vic.
"Here, give me the dog. You go inside," he said.

She rushed to the house. A patrolman stationed at the entrance held up his arm.

"I live here," she declared. "What's going on?" She looked over his shoulder into the foyer to the grand stairway that split into two at the landing. Down one side, she saw two emergency medical technicians balancing a stretcher as they descended carefully. She couldn't tell who was strapped down. But she saw Noreen bringing up the rear. Her face was pale, her hair askew in a low ponytail.

Mimi muscled past the policeman, raced across the carpet and pounded up the stairs. She flattened herself against the railing and peered down as the EMTs maneuvered past her. Another policeman helped Noreen.

It was irrational, she knew, but Mimi half-expected to see her mother's body.

Only, it wasn't.

CHAPTER TWENTY-TWO

AN OXYGEN MASK COVERED her father's face. His skin was waxy gray.

Mimi reached out to touch his arm. "Father, I thought you were in New York with Noreen?"

Conrad lifted his hand to remove the mask. "This happened after we came home. Something untoward… I…I can't talk of it now…" The effort seemed to sap his strength, and the EMT replaced the plastic device to aid Conrad's breathing.

"We should really get going," the emergency medic said.

Mimi nodded and moved to the side. "Of course." *Untoward?* Her brain focused on her father's vocabulary. It was so Lodge in its formality—a microcosm of their distant relationship.

She waited until Noreen reached the same step, then stumbled along next to her. "What happened?" she asked.

Noreen barely glanced her way. "We'd just gotten back from New York City and were up in the bedroom changing when your father got these chest pains and had difficulty breathing. I called 9-1-1."

"His heart?" Mimi held Noreen by the forearm

as they stepped down to the entrance hall. They stopped as the paramedics flipped the legs down on the stretcher. The wheels moved silently on the massive Oriental carpet.

"They're not sure," Noreen answered in a daze.

The EMTs hustled outside. One of the policemen turned. "Mrs. Lodge, you can travel with Mr. Lodge or come with one of us."

"I'll ride with my husband," Noreen answered, ghostly pale.

"Do you want me to come with you?" Mimi asked.

Noreen shook her head. "No, I'll be fine. Brigid is due back from a friend's house any minute now, and you could do me a favor and be here for her. I wouldn't alarm her, though. I'd ask Press, but I'm not sure where he is at the moment. And I tried to call you earlier, but you didn't pick up."

"I didn't have my phone with me." That's how nervous and excited she'd been about the picnic with Vic. That seemed like a lifetime ago. "Don't worry. I can handle everything. Do you have your phone?"

Noreen fumbled in the pockets of her linen slacks. "I...I..."

"Maybe it's in your bag?" Mimi suggested softly.

Outside in the driveway, the noise from police radios filled the air along with the rapid-fire conversations of the paramedics doing their job.

Noreen looked down as if surprised to see her Birkin bag in the crook of her elbow. "Of course.

took it because it has all the insurance information."
She bit down on her lip.

"Mrs. Lodge? We're ready to go now," one of the
paramedics called.

Mimi squeezed her arm. "It'll be all right."

Noreen nodded stiffly, then with the help of one of
the policemen climbed up into the ambulance. The
doors shut with a decisive finality. Mimi stepped back
and watched the vehicles circle around the drive and
head for the gate. The police cars were out front, sirens going, lights ablaze.

And then there was silence. The sirens growing
fainter as the cavalcade sped toward the hospital. Silence, that is, except for the buzzing of the cicadas and
the chirping of crickets. Nature had decided to take
back the night. Mimi stood in front of the house, doors
open, light pouring out. It was profoundly empty. She
wrapped her arms around herself. That cold feeling
that she never really lost enveloped her like a tight
bandage.

"You going to be all right?" Vic was standing on
the edge of the driveway. An enormous rhododendron
hovered over him.

Roxie cowered fearfully behind him, trying to look
small. Her head sunk into her hunched shoulders as
if waiting for the giant leaves to attack or the sirens
and strange men to return. But when she saw Mimi
turn their way, the dog braved a tail wag.

Mimi lowered herself step by step off the front portico and walked slowly toward them. "It's my dad."

"I gathered. Heart attack?" Vic asked. He stood still.

"They're not sure. Something about him having difficulty breathing. I'm supposed to stay here and take care of Brigid when she comes home." Mimi waved toward the house.

He moved closer. "Probably just as well. There's nothing worse than sitting around an emergency ward. Do you want me to stay with you?" He put out his hand and rubbed her shoulder. "It's not a problem, you know."

"No, no, that's not necessary. I know you have work tomorrow." Of course she wanted Vic to stay, but she wasn't going to admit it. Out of politeness. Out of pride. Out of fear.

Roxie rubbed her flank against Mimi's leg, and Mimi squatted down. "Oh, sweetie, you're the best. I'm sorry you got scared with all the commotion." She snuggled close to the dog's head, closed her eyes and let her cheek rest against the silky fur. After a moment or two, she squeezed a little harder, then stood up.

"Okay. I won't keep you," she reiterated. "I'm fine here, really. It was a shock—the ambulance and stuff, but it's not as if my father and I are all that close."

Vic shook his head. "It doesn't matter. No matter what, he's still your father." He placed his hand gently against her cheek and bent down to be eye to eye. "Promise that you'll call when you hear what's up?"

She braved a smile. "It could be late."

"It doesn't matter."

She nodded. "Okay." She looked up into his eyes. He looked worried. Nobody ever worried about her.

"I can stay. Give me coffee and I can move mountains."

She shook her head. "The mountains are fine just where they are, thanks. And I'll be okay. I can do this."

"I know you can. That's not the point."

She nodded in acknowledgment. "I know. But I have to do this. It's important to me." If she was going to move on, going to turn the page on her fears and be open to the possibility of happiness in her future, she needed to know she could stand on her own in a time of crisis. "You understand, don't you?"

He hesitated, then nodded. "Yes, even though I don't like it."

She knew he spoke the truth. Knew that he respected her enough to make her own decision. "We should get together tomorrow, but maybe it's better to see what happens here?" Mimi suggested.

"Sure. But make no mistake. If it turns out to be serious, I'm seeing you tonight."

"If that's the case, it won't be like I'll be all bubbly and ready to party."

"I don't need bubbly and party. You'll need help—"

Mimi started to protest.

He put his fingers to her lips.

"Don't object. Just say yes."

"Okay, for your sake."

Vic breathed in. "No, for yours." He brushed a light

kiss on her lips, then, jingling Roxie's leash, the two walked down the driveway to his car parked in the street.

Leaving Mimi alone. She turned, trudged up the steps to the house that had never felt like a home. Something stopped her from crossing the threshold.

The picnic basket.

CHAPTER TWENTY-THREE

LATER THAT EVENING, Mimi began to realize how much space a sleeping eight-year-old could take up in a bed.

"Mom took Dad to the hospital for some tests," Mimi had explained when Brigid arrived home. It was technically true. She wasn't going to lie to her sister, but there was no need to alarm her, either.

Brigid had shaken her head, her silky reddish-blond hair swinging beneath two blue barrettes. "I don't understand. Why would he get his tests at night? Why can't he go to the doctor during the day?"

The kid was clearly no dummy, Mimi thought. They sat on Brigid's double bed. A fairy princess bed, with a pale pink duvet of tufted cotton, and mounds of pale pink pillows with Irish lace—what you'd expect from an Irish mother, right? Overhead, miles of blush-colored organza were draped over the four posts, anchored by a headboard painted with butterflies and fairies. The latter held wands and were tapping the heads of frogs and other woodland animals, all prepared to turn them into princes or at least happy creatures.

Mimi took Brigid's small hands in hers, looking down at her gnawed fingernails. What anxiety could a girl who slept in a fairy princess bed have? Clearly, some that Mimi didn't know about. She hesitated, wanting to choose her words carefully. She knew the cost of lying to children firsthand.

Instead, she looked Brigid directly in the eye. But she spoke in the tender voice of…of…a big sister. "You're right. Most tests can be done in the doctor's office. But this kind couldn't, and it needed to be done right away."

Brigid's eyes opened wide.

Mimi didn't know what to do if she started to bawl.

"Something's wrong, isn't it?" her sister asked. Her determined jaw quivered.

"We don't know for sure. But whatever it is, your mom called the hospital right away, and he's having the best possible care." Mimi hoped she sounded re-assuring.

"He's going to die, isn't he?" Brigid's eyes welled with tears.

The kid didn't muck around. And in Brigid's fear, Mimi recognized the same fear she had experienced when her father broke the news of her own mother's suicide. It seemed cowardly, but for a split second, Mimi wanted to run and hide in the closet of her own bedroom—the way she used to when her mother and father fought, or later when he brought her back for the funeral, and Mimi had refused to come out for the service.

But Mimi wasn't a child anymore. If she were, she could have told her, "You're lucky. He's too mean to die. Not like my mother." But she didn't. Because she was the adult in the room, and Brigid deserved to have a glowing picture of their father until she decided otherwise.

So, instead, Mimi pulled Brigid into her arms. "What do I think? I think that he's going to be all right—and I'm not just saying that. I think it's not his time to die, not yet." She held her sister close, rocking her gently.

Brigid cried softly into her chest, and Mimi felt the salty wetness grow into two round circles on her thin sweater. Finally, the tears diminished and the sniffling stopped. Yet, Mimi didn't let go. She dropped her chin to the young girl's head, breathed in the smell of herbal shampoo and murmured, "You know, I think that at a time like this, the best thing is to have some ice cream."

Brigid's narrow shoulders heaved a deep sigh. Hesitantly, she raised her head and gazed at Mimi, her eyes red and swollen from crying. Her skin had blotches from the wet tears. "Mummy doesn't let me eat after seven," she said between hiccups. "She says it's not healthy. It's one of her rules, and she's very strict about her rules."

Mimi fingered back a loose strand of Brigid's hair and tucked it behind her small, perfect ear—a fairy princess ear. "Well, I'm sure your mother's absolutely right. But you know, every once in a while you just have to bend the rules—especially in the case of an emergency. And this is one of those cases."

Brigid frowned in thought. She blinked, her eye-lashes clumped and dark with wetness. "I think you're right. And maybe because it's such an emergency, I could have chocolate sauce on the ice cream, too?"

"It might have to be carob, but we'll make do."

Vic was right, Mimi realized. In the end, it didn't matter. It was family.

CHAPTER TWENTY-FOUR

MIMI WOKE WITH A START at the sound of the phone ringing. She shot upright on the bed. Disoriented, she looked around. Brigid's room, she realized.

Her little sister lay on her pink duvet, curled in a tiny cocoon. She was still wearing her leggings and T-shirt from during the day. Her thumb was jammed in her mouth, and she cradled a plush rabbit up against one nostril.

Mimi patted around the coverlet looking for her phone. It must have slipped out of her jeans pocket when she'd dozed off. She found it under her hip. The time on the screen read two in the morning.

Mimi pressed Talk. "Hello," she said softly and rose off the bed, careful to untangle herself from the covers and the army of pillows.

"It's Noreen. Everything all right with Brigid?"

Mimi lifted a pink mohair throw—an airy, spun confection—and leaned over to cover Brigid. The throw rose and fell with each of her sister's deep breaths.

Mimi backed away from the bed and out of the room before answering. "Yeah, fine. Brigid's asleep." She closed the door quietly behind her and moved to the table in the upstairs hallway. She turned on a small crystal lamp and the soft glow illuminated photos of smiling children and women in a jungle setting. Mimi recognized the decidedly unglamorous one as Noreen, towering in the background. They were pictures from Noreen's work in Congo with Lilah, she realized.

"Brigid was concerned, but I told her that Father was having good care." She paused. "So what's the story?"

"It seems that his guardian angel was near," Noreen expressed with a sigh, her Irish brogue coming out with the tiredness and stress. "It appears that it was no more than a panic attack. Just the same, they'll keep him overnight for observation—to be on the safe side."

Mimi was confused. "Panic attack? Why would he have a panic attack?"

"He had a…ah…a rather stressful time at work earlier in the day. In fact, that's why he asked me to join him in the city." She didn't offer any more details.

Mimi wanted to know more, but given the strain Noreen was under, she held off on a full-scale interrogation. Soon enough, the details would come out—they always did. She wasn't about to start feeling sorry for the insensitive jerk in any case.

"So do you need me to come and get you?" Mimi asked, trying to do the right thing. After all, her beef wasn't with Noreen.

"No, thank you. I think I'll just stay here. I couldn't get to sleep anyway—not after all the excitement and the bad coffee from the hospital cafeteria. And there's a comfortable chair in Conny's room, so that should do me fine. And if I really need a treat, they have Jell-O in the nurse's refrigerator for visitors. Green Jell-O. It's totally against my dietary philosophy, but at times like this it seems the perfect thing."

Mimi was about to mention the ice cream with chocolate—sorry, carob sauce—sprinkled with almonds, raisins and organic Gummi Bears—but Noreen continued unabated. She was definitely a bit wired, Mimi realized. *Wait till she crashes.*

"Anyway, since I'll stay until Conny's discharged, which heaven only knows when that will be, I have another favor to ask of you. Could you make sure Brigid gets to school on time? I suppose she could miss one day of school, it being Friday tomorrow and all, but I think it's important to maintain her regular schedule. Children thrive with order, you know."

Mimi thought back to the way her mother would sometimes spontaneously decide that Mimi should play hooky, just to have tea at the Plaza Hotel or go skating at Rockefeller Center. Once they'd even hopped on a plane for Bermuda. "You must see pink sand," her mother had exclaimed. "It'll be our secret, our ounce of naughtiness," her mother had said conspiratorially, kissing Mimi on the brow. In the end, her father had to come and bring them home when her mother had lost her passport. The adventure had ended in tears and recriminations.

"And as soon as we finish here, I'll text you a

schedule of when she should get up and dressed and have breakfast, as well as when the bus comes," Noreen rattled on, bringing Mimi back to the present. "Cook left last night for a long weekend. I always give her off Reunions since we rarely eat at home then. So it will be up to you to make Brigid her porridge in the morning as well as fresh-squeezed orange juice. If you need to make more, the juicer is in the cupboard next to the sink. And if she wants a piece of toast, could you make sure it's from the loaf of spelt bread?"

Mimi wasn't sure what spelt was, but it sounded so earthy that it had to be exceedingly healthy. "No problem. I might even have some myself." *Not.*

"What a good idea," Noreen chimed in.

Clearly, the lack of sleep was affecting Noreen's sarcasm-detection radar.

"Oh, you know where the bus stops, right? You were with me the other morning, but just in case, I can send you a Google map—"

"Noreen?"

"Yes?"

"I remember, and even if I didn't, I think Brigid might be able to tell me."

"Yes, of course. I don't know what I was thinking."

"I think it's more that you've been thinking too much for the past six hours or so."

Noreen emitted a shrill laugh.

"And you don't normally drink coffee, do you?"

"No, does it show?"

"Kinda." An understatement if ever there was one.

"Listen, thanks for the update, and I'm glad the news is good. I really am." She had to be getting soft in her old age. Either that, or Vic was once more correct. In the end, family was family.

Speaking of Vic, Mimi knew whom to call next.

VIC PICKED UP THE PHONE immediately.

He hadn't bothered to go to bed, but instead sat in the second bedroom that served as his office, staring at the computer screen. He had been nominally checking the sales figures of the past quarter and catching up on overseas emails. With offices in Asia, there was no such thing as downtime.

And while he had a remarkable—Joe would even say inhuman ability, though in words far less refined—to concentrate on the task at hand despite total chaos going on around him, that focus was sorely tested tonight.

Roxie, he noticed, was antsy, too. Instead of simply curling up on the dog bed by Vic's desk, every twenty minutes or so she'd get up and wander down to the kitchen where he'd hear her lapping water from her bowl. Then, she'd pad up the carpeted stairs and check out his bedroom before coming back to the study. At which point, she'd give him a soulful look, step on her soft bed, circle several times before settling into a donut shape, only to repeat the whole process twenty minutes later.

Now as the ring tone of Vic's cell phone cut through

the dead of night, Roxie pricked up her ears and raised her head.

"Mimi," Vic answered, recognizing the number on the screen. He swiveled his desk chair away from the desk and crossed his free arm over his chest.

At the mention of Mimi's name, Roxie got up and stood next to Vic. She rested her head on his thigh.

Vic shifted his arms so he could rub her behind her ears. "So, what's the news?" he asked.

"You wouldn't believe it, especially after all that drama with the ambulance and the police. Apparently, all he had was some sort of panic attack. I guess those symptoms can mimic a heart attack. Anyhow, he's sedated now and resting, and will be released tomorrow."

From the sound of irritation in Mimi's voice, Vic could sense that she had come down from the initial shock. "I'm glad it wasn't more serious."

"I suppose I am, too. But, you know, it's just so typical. Complete attention-seeking behavior. All this fuss. Everybody worried sick. And he doesn't even have the decency to have a heart attack."

"I don't think a panic attack is something you can plan."

"I wouldn't put it past him. You don't know my father. He can manipulate anyone and everything to get what he wants. I am *not* exaggerating. Please, if his own mother were still alive, he'd sell her out if he could gain something by it. And I wouldn't be surprised if he's used me from time to time for his own ends. The man is amoral."

Vic stilled his hand atop Roxie's head. He thought about the bargain he'd made with Conrad. He wasn't convinced it was manipulation, but that still didn't allay the fact that he'd need to come clean with Mimi before the secret dragged out any longer.

Now is probably not the best time, he told himself. She'd just been through a traumatic night. It was late. Clearly she was exhausted. Hell, he was exhausted. And besides, it was not the kind of confession you made over the phone—especially not to Mimi, whose first reaction, given her low opinion of her father, was bound to be outrage. Besides, he didn't feel like having to regain her respect all over again.

Tomorrow. Definitely tomorrow. What he needed was to have her in a good mood, a lighthearted mood. Not weighed down by family dramas or her own demons.

"You should try to get some sleep," he said softly.

"I know I should, but I'm wide awake, so maybe I'll catch up with my email. I've been neglecting my colleagues, and it's time that I touch base, maybe make a few appointments."

"Don't you think that can wait until tomorrow? I doubt anyone's awake," he pointed out.

"I know, I know. It's irrational. But that's the problem with being up at this time. You kind of think you've slept enough or gotten past that time when you really did feel tired. Does that make any sense?"

"Perfect. You're talking to someone who rarely gets more than five hours of sleep a night. I just wake up, and that's it for me."

"Me, too," she said with surprise in her voice.

"You see. We have more in common than you might have thought." Speaking of thoughts, Vic had one of his own. He quickly swiveled around to the desk—apologizing to Roxie for disturbing her chin rest, and with the phone tucked under his chin, typed in Grantham University and found the Reunions website. He scanned the events listed for Friday. And then he saw it. *Perfect. Talk about silly, non-traumatic, definitely not tragic.* He checked the availability. *Good.*

Then he leaned back in the desk chair, very pleased, very pleased indeed. "Tomorrow, we're on, then, right?"

"You bet. There is no way I'm sticking around here. I don't want to get roped in to having to get hot cocoa or slippers for the imaginary invalid."

"In which case, I'll pick you up at—" he looked over his shoulder at the screen again "—seven o'clock." He suddenly remembered. "Is riding in my car going to be all right?"

"You know what they say. Second time around is the charm."

That's exactly what Vic was hoping.

CHAPTER TWENTY-FIVE

MIMI STUCK HER HEAD in Brigid's room. *Good.* Her sister was out like a light. She tiptoed across the room to turn off the lamp on the nightstand, and noticed their dirty bowls lying on the hook rug. Mimi scooped them up. The spoons rattled against the porcelain—Brigid had insisted on using her baby Royal Doulton Bunnykins china bowls. Mimi rested her thumbs on them to dampen the noise. Then she bent back to the lamp and turned it out. A nightlight in the center of an elaborate carousel on Brigid's dresser cast a dim, reassuring light.

Mimi closed the door behind her and descended the staircase to the kitchen. The under-cabinet lights cast a soft-white glow over the granite countertops and polished hardwood floors.

She put the dirty bowls and spoons in the farm-house sink, but when she went to turn on the water realized she had no idea how to work the gooseneck faucet. She sniffed and arched her neck, looking for a handle but didn't see any. "Oh, come off it." She held up her hands in exasperation and accidentally bumped the side of the faucet. Instantly, a stream of water gushed out.

Mimi stared speechless. She guardedly touched it again. It turned off. "Wow!" She repeated the process a bunch more times, each time mystified. "What is the world coming to?" she wondered. She rinsed the bowls and silverware and placed them in the dishwasher. No doubt she was loading it all wrong, but such was the price of delegating authority to the prodigal daughter.

Satisfied with this tiny bit of domesticity, she straightened and rested the small of her back against the counter. Then she crossed her arms. She was bored, not really hungry, but searching for something to occupy herself.

The expansive country kitchen didn't really inspire her. The bowl of fruit was too virtuous. She pushed away from the counter and checked out the commercial-size refrigerator. There, too, nothing caught her fancy.

"Maybe herb tea," she said out loud. Isn't that what people drank to relax themselves? Surely that's something that Noreen would have. Barring that, she'd just have to hit the liquor cabinet. But first, she'd look for the tea.

Mimi padded in her bare feet to the adjoining pantry and turned on the light. Talk about herb tea. The choices seemed to span several continents and flavors including exotic fruits she'd never heard of. Mimi studied the labels, deciding in the end that chamomile sounded like something that a kindly grandmother would suggest in moments of stress. She jimmied off the lid and discovered that the tea was loose and not bagged. *Of course. Proper tea, not that wimpy American sort.*

Back to the kitchen, tin in hand, she searched through the drawers, looking for a tea ball.

Silverware, pot lids, plastic storage containers. She switched to the drawers under the center island. More silverware, a drawer with plastic spatulas and serving spoons. She was getting warmer.

She had her hand on yet another drawer when she heard a rattling of the back door. She stopped, the drawer half open. The door creaked open on its hinges. Her throat tightened. Then she grabbed the first thing her hand could reach.

The door slammed shut. Footsteps came closer. Mimi raised her hand, adjusted her grip. The metallic taste of fear flooded her mouth. An overwhelming sense of anxiety threatened to engulf her.

Mimi remembered trying to fight her attackers on the streets of Grozny. She remembered attempting to keep them from dragging her into the waiting car— her reaching for a lamppost, her fingers finding cold metal, her hand being ripped away at the wrist…and finally the snap of bones breaking, followed by white-hot pain shooting up her arm.

A surge of nausea and the impulse to blackout struck her anew. She could practically feel how the gloved hand had clamped over her mouth before bundling her headfirst into the backseat of the car. Once more she smelled the moldy upholstery and diesel fumes—followed immediately by the sensation of having her neck yanked backward, and a rag thrust down her throat. And then, most chilling of all—the realization that quite possibly, there was something worse than death.

But not now, Mimi told herself despite her ragged breathing. She forced herself to exhale slowly. No matter what, this time…this time, she would not surrender….

The bill of a baseball cap was the first thing she saw. She took a step forward, ready to strike.

He turned. And did a stutter-step. "Geez, Mimi, you scared me to death," Press proclaimed. "What're you doing in the dark?" He reached over to another bank of switches and turned on the overhead recessed lights. "What the hell? You planning on assaulting me with a turkey baster?"

Mimi looked at her raised arm and realized what she'd grabbed. Sheepishly she lowered it to her side and willed herself to calm down—or at least to quell the panic. "I was looking to make some tea," she bluffed.

"Might be tough with that."

"I know. I was looking for a tea ball because Noreen only has loose tea leaves."

Press marched over and opened an upper cabinet that contained mugs and pulled down a teapot from a middle shelf. Then he reached in a drawer for a metal strainer. "You brew the tea in the pot and then strain it with this. See, it even has a bottom thing to catch the water." He pointed to the metal saucer that fit beneath the strainer.

"How civilized."

Press glanced sideways at her. "I presume you can figure out how to boil water. The tea kettle is on the stove."

"I'm sure I can manage that, especially now that I've mastered the faucet." She reached for the kettle and filled it with water. "Can I get you a cup?"

"No, thanks." Press launched an attack on the fridge instead. He grabbed the freshly squeezed orange juice and drank right out of the bottle. After a long swig, he turned and looked at her. "What?" He seemed to be looking for a fight.

Mimi shook her head. "Nothing." She put the kettle on and literally watched the water boil. "Hey, where've you been anyway?" Her back was to him. "I've been leaving messages on your cell, but it goes right to your mailbox."

Press reached for his phone. "Looks like the battery's dead. I need to charge it. Besides, it's not like any of my so-called friends are so hot to get in touch with me anyway." He slipped the phone back in his pocket.

The kettle started whistling and Mimi turned off the burner. She dumped some leaves in the pot and added the hot water. Then she looked at him over her shoulder. "Well, I'm not one of your so-called friends, and I was trying to get you. It may interest you to know there was some excitement here today."

Press shrugged and took another swig of juice. "What? Did Brigid throw a tantrum when she wasn't allowed to get a pony even though she promised to feed it nothing but organic oats?"

Mimi chuckled and reached for a mug, selecting one that was hand painted with tulips. "No, though that is pretty funny." She placed the strainer over the top of a mug and gingerly poured the tea through it. "Cool. This actually works, though it's pretty strong."

Press came closer. "That's because you put too much tea in the pot. You only need a small amount. Just add some hot water to dilute it."

Mimi frowned. "Who died and made you the tea guru?"

"Unlike some people I could name, I have actually suffered through tea parties with our stepmother and half-sister. Let me tell you, you haven't lived until you've had Earl Grey and scones with strawberry jam and clotted cream—with fancy pink cloth napkins."

"I don't think you suffered too much." Mimi blew on her tea to cool it down. "The reason I was trying to reach you was that our father was whisked away in an ambulance this evening."

Press stopped with the orange juice halfway to his mouth. "And?"

"He's fine. Turns out that even though he was showing symptoms of a heart attack, he was just having a panic attack."

Press shook the orange juice bottle, then brought

the jar up to his mouth and finished it off. "I suppose I should feel relieved."

Mimi nodded. "I know. It's confusing. I thought I'd feel nothing, but I was actually worried at the time."

He seemed to think about her statement. "So what set it off? The panic attack?"

Mimi shrugged. "I don't know. I mean, what kind of stress could he possibly have that's different than usual? He always seemed to thrive in the cutthroat world of finance. Noreen hedged, and then mentioned something vague about problems during the day. It has to be personal. Maybe he was shunted to a back table at the Jockey Club?"

Then Mimi had a thought. "Wait a minute. You don't think Noreen told him she was leaving him, do you? I mean, she always seemed content to play the perfect trophy wife of the successful husband, but now with her work in Congo she seems less interested in hanging on his arm at charity galas. And I haven't heard her once mention her book group." Mimi mulled over the possibility.

"You think she plans to take off for Africa full-time?" Press asked. He was clearly taking her suggestion seriously. "Not that I blame her. After all, I took off for Australia just to get away from this family."

"Not that I felt slighted or anything," Mimi replied sarcastically. Actually, she did feel a little slighted. She focused on the topic at hand. "She'd never walk away and leave Brigid here."

"Why not? She'd just be like everybody else in

this family—not there for you when you need them," Press said bitterly.

"Gee, someone took his negativity pills today," Mimi cracked. She freely accepted her own bitterness. Yet it bothered her to hear how jaded Press had become. "Anyway, all of this is guesswork. We don't really know if they're breaking up, for a fact."

"Speaking of facts…where were you earlier this evening? I came back around seven and waited around for you to get dinner together. I'd already gotten the text from Noreen, saying she and Father had to back out, but I thought we were still on."

"Oh, my God, I never even thought about you," Mimi said truthfully. "I'm sorry. But when Noreen cancelled, I just assumed… I mean, I can't even remember the last time we had dinner together, just the two of us, beyond getting hoagies, that is."

"Well, I do. You gave me a birthday party. I was like Brigid's age, and Father and my mom had gone to New York for the evening—totally oblivious to the fact that it was my birthday, and it was Noreen's night off, too. So, I was all alone—except for Cook over the garage."

"Watching *The Simpsons* on TV," Mimi supplied.

"Yeah, she always liked that show." Press chuckled quietly.

Mimi sipped her tea. "I remember getting your call. It was in the summer, and I was a counselor at the water polo camp at the university. I'd been staying in some dorm—one of the disgusting modern ones that have since been torn down. It was like an oven—no air-conditioning, maybe one hundred degrees with one hundred percent humidity—typical New Jersey summer."

"Excuse me, but this is my sob story not yours," he reminded her.

"You're right. And you were crying up a storm."

"I wasn't *that* bad," he protested.

"Oh, yes, you were. And you had every right to be."

"And then you came home and you brought me this Hostess cake with a candle stuck in it. Only, you'd dropped the bag when you biked over, and it was kind of squished."

Mimi struck her forehead with the palm of her hand. "I didn't just bike over—I biked over it. I was so mad at what they'd done that I borrowed somebody's bike and raced to the convenience store by the Link Station. It was the only thing open that time of night, and the selection was either that or a bag of Chips Ahoy. So I went with the cupcake. And then I put the paper bag in my mouth so I could keep both hands on the bike—it was already dark and it didn't have a light, and I wanted to be as careful as possible. I don't know what happened, but somehow the bag fell out my mouth and the front tire went right over it." She gripped the mug of tea with both hands. "What a disaster."

"No, I thought it was great. I thought you were a god."

"I guess the bubble had to burst some time," Mimi mused.

Press turned away. "I don't know why I even bother to come back."

"I thought you were all excited to get together with your friends?"

Press narrowed his eyes. "Excited? I'm not even sure I have any friends." He grumbled the last statement. "When you were a no-show, I ended up hanging out at Lion Inn, helping out Tony, the manager. The kids who are supposed to be working Reunions this year are total losers, and Tony was going out of his mind. So I brought in kegs for him and set things up. You go away for one year, and you come back, and things are totally screwed up. He said as much." Press sighed with disgust.

He was becoming a bitter, old man fast, she realized. But Mimi held her tongue. Normally, she would have chided him about this. But it was hardly a "normal" occasion. Instead, she put her mug of tea on the counter and attempted to do the mature, empathetic thing. It wasn't easy. "I'm sure that Tony appreciates your efforts. But speaking of Brigid, since Noreen stayed at the hospital tonight, she asked me to take care of Brigid in the morning, getting her off to school and stuff. And, trust me, *I* could really use some help in that department."

Press snorted.

"I'm glad you agree." She raised her eyebrows and

set her mouth. "If it were left up to me, I'd feed her high-fructose sweetened cereal for breakfast and give her a dollar to buy a slice of pizza at lunch. So, will you help me?"

Press shrugged one shoulder. "Sure, it's probably the closest thing I'll get to female company this trip. Anyway, clearly you're clueless around the kitchen."

"You're right. I only figured out how to turn on the faucet by accident."

"And she'd need at least three dollars for pizza," Press continued seriously. He didn't seem to catch on to his sister's self-deprecating humor. Instead, he picked up the empty juice container and like a well-trained boy, walked over to the sink, rinsed it out and placed it in the dishwasher.

Mimi smiled sadly. He was too nice a kid to feel slighted by the world and everyone in it. "Press?"

He looked up.

"I may be getting soft in my old age, as you put it. But, no matter what—I'm still your sister. And while we may be apart most of the time and I may forget dinner engagements, I'm always here for you."

"No, you're not. If you were always here for me, you would have done what you promised."

Mimi furrowed her brow.

"You would have taken care of yourself in Chechnya."

"It wasn't my fault," Mimi protested. "There was nothing I could do to stop it."

"Yeah?" He didn't look like he believed her. "Well,

you left me—you left me alone, that's what you did." He pushed past her and hustled out of the kitchen.

Leaving Mimi confused and alone with her half-empty mug.

CHAPTER TWENTY-SIX

EARLY FRIDAY MORNING, well before anyone else was in, Vic unlocked the front door to GSI's offices in Edison. It was overcast and chilly. June, which usually was the nicest month—mild, low humidity, sunny—was shaping up to be really lousy. The forecast had called for rain today, and tomorrow was supposed to be wet, as well. They were even calling for thunderstorms on and off the whole day.

The organizers of Reunions must be ticked, Vic thought. He held the door open for Roxie, and she trotted through, holding her leash in her mouth. Without prompting, she took the first left before the reception desk and headed down the row of offices along the wall. Then she stood and waited as Vic flipped on the lights.

"I'm coming, I'm coming," he told the dog. It was their routine every weekday. Oh, who was he kidding? It was their routine practically every day of the week since Vic frequently came into work on the weekend, too.

He unlocked the office and pushed in the door. "There you go." He stepped back and let Roxie lead the way.

She headed to her bed near his desk, sat and barked. She wagged her tail expectantly.

"What makes you think you deserve a treat?" he addressed her. This was also part of their routine. Somehow it never seemed to get old, which no doubt said a lot about what made a dog happy, but even more about his own simple pleasures. Vic set his canvas briefcase atop his desk and fired up the desktop. Then he reached for the bottom drawer on Roxie's side, pulled out a bone-shaped biscuit and tossed it in the air.

Roxie caught it in one swift motion, chewed loudly, then looked up for more. She batted her thick eyelashes. She was killing him and she knew it, especially when she cocked her head and batted those same lashes some more in all innocence.

"You must think I'm a sucker," Vic responded. "Yeah, I guess I am." He dug into the drawer and pulled out one more. "Here. But that's it. Otherwise you'll get fat, and I won't love you anymore." He tossed the biscuit, and the dog swiped it in midair before chomping loudly.

Vic shook his head and returned the bag to the drawer.

Roxie sniffed around the floor for escaped crumbs, finally giving up before inspecting her stainless-steel water bowl. It was empty, and she made a pathetic attempt to lick up a bead of moisture, causing the bowl to bang repeatedly against the wall.

Vic shook his head. "I get it. I get it. You stay here,

and I'll get you something to drink." He picked up the bowl and headed toward the water fountain by the side door. His footsteps echoed on the marble floor of the empty building.

Vic usually enjoyed getting into the office early and having the place all to himself. Usually. Today he found he was antsy. He had come in on purpose to get a head start on his phone calls, especially to his people in India. This proposal for Conrad Lodge's new office in Australia was getting to the crunch stage, and he wanted to make sure that his suppliers could deliver on the mammoth order on time and at the cost he had estimated. With the decision seemingly stalled for some unknown reason, he wanted Joe to be able to come back with a supply dateline that other competitors couldn't match. His brother had been in close contact with the female project officer at the firm and had wielded his considerable charm to keep him in the loop.

Given the time zone changes, early morning was the best time to get a hold of people, but for the first time in a long time—forever, really—he found it difficult to concentrate on work. And he knew why.

He held the dog bowl under the water fountain and depressed the side button. A steady stream arced into the center of the bowl, and he stared as it filled the container. Actually, he didn't stare. He spaced out.

Mimi Lodge. Who'd have thought it? He pressed the tip of his tongue against his top lip. He hoped she'd like the show this evening. He'd ordered the tickets online, and he wasn't really sure. The last show he'd been to had been when he was married. It had been in Vegas. Some Canadian female singer. Tall. Huge voice. Shauna had loved it. He'd been nursing a dislocated shoulder at the time and couldn't remember much of anything through the fog of painkillers.

Somehow Vic couldn't see Mimi going to Vegas. She didn't look the glitz-and-glamour type. Come to think of it, he'd only ever seen her in loose pants and sweaters. The woman sure covered up her body. He wondered if she had good legs. He frowned. Probably. She'd been a jock, after all, and no amount of loose fabric could hide everything—especially when a woman was lying on top of you. Vic opened his mouth wider and—

And jumped. Cold water had run all over the side of the dog bowl and down his hand, traveling up the sleeve of his blue Oxford button-down shirt, what else? He jumped back, swearing and banging the bowl against the stainless-steel basin of the water fountain. The metal-on-metal impact made a loud clang that echoed off the painted cinderblock walls.

The outside door opened. Vic looked over. And saw his father poke his head in.

"Vic," Gus Golinski said, startled. "I heard a noise." He stepped into the hallway but kept the door open behind him with his back.

Vic rubbed his mouth, embarrassed. "Sorry, I was filling Roxie's dog bowl and accidentally dropped it in the water fount—" Vic stopped midsentence.

"Wait a minute, don't you play racquetball with your group today?"

His father frowned. "Something came up and I had to cancel."

"I can't remember you ever skipping racquetball."

"Gus, is everything all right?" a woman's voice asked from outside the open door.

Vic lifted his chin to get a better look at who was standing behind his father. Not that he really needed to. The larger-than-life, strong Jersey accent was unmistakable. "Abby. I didn't know you were here, too," Vic said, acknowledging the firm's receptionist.

"Yes, well…" She stepped closer to the open steel door and sniffed.

Vic looked down and saw she had a wad of tissues in her hand. Her jet-black mascara had run under her eyes. "Is everything all right?"

"Fine, fine." She shook her head.

"You don't look all right."

"Why don't I just wait outside?" she suggested, then ducked away.

Vic watched as his father let the heavy door close behind him. "I don't get it. Anyway, she shouldn't stay outside. It's not very pleasant."

"She'll wait in her car," his father assured him.

Only, it wasn't reassuring at all. Vic looked at his father. "What's going on here?"

"It's not what you think," Gus said quickly. A little too quickly.

Vic opened his eyes wide. "You have no idea what I'm thinking. I don't even know what I'm thinking."

"It's just that Abby and I…we talk to each other."

"Talk?"

"About things."

"Things?"

"Witek, don't act that way," his father ordered.

His reprimand didn't make a dent. "What way should I act?" Vic asked.

"We're not having an affair, if that's what you're thinking. More a support thing. Abby tells me her problems—like how her oldest son told her late last night that he's decided to leave his wife. He's met someone online. Claims he's never been in love with his wife. Can you believe it? Married going on eight years. Two kids, the youngest with Down's syndrome and everything, but cute as a button. What kind of a man does that?"

Vic had absolutely no idea—about a lot of things at the moment. "How long has this been going on?" He waved his hand toward the closed door.

"What?" His father stuck up his chin. He was still a powerfully built man, with wide shoulders and a barrel chest. Hands like hams. But middle age had brought a small stoop, and his once black hair was more salt than pepper and thinning on the top. His legs, from years of laying tile and brick, now gave him trouble, and he wore elastic knee braces when he played racquetball. Not that he would ever give it up. They'd have to drag his cold, dead body off the

court before he'd stop. "It keeps me young," he liked
to boast.

Young enough for more things than racquetball,
Vic had to think. He didn't buy this mutual support
baloney. Even if they were not having sex—geez, he
didn't want to think about that—there was clearly
something going on, something that he had hidden
all these years. Speaking of which. "How long has
this been going on?" Vic repeated.

Gus set his jaw. "Fifteen years."

Vic did the math. "Was that before or after Tom
died?" His voice was stone cold.

"After." His father looked away.

"So when you recommended that I hire her to work
here?" He let his voice trail off.

His father nodded without looking at Vic directly.

"What would Mom think?" Vic asked accusingly.

Gus looked up. "You really think your mother
doesn't know? Your mother and I haven't had a real
marriage in years—ever since…ever since…"

"Ever since you took Tom fishing and he died."

"It was an accident," his father pleaded. Then he
dropped his head. "Your mother will never accept
that. She'll blame me forever. Even now she can barely
stand to be in the same room with me."

"But…but…you live with each other. We get together every Sunday—the whole family." Vic was
confused.

"That's different. That's family," Gus explained as
if that one word said everything.

Maybe, but not to Vic. "But if it's all a farce, why don't you get a divorce?"

"Your mother would never agree to a divorce. Marriage is a holy sacrament."

Vic was dumbfounded. He tried working through all the thoughts racing through his head. "And Abby? She's content with this...this...I don't even know what to call it." Vic felt dirty just searching for the word.

"She understands. Life isn't so simple. She's been through a lot, too. A lousy divorce. Raising kids on her own. It hasn't been easy."

Vic narrowed his eyes. "Do you support them, too?"

Gus balled his fists. "You've gone too far now."

"*I've* gone too far?" Vic bellowed.

There came the clipping sound of toenails.

Roxie had gotten up to see what was wrong. "It's all right, girl. Go lie down," he ordered. Somehow he didn't want her getting close, didn't want her tainted.

The dog hesitated, then turned back to the office.

Vic rubbed his forehead.

"From all the shouting, Abby's probably worried like crazy that you're planning on firing her," his father criticized.

"Maybe you should have thought of that before you began screwing her?" Vic looked at him askance.

Gus breathed in sharply. "You apologize for that remark."

"Why?"

"That's no way for a son to talk to his father. We're family."

"Wow, some family." Vic stormed back to his office. He completely forgot about the water bowl.

CHAPTER TWENTY-SEVEN

VIC SHOWED UP at the Lodge house at seven o'clock focused on only one thing.

To put any thought of his family out of his mind.

Well, that—and sex.

He reached for the brass knocker on the massive front door painted a glossy black to match the shutters. There was also a very discreet—what appeared to be mother-of-pearl—doorbell. He wasn't sure whether he was supposed to use that, too. Frankly, he wasn't sure anyone was supposed to even touch it. As he considered his options, Vic let his eyes peer upward and saw a security camera pointed to exactly where he was standing. He hadn't noticed it the night before. But today, now that he recognized the extent to which old money made sure of the safe continuation of the dynastic line, he fully expected armed guards to descend on him if he made the wrong move. Talk about Big Brother.

The door opened. He was spared the quandary.

And it wasn't Big Brother.

It was more like little sister.

"Hi, you must be Mimi's friend." An extremely confident young girl with red pigtails, wearing a black

T-shirt and jodhpurs, held out her hand. "I'm Brigid, Mimi's half-sister. She asked me to invite you in."

"Vic Golinski. Pleased to meet you." Vic solemnly returned the handshake—Brigid's hand dwarfed in his much larger one—and noticed the dirt along the side of her riding pants. Clearly, they didn't serve as a fashion statement, and she'd actually been in close contact with horses. Probably her own horse, Vic thought. *The rich are definitely different.*

"Mimi should be down shortly. Would you care to sit in the living room?" She sounded like a highly trained, miniature etiquette expert.

Then Brigid leaned toward him conspiratorially. "I'm supposed to ask you that, but the furniture's really uncomfortable. I always slip off the chairs. You want to go to my room instead and see my Barbie collection?"

"Brigid, Vic probably doesn't want to play with Barbies." Mimi called out from upstairs.

Vic glanced up as she ran lightly down the stairs, her hand skimming the railing. "Sorry I'm running late, but we just got back from Brigid's riding lesson at Daisy Hill stables."

Brigid pulled on Vic's pants leg. "It's not called Daisy Hill. It's Colonial Hall. Anybody knows that." The little girl rolled her eyes, then turned to the grand staircase. "And I don't know why he doesn't want to play Barbies. Press plays Barbies with me, and he's a boy."

"Press is your brother. He's forced to play Barbies out of love and devotion."

Vic smiled and refocused on the stairway. It wasn't an exaggeration to say his jaw dropped.

Mimi had stopped on the landing. She had her head tucked to one side as she was fastening an earring. She wore a lush, teal-blue dress that clung to her top and draped seductively around her hips, falling just above her knees. The wrapped dress was tied on the side, and the front V-neckline was opened deep enough to split the high rounded mounds of her breasts.

Vic gulped. And watched her watching him as he gazed on her. A pleased smile spread across her face, and she rested a hand on the polished rail and descended the stairs slowly, her hips swaying gently as she placed one sandaled foot after the other.

"You'd be surprised what a man will do for love and devotion," Vic finally replied. He breathed silently through his mouth.

She arrived at the bottom of the stairs, let her arm drop to her side and walked straight for him, her shoulders back, her chin high, her eyelids narrowed. Stopping a bit too close for comfort, she stood staring at him. The heels on the sandals brought her mouth closer to his full height. "I'm counting on that," she said.

Wow. He could actually feel molecules move. She pushed forward, reaching out with her arm, her breasts lightly pushing against the sleeve of his blazer.

What the...

She stretched to pick up a small clutch bag on the narrow hall table behind him. When she straightened up, she leaned even closer.

Vic couldn't help noticing that she definitely was *not* wearing a bra. And he could only hope that he wouldn't do anything too embarrassing.

HOLDING THE SMALL CLUTCH BAG next to her nervous stomach, Mimi looked over at Brigid. "Now, you promise to have a shower before the pizza is delivered, right?" She took a step back into the central hallway and shouted, "Press, I'm about to leave. Could you come take care of things?"

Then she turned back to Vic. "My half-brother's in charge tonight since my father and Noreen aren't back yet."

He stopped adjusting the knot of his rep tie. "Your father's still in the hospital? I thought it was just a panic attack." She could hear the concern in his voice.

"It took longer to check out than they'd hoped. Something about the cardiologist being tied up in the morning. I'm sure my father had kittens, reminding everyone how much money he's donated to the place over the years."

The sound of footsteps chugging up a flight of stairs could be heard, then the slamming of a door. Press appeared from behind the grand staircase.

"Sorry, I was just looking for a bicycle pump. It looks like a tire on my bike is flat and I was hoping it's just from lack of use."

Mimi coughed into her hand. "I might have gone over a nail when I borrowed it the other day. I was going to get it fixed."

"Yeah, right. Like that's about to happen." Press gave her an annoyed look.

Mimi held out her hand. "Vic, I think you met Press the other day. As you can see we have a mutually supportive relationship."

"Sounds similar to the relationship between my brother and me."

Press gave a curt wave, then slammed his hands in the back pockets of his jeans. "I remember you from the other day at the Palace. Good to see you again," Press said with a nod. Then he directed his attention to Mimi. "So any idea when Dad and Noreen are getting back?"

Mimi shook her head. "I'm not sure. Noreen said the counselor was squeezing them in at the end of his regular schedule of clients."

Vic raised his eyebrows. "Counselor?" he asked quietly, mindful of Brigid standing next to him.

"What? They're going to go to camp and I don't get to? That's not fair," Brigid pouted. "Mummy says I'm too young. You don't think I'm too young, do you?" She looked up at Vic.

Vic looked stricken.

"Ignore her. She's a master of manipulation," Mimi advised. Then she regarded her sister. "It's not that kind of counselor."

"Probably M-A-R-R-I-A-G-E," Press spelled out rapidly.

"Mar—Mar…" Brigid tried to form the words.

Mimi raised her eyebrows. "Careful. Little pitchers have big ears."

"And very good spelling skills." Vic looked impressed.

Press scooped up Brigid and threw her over his shoulder. "Okay, half-pint, into the shower with you. Otherwise there's no pizza and I'm hungry. And when I'm hungry, I eat children for dinner." He made loud munching noises.

She squealed riotously.

Then he made a theatrical sniff of her pants legs. "Whew! You smell like a stable. It's definitely shower time." He turned and headed for the stairway.

"Thanks, Press," Mimi called out.

"Have fun, you two." Press waved over his shoulder. "And don't do anything I wouldn't do." He continued his march up the stairs.

"We're going to paint each other's nails," Brigid announced, her head bobbing as Press went up each step. She waved goodbye and giggled.

Mimi looked across at Vic. "I presume you didn't have pedicures in mind."

Vic shook his head. "The thought never occurred to me. It's something much more conventional." He glimpsed his watch. "Actually, we should get going."

"In that case, shall we?" She preceded him out of the house, waiting for him to close the door behind them.

He did so carefully, then stopped, hands on hips. He cocked his head to one side and let his eyes drag downward, giving her legs an obvious appraisal. "You know, I probably shouldn't be doing this."

"Why? You think I'll object on sexist grounds?"

"I hadn't thought about that. No, it's just that I'm not particularly keen on having my actions recorded for posterity." He pointed up toward the camera.

"Well, there's more than one way to skin a cat." Mimi stepped nearer and raised her clutch to cover the camera lens. "As to my feminist sensibilities, what can I say? Vanity wins out. Stare all you want." She went on tiptoe and gave him a deep kiss. When she finished, she sank back on her heels. "And I must say, as well, that you look very natty tonight." She brushed her fingers across his lapel—a blue blazer, naturally. "I like the tie, too. Pink suits you."

"A present from my sister. She says I should be secure in my masculinity. But enough about me. *You* look great, too. The dress. It's…it's…"

Mimi laughed. "It's so not me?" She leaned up again and gave him a quick kiss before skipping down the steps to the red pebbles in the drive. "I asked Noreen when I was talking to her on the phone if I could borrow something, and she said go ahead. I'm sure the dress looks better on her, but I thought…whatever?"

"No, whatever." He took the steps in one stride and

caught her by the hand. Then he grabbed the other and held her away to look at her. "You know, I was wondering what your legs looked like."

She went *en pointe* on one foot. Her calf muscle tensed. "Disappointed?"

"Are you kidding me? Definitely A-plus."

"It's all the swimming. Develops the leg muscles, not to mention the gluts."

He cocked his head to get a glimpse at her backside. "You-know, if someone had asked me, I would have thought it was mostly upper body strength."

"On the contrary, most of the action takes place below the water."

"You don't say?" He pulled her up against his chest. This time, he was the one to lower his head and offer the deep kiss.

When he pulled away, she sighed loudly. "So, the start of our second date. I can't wait to see what comes next."

"I hope it lives up to your expectations." He held open the door to his parked car. "You know the Quadrangle Club?"

Mimi slipped into the passenger seat and looked up. "You mean the undergraduate musical theater group? The one that does the satires?" She did up her seat belt and watched him circle the front of the car and get into the driver's seat.

He put the key in the ignition. "Yeah, they're having a show tonight to kick off Reunions. Something called 'My Big Fat Grantham Wedding.'"

"That's pretty awful. You do know that no matter what the play's about it always ends with a kick line with guys in drag?"

"You think I'm not open to a little cross-dressing?"

Mimi put the back of her head against the headrest and considered her answer. "Somehow I just can't imagine a female version of you. Even in pink, you exude testosterone."

"Is that good or is that bad?" He looked unsure.

She leaned sideways. The wraparound dress slit open at the bottom, exposing a fair amount of leg. She wondered if he'd noticed. "In your case, definitely good."

From the way he was moving his jaw, he'd noticed all right.

"So dinner and a show?" she asked, feeling powerful.

He started up the car and slowly drove to the gate. "More like a show and dinner. I got tickets for the early performance. The later one was sold out."

She reached out to touch his arm to stop him. "You know, I have a confession to make."

"You've met someone else at the Daisy Hill stables?"

"Its Colonial Hall, as you know only too well—so stop teasing me. And, no, I didn't meet anyone—at least no one over the age of twelve. It's just that… that…I've never been a huge fan of musical comedies—of any sort. I know that's practically un-American, and I could probably recite most of the songs in

'The Sound of Music' but that doesn't mean I really like them. I know you went and got the tickets. And I'd be happy to reimburse you. Not that it wasn't a spark of genius thinking to buy them—under normal circumstances that is."

Vic put the shift in Park and turned to face her head-on. "But this isn't normal."

"It's more like I'm not." She wrinkled up her face. "Is that bad?"

He let his shoulders relax. "No, in your case that's definitely good. And to tell you the truth, I'm not much into kick lines. I never got them, even when it was a line of football cheerleaders. It just seemed so cheesy. So obvious."

Mimi grinned. "I always thought you were a subtle kind of guy."

"No, you didn't. But that's all right. So what do you suggest?"

"First a question. Are you really hungry?" She was starved, but she wasn't going to admit it. In fact, she'd been hungry for the past few days in ways she hadn't been for months.

"Not particularly. Why?"

"But you made a reservation, right?"

"At the new place in town called Sustenance. Well, relatively new. A couple years old, maybe. I've never been there, but my brother, Joe, swears by it for dates."

"I'm sure it's just wonderful, but I have a favor—another favor, I guess, technically."

"Another favor?" He lowered his chin and gazed at her from under his eyebrows.

"Do you think you could cancel the reservation?"

Now he looked confused. "I suppose. You have somewhere else in mind?"

"Do I need to spell it out?"

"My place, then?" he asked, ever the quick study.

"If we go back to mine, you run the risk of having to play Barbies."

"I'd rather play with you."

Mimi felt a tingle in her gut that had nothing to do with the dozen organic Gummi bears she'd had for lunch.

CHAPTER TWENTY-EIGHT

VIC EXITED THE GATE and turned left on her street. At the intersection by the Y, he went through a yellow light.

"That was a bit risky," Mimi noted, even though three cars behind him did the exact same thing, the last when the light had already changed.

"In case you hadn't noticed, I'm in a hurry." He glanced over as they approached the public library. "Are you okay?"

"If you mean about riding in the car—I'm nervous." She pursed her lips. "But not that much. More nervous in a good way." *Strange, how the mind works.*

She glanced to the left at an old Victorian house that was divided into apartments. It was where Lilah and Justin used to live before they bought their own house on the other side of town. She remembered the good times there—lots of laughter and probably a little too much wine. Definitely too much wine.

He cut past the shopping center and turned right at an office complex of medical doctors on the corner. The hilly road gradually gave way to suburbia with its Colonial and split-level houses, the sprawling lawns and sweeping Norway maples.

The road dipped and Vic took the first left. The private drive was lined with flowering cherry trees on both sides and the ground had been artificially contoured into flowing hillocks to provide the maximum privacy for the town houses over the ridge.

Mimi had been to the complex once years ago, and then only because she was curious about what had happened to the wooded hill that she used to sled down as a kid. The hill was gone, replaced by an intimate cluster of Georgian town houses. Eye-level brick walls delineated small private front gardens. Wrought-iron plaques displayed the house numbers and Colonial-looking lampposts stood sentry on every street corner. It was like a bit of eighteenth-century Inner City Philadelphia transported to the countryside. And now that the years had passed and all the landscaping had matured, the small complex had lost that fresh, almost naked feeling, replaced by a quiet sense of comfort.

Vic circled around the block and pulled into a short driveway large enough for two cars. He had an end unit. "We're here," he announced, cutting the engine.

Mimi got out and looked around. "That's great to have the woods on one side. Makes it really private."

"Yeah, Roxie loves it."

Mimi glanced at the other units. They all looked approximately the same size—three floors, double garages—a planned development, but definitely not a development for poor people. Then she noticed a white curtain flutter in the second-story window of the town house next door. "Why do I get the feeling that someone is watching us?"

"Because someone probably is. My mother, to be exact. I'm not sure if you remember, but I think I told you I bought them a place next to mine? Anyway, she usually goes out on Friday nights with my aunt, so I'd hoped we'd miss her surveillance." He guided her through the opening in the brick wall, and they walked down a brick path lined with low boxwoods. He unlocked the front door and held it open for her.

"Always the gentleman." She stepped into the vestibule, which popped with a black-and-white marble floor. "Let me see. Perhaps I can guess what business you're in?" She admired the dramatic diamond pattern.

"It was my housewarming gift from the company. My dad even insisted on laying the stone himself." He laid his keys in a small ebony box on the side table. A gilt mirror reflected his face, but he didn't seem to notice. He barely glanced at the large abstract painting on the facing wall before turning back to Mimi. "I let my mother decorate the place. I think it represents her idea of a masculine statement."

Mimi peered into the living room. "I can see that. Lots of leather and dark wood paneling."

"Not really my style, but it made her happy."

"You're a good son."

Vic shrugged. "I try."

Mimi startled when she heard a thump from the second floor. Then she heard the by now familiar clipping of nails. "Roxie? Is that you, girl?" She crossed to the stairway and rested her hand on the newel post. The dog waddled to the top of the stairs and stood there wagging her tail.

Vic joined Mimi. "Were you on my bed again? You know you're not supposed to be."

Roxie wagged harder.

Mimi turned to Vic. "How can you deny her anything when she greets you like that?"

He shook his head. "I'm convinced she practices that greeting when I'm not home to get it just right. Besides, if I always gave into her—like with how many treats she gets—she'd be a Butterball Turkey incapable of jumping up on my bed." He looked up at the dog who remained at the top of the stairs. "You see? I only have your best interests at heart."

Mimi turned to Vic. "Not to change the subject, but to change the subject—how come your mother was staring?"

"That's what she does. She's a very suspicious person." He stepped back. "And speaking of subject changes, can I get you something to drink? Wine? Beer? Water?" He frowned. "Actually, I'm not sure I have any wine."

"I'm fine, thanks." Mimi was not going to be deterred. "Does she have a reason to be? Suspicious, I mean?"

"My mother was born suspicious. Actually, that's not quite true. It was an acquired trait. She's not a very happy person."

"I suppose I should feel relieved. I don't know why, but I was going to take it personally."

"It was—kind of. She warned me about you." He cocked his head to the side as if to gauge her reaction.

Mimi raised her eyebrows and clasped the banister tighter. "Anything in particular she didn't like?" she asked. "My hair? My clothes? You'd be surprised the number of emails the network gets about my clothes." She was suddenly feeling defensive despite the lightness to her tone.

"Who knows?"

Mimi leveled a glance at him. "C'mon. You can tell me."

"Uh, all right." He paused. "She doesn't like your family."

"She's got good judgment. *I* don't like my family— more like my father. Press's mother, my nanny—and later first stepmother—was also pretty disgusting. But thankfully, she's out of the picture and Noreen's come along. But then that's *my* take on the situation." She raised her arm and placed a hand on Vic's chest. "But pray tell, why exactly doesn't *she* like my family?"

Vic stared down at her hand. A tiny muscle moved at the back of his jaw. "She says your father killed your mother." He glanced up.

Mimi didn't reply.

"But then people say a lot of things that aren't true," he added hastily.

Mimi gave a pat to his chest, then walked away. Rubbing her arms, she wandered toward the large wall of windows in the back of the living room. They looked out on a stone patio. A man-size grill stood in one corner. A glass-topped patio table and chairs occupied the center. It all looked very efficient, very angular. "Well, maybe she's right there, too," Mimi answered softly. "I mean, he didn't physically open the bottle and hold the pills that she overdosed on. But he might as well have." She kept staring outside. Rows of azaleas were planted in front of the walls, but the boxlike space still resembled a well-manicured prison.

Vic came up behind her and put his hands on her shoulders. "Let's not talk about this."

He pressed gently to turn her around, and she complied, giving him a sad smile.

She sighed. "Gladly." Then she cocked one ear at the sound of Roxie mewing from the top of the stairs. "I think Roxie is trying to tell us something, but she refuses to come downstairs."

"You're right. It's almost her bedtime, and she expects her cuddle upstairs. I'm afraid that despite my earlier protests, I spoil her rotten—or at least, that's what the rest of my family says."

Mimi smiled slyly. "You know, a girl could really fall for someone like you."

"Any girl?"

"Well, if I had to hazard a guess, I'd say some girls in particular."

"Anyone I know?"

"I tell you what. How about we oblige Roxie and

go upstairs. That way you can show me your cud-dling technique."

He grinned. "You appreciate a good ear rub, then?"

"That's not bad, but I can think of other places I'd like more."

He slipped his hands from her shoulders to her back, massaging her lightly and drawing her near. "Such as?"

Mimi wet her lips. "My feet. I really like a good foot massage."

Vic blinked. "Somehow that wouldn't have been my guess."

"I guess I'm unpredictable."

He angled his face one way and then the other. "One of your more endearing qualities." And then Vic did the unpredictable. He swooped her up in his arms, crossed the living room and the hallway, and began carrying her upstairs.

Mimi let her head fall back. "This is all very Rhett Butler of you. I'm not exactly a small person." She laughed.

"Honey, I bench press women like you for break-fast." He was almost to the top and not even panting.

"But it's closer to dinnertime," Mimi noted.

"Then I'm truly just getting started." He reached the top landing.

Roxie got up and danced a four-pawed jig around his feet.

"Okay, girl, you can come into the bedroom—for

five minutes tops. And then it's private time," Vic announced to the dog.

"You think she'll understand?" Mimi asked, quite enjoying the feeling of a hunky male effortlessly transporting her down the short hallway.

"Trust me. She'll get the message." Vic kicked open the door to his bedroom and crossed the carpeting to the bed. He deposited her at the end, allowing her to sit with her legs hanging over the edge. He sat next to her, and Roxie trotted in to face them both. "Five minutes," he warned again, pointing to his watch.

It was bizarre, but Mimi could have sworn that Roxie nodded. That was just *before* she jumped on the bed, somehow wiggling her way in between the two of them.

She gave Vic a slobbery kiss on the face, then did a twitch jump, sending Mimi falling backward. The dog landed with her front forelegs on Mimi's collarbone and proceeded to nuzzle her cheek, kiss her chin, finally rolling over lengthwise between Mimi and Vic and exposing herself with no inhibitions.

Mimi laughed. "I can see why people have dogs to greet them when they come home."

Vic leaned back and gave Roxie a good tummy rub. "You're shameless, you know that?"

Roxie leaned her head toward Mimi.

"And you're also incredibly disloyal," Vic chided. "Who feeds you? Who walks you? Who takes you to the vet?"

At the last question, Roxie whined.

Mimi chuckled. "Maybe you should have omitted the vet part?" She gently ran her hand down the silky fur of the dog's ear, mesmerized by its softness. "You're some lucky dog, you know that?"

Roxie emitted a gurgling sigh, simultaneously moving a hind leg rapidly back and forth as if scratching her tummy. The movement caused her to brush up against Mimi.

"Hey, you're tickling me," she protested.

"I think you found her sweet spot," Vic said with a catch in his voice.

Mimi looked over.

Vic was resting on an elbow and staring at her.

"What?" she asked. Then she noticed his eyes focusing downward and she craned her neck to see. "Oh, I see." Roxie's scratching had loosened up the self-tying belt on the dress. One side of the bodice hung open, exposing only her thin, flesh-colored camisole. "Oh," she repeated again. Under his intense scrutiny, her nipple hardened into a tight point.

"Roxie, I think your five minutes of fame are up," Vic commanded.

The dog tried wagging her tail. It flopped back and forth on the quilted bedcover.

Vic stared sternly.

Roxie went for batting her long, lush lashes—the ultimate in guilt-inducing-cuter-than-cute behavior.

"Roxie." His voice became more disapproving.

The dog scrambled to her stomach, then hopped off the bed, stepping on Vic in the process.

"Oomph," he exclaimed and grabbed just above his crotch. "That was close."

Mimi watched the dog pad out of the room, then turned on her side to look at Vic. "Any commands for me?"

"Like you'd take commands." He gently inched his index finger to open the top of her dress, revealing both breasts. "On the other hand, if you have some directives..." He lowered his head and rubbed his cheek against one breast through the silky material. Then he shifted the fabric and began feathering light kisses around the small mound, before using his tongue to lathe her nipple to a sharper peak.

Mimi caught her breath when he took it completely in his mouth and suckled deeply. When he moved to the other, she pressed her eyelids shut, absorbing the sensations. And when he finished, he straddled her body and shimmied up, his head even with hers. Feeling his cool breath on her face, she reluctantly opened her eyes.

"Nothing to say?" he asked playfully.

She swallowed. "I think you're doing pretty well all on your own."

"In that case." Vic sat back on his haunches and slipped off his jacket and began methodically undoing his buttons.

Mimi saw that his pupils were dilated and her chest rose and sank as she watched him undress. He didn't disappoint. Muscles contoured his chest and sculpted his arms. A smattering of brown hair formed a triangle, setting off his light brown nipples.

Vic moved for his belt, and Mimi reached up to help him. Together, their fingers fumbled with the button at the waistband. She pushed his hand aside, and lowered the zipper herself. "Bossy," he exclaimed.

His erection jutted out against his boxers. She ran her hand up and down the length through the knit material. Then she looked up. "Are you complaining?"

"Hardly." He pressed his hand atop hers before moving aside to kick off his shoes, trousers, socks and finally underwear.

Mimi swallowed as he came back to her completely naked. "You're quite...ah...coordinated."

"As a football player, I was particularly known for my hands and my timing." He began to methodically strip the dress off her body.

Mimi raised her arms and wiggled out of her camisole. But when she lowered her hands to take off her bikini briefs he stopped her.

"Let me." Slowly, tortuously, he slid them down her legs, slipping off her sandals as well when he reached her feet. Then he snaked back up and stopped with his hands on her hips. He used his thumbs to gently massage the juncture of her legs, the circular motions finding her most sensitive area.

Mimi gasped. "You're right about your hands."

"Well, that's only the start of things." He lowered his mouth to tease her intimately.

And after that, she forgot all about football.

CHAPTER TWENTY-NINE

THE NEXT MORNING, Mimi sat on a stool in Vic's kitchen munching a piece of toast with peanut butter and nursing a mug of strong black coffee. She crossed her bare legs and lazily swung one foot. She wore underpants and his blue Oxford cloth shirt, buttoned haphazardly.

Vic definitely thought that was two garments too many—especially as he watched her lick the peanut butter. He stifled a groan.

He ignored a nudge against his leg, right below the hem of the pair of gym shorts he'd slipped on.

The nudge came again.

Vic reluctantly tore his eyes away from Mimi and glanced down. Roxie. Who else? He reached for the jar of peanut butter and used a knife to scoop out a small amount. Then he got off the chair and plopped the dollop into Roxie's stainless-steel dog dish.

Mimi leaned to the side and watched, holding on to the counter top—Absolute Black granite in a honed, matte finish. "Very masculine," had been his mother's assessment.

"You know, beneath that gruff exterior lies a very tender being," Mimi said.

"If you're implying I'm a sucker for big brown eyes and a few strategic prods, you've got that right."

"I noticed," she said, pursing her lips.

Vic immediately abandoned the dog for Mimi. Leaning over like that, he couldn't fail to notice how the shirt gaped open. He caught a tantalizing glimpse of her breasts. Mimi's lanky, coltish figure, with her narrow hips and small breasts, seemed more luscious—more real—than the surgically and cosmetically altered women who usually latched onto football players.

Vic always thought there was something desperate about the way they tried so hard to look sexy. Whereas Mimi wore no makeup, barely brushed her hair and clearly didn't give one wit about her wardrobe. She wasn't even self-conscious about the small chip on the side of her top tooth.

"Oh, that," she'd replied some time last night. "I got that from one of our first matches when I was a freshman. After that, *I* learned how to play dirty, too." She'd laughed and rolled over on top of him.

She was right, Vic thought, recalling their lovemaking. She had learned how to play dirty, all right.

Never mind whom he'd been involved with in the past—she was the sexiest woman he'd ever met. But it was more than her look—or lack of caring how she looked—that made her so fantastic. It was her attitude—the mixture of fearlessness and vulnerability. And over the course of the past few days the fearlessness that she always displayed on camera was coming out more. Still, though, the vulnerability, the sensitivity was there—no matter how hard she tried to mask it with smartass comments or her take-no-prisoners attitude. And that was probably the part of her that Roxie responded to, Vic figured.

Just as Vic took a sip of coffee from his mug—the Best Uncle mug that Tommy had given to him for his birthday—he had a lightbulb moment. His dog? His dumb dog? And he wasn't being cruel here—Roxie was not the brightest—but in this instance, she was a lot quicker than he.

Mimi Lodge was The One. Okay, so he didn't know her in fine detail—well, he did, but not in that sense. But in his gut—a part of his body he rarely called upon for advice. Somehow, someway, she was his soul mate. Someone he could spend the rest of his life with. Because she made him realize that he didn't need to always wear a blue Oxford shirt. Maybe there was even a world beyond blue? And maybe he could get close to someone and not always feel responsible—not that he didn't want to share. But he knew that when push came to shove, if bad times surfaced amidst the good, she would be able—no, she'd jump at the opportunity—to do her share.

This realization had hit him in a flash. Just long enough—and radical enough—for the coffee to go down the wrong way. He pounded the mug to the table, sputtering and coughing.

Mimi immediately sprang from her stool and came

over. "Raise your hands. Open your airway," she ordered, then started slapping him on his back.

He did what he was told, and the spasms petered out. At last, he breathed in deeply.

"Are you okay?" she asked, clearly worried.

He coughed. "Better than you could possibly imagine." The truth was, if he had to die right now, he'd die a very happy man—the happiest he'd ever been in his whole life.

On the other hand, he had no intention of dying. Not by a long shot.

Vic turned toward her and looked down at his shirt, buttoned with only a minimum of modesty. It was too inviting to pass up. He wiggled his fingers mischievously and snaked his hand inside the slit. "Care for some morning exercise?"

"I'm usually more a water person." Mimi gulped when his hand found her breast. "Though I could be persuaded."

"How would you react if I told you I have a very large bathtub, with all sorts of jets and whirlpools that I've hardly ever used?"

She pressed her body up against his. His hands rested between them. He could feel her heart racing through his palms. His own doing a rapid tattoo.

"It sounds very therapeutic," she said, her voice smoky. She went up on tiptoes and kissed the underside of his chin.

Vic wasn't sure he could make it to the second floor. "I can think of several other areas that could use that kind of kissing ministrations. Old football injuries."

"I've never thought of myself as having healing lips."

"Honey, you don't know how therapeutic you are." Vic rubbed his body against hers, letting his jutting arousal inside his shorts tease her stomach.

"Uncle Vic, Uncle Vic. It's raining. It's raining," a high-pitched voice shouted. A door slammed shut. "No Parade. No Parade."

Vic and Mimi jumped apart.

"What?" she squeaked.

Vic barely kept from swearing.

"Uncle Vic. Uncle Vic." The shouting and the stamping of rubber-soled feet grew as their owner approached the kitchen in the back of the house.

Tommy, all three feet of him, stopped at the threshold with his eyes wide and his yellow rain slicker dripping in a circular puddle around his green rubber boots. He raised his arm and pointed. "Who are you?"

Vic rubbed a hand across his bare chest. "Tommy, it's not polite to point. This is Mimi." He nodded toward Mimi who was rapidly buttoning up her shirt and pressing the shirttails flat against her long legs. "Mimi, this is my nephew, my sister Basia's son, Tommy."

Mimi stepped from the safety of the island and held out her hand. "Hi, Tommy. I'm a friend of your uncle's."

Tommy shook hands solemnly, his head bobbing

up and down in rhythm. "How come you're Uncle Vic's friend? You don't look like a boy."

Mimi blinked. "I'm not. Boys can be friends with girls, too."

Tommy nodded as he took in the information. "There are girls at nursery school." In Tommy's version, "nursery" came out "nussry." "One has a cubby next to me."

That seemed to be the end of the discussion because the next moment, Tommy went running to Vic and gave him a bear hug around his knees. Then abruptly, he pounced on Roxie who was lying on the tiled kitchen floor in front of the humming refrigerator. The dog heaved a large sigh but otherwise tolerated being smothered by thirty pounds of boy.

"Mommy says no Parade," Tommy announced without letting go of Roxie's neck.

Vic decided to take pity on Roxie and opened a lower cupboard. He pulled out a box of dog biscuits. "Hey, bud, I bet Roxie would like some treats. How about you come over here and get some? And then you can tell me how you got in here." He looked skeptically at Mimi, who shrugged.

Tommy reluctantly let go of his death grip and ran to Vic. He held his hands out. "I took Mommy's key ring from the key basket. I know your key 'cause it's blue." He looked at Mimi. "I know my colors."

"That's fantastic," Mimi answered. She crossed her hands across her chest.

Vic placed three biscuits in Tommy's hand. Usually,

he only gave Roxie one, but he figured that the dog deserved hardship pay. "Where are the keys now?"

"In the door," Tommy answered with a slow shake of his head.

"Okay, you give Roxie these and then you better run back home and return your mom's keys. I'm sure she'll be looking for them—and you."

Tommy gazed at the biscuits. "One, two, three. See, I can count, too," he said proudly.

"That's great. See if you can give all three to Roxie. But then you better go home."

Tommy turned and looked up at Mimi. "You can give her one, if you want?"

"Oh, thank you," Mimi said and knelt next to Roxie.

Tommy handed her one. "You've got boobies. Not big like Mom's," Tommy told her in a very serious voice.

"Tommy." Vic raised his voice.

"That's all right," Mimi said in a normal tone. "Girls have breasts, especially when they get older."

"Then you must be old," Tommy said, intently staring at her.

"Not that old, but old enough." Mimi held out the biscuit for Roxie and let her lick it greedily off her hand.

"You gotta make her sit first," Tommy instructed. He held his arm up stiffly. "Sit," he commanded loudly.

Roxie lumbered up, then sat. Her lips sagged on the side.

Tommy rewarded her with one biscuit, and the dog crunched loudly.

"High five," Tommy commanded when Roxie sniffed out the remaining treat.

The dog lifted a front paw and shook hands with Tommy.

Mimi clapped. "Good girl. You're a clever dog. And you're a very good dog trainer," she complimented Tommy. Then she looked at the refrigerator doors and studied the snapshots stuck to the stainless steel with various magnets. "Hey, is that you in the picture?" She pointed upward toward a photo of Tommy blowing candles on a cake. A young woman hugged him from behind and helped with the candle blowing.

"It's not po-po—"

"Polite?" Mimi suggested.

"Yeah, that. You shouldn't point."

Vic came over. "That kind of pointing's okay. It's just at people that's not good."

Tommy accepted Vic's explanation and looked up at the photos. "Yeah, that's me with Mom at my birthday party this year. I'm three." He held up three fingers.

"Yes, I can see you can count." She studied the photo. "Your mom's very pretty."

Tommy didn't seem to listen because he'd already moved to other pictures. "And that's my Grandma and

Grandpop at Christmas in their house. Santa comes to their house 'cause that's where I live with my mom."

Mimi squinted. "That makes sense. And who's that with your Uncle Vic?" She pointed to the photo next to it.

"Oh, that's Uncle Joe. That's at the office, right, Uncle Vic?" He looked up for confirmation.

"Yes, that's right. That's when we opened the new company headquarters in Edison."

Mimi peered closely. "He's very handsome, your Uncle Joe." She glanced up slyly at Vic.

"He's too young for you," he said back, not completely joking.

"Maybe I like 'em young?"

"Yeah, he's not old like you," Tommy rattled on, oblivious to the adult interchange, let alone the undercurrents. "He acts like a kid. That's what everybody says, 'specially Uncle Vic."

Mimi raised her eyebrows. "Oh, does he?"

"Joe has maturity issues," Vic said with the tone of an older brother.

Mimi processed that information before looking back at the photos. "And who's that?" Mimi asked Tommy, pointing to an old snapshot. It showed an adolescent boy all suited up in a football uniform, holding his helmet against his hip. His thick chestnut-brown hair hung around his ears, a large smile spread across his face. Dimples marked each cheek. She raised her chin. "Don't tell me that's you, Vic, from high school or even earlier? You look so young."

"No, silly, that's my uncle," Tommy corrected her impatiently.

Vic reached over and picked up Tommy. "Okay, buddy, it's time you headed home before your mother starts to worry." He carried him to the front door, gave him the blue keys and opened the door. He set him down and patted him lightly on the rump to send him on his way.

"Boo-bies, boo-bies," Tommy sang loudly, laughing in between syllables as he skipped down the path.

Vic waited until he saw his nephew run next door before walking back to the kitchen. Mimi was standing now, studying the photos. "Sorry about Tommy barging in and the whole 'boob' thing," Vic apologized. "He's three. Three year-old boys' favorite words are boobies, poopie and pee pee."

Mimi turned to face him. "Well, I'm not sure that boobie fascination stops at three years old." Then she pointed over her shoulder. "Speaking of getting older. That photo from high school? The football one? It's strange, but I would have sworn it was you. I mean, your brother, Joe, must have changed a lot as he got older."

She moved her hand to a newer picture taken of Vic and Joe standing side-by-side at a ribbon cutting ceremony. Joe a cocky smile. Vic a serious expression. Vic's hair dark, Joe's a golden blond. She looked from one picture to the other and back again. "Of course, he could have highlights. You'd be surprised the number of men who highlight their hair these days. Did I ever tell you about the rebel leader in Kosovo?"

Vic shook his head and reached for her hand. "That's not Joe. That's my twin, Tom."

CHAPTER THIRTY

"You have another brother?" Mimi looked at him curiously.

"Had. Tom was my twin. He died in a boating accident when he was in middle school."

"Oh, I didn't realize…" She thought she'd felt embarrassed after Tommy barged in. Now she really felt like she had put her foot in her mouth. "Here I rattled on and on the other night, a real pity party about my own childhood. Why didn't you stop me? Say something? I feel foolish." She held her hands up in the air.

He rubbed his mouth, then his chin. "It wasn't about me last night. Besides, it's not something I talk about all that much."

"What do you mean it's a question of not talking? You let me bare my soul to you the way I've never done to anyone one else, and you don't think it might be relevant to mention somewhere that you lost your twin brother?" She stared at him and waited.

And got nothing in return.

She breathed in. "Tell me."

"Tell you what?"

"Vic, you of all people are ill equipped to play dumb."

Vic rested a hand on the kitchen's center island and looked down. "I wasn't there when it happened," he said with resignation. "But I was supposed to have been." He glanced up. His face was clearly marked with sadness.

Mimi sat down on one of the kitchen stools, pulling out another next to her. She patted the seat. He relented and straddled the cushion. He rubbed his fingers across the smooth black countertop, his eyes not really focused on anything in the room.

Roxie got up and rubbed against his leg. He reached down and patted her silently.

"Vic?" Mimi ducked her chin and tried to get his attention. "If it's too difficult, you don't have to talk about it. I understand, you know."

He swallowed and turned to face her. "I know. But it's all right. I mean, it happened a long time ago." He massaged Roxie's bigger ear. "Tom and I were really close, which you'd expect from identical twins. When we were little, we even had our own twin language. But as close as we were, we were also really competitive."

He laughed philosophically. "No more so than on the football field, even back to the Pop Warner League. Anyway, we always had this thing in our family—whoever had a better game that Saturday got to go fishing with my dad on the Delaware River."

"This particular weekend, I had the better game, but it was raining, and I really didn't feel like going. But tradition is tradition in my family."

Why did that phrase sound so familiar to Mimi?

"Anyhow, I claimed I had a sore throat and that Tom could take my place—I made it sound like I was really bummed and being all magnanimous." He stopped.

Mimi skirted her hand across the island and rested it atop his. "It's okay. It was an innocent act."

Vic frowned. "Is anything an innocent act?" He shook his head, obviously not in the mood for a philosophical discussion. "Anyway, the river was swollen from the rain storm, and the water was running fast. My father couldn't see a tree trunk that had gotten snagged on some rocks. They capsized. Dad made it. Tom didn't. They found his body two days later washed up downstream."

Mimi was horrified. "Wasn't he wearing a life jacket?"

"Yeah, but—" Vic held up his hands in frustration. "He didn't make it." He stood up, wandering to the refrigerator. He opened one of the double doors and stared inside.

Mimi still sat. "Your family must have been devastated."

Vic shut the door without removing anything and turned around. "Tell me about it. I don't think they've ever fully recovered."

"And what about you? Have you fully recovered?"

Vic bit down on his lower lip. "For a while I was pretty angry. But then I learned that if I just kept everything in check, lived a very orderly, well-regulated existence, I could put it behind me." He made an exact chopping motion with his hand. "I learned to focus on the tasks at hand, work hard and try not to screw up. I figured that was the best way to make sure there were no more family tragedies."

Mimi digested what he'd said. It explained so much about him. "So that's how you acquired your overdeveloped sense of responsibility?"

He shrugged. "Perhaps. But that's just what the oldest is supposed to do."

"Then I must have missed that gene," Mimi admitted. "And what about the anger? Does it ever get out?" Not that she was personally worried. The man was intrinsically gentle. Why else would the world's most fearful dog feel the need to wander over and entwine herself between his feet? No, Mimi was more concerned for him.

"Anger? No, not really. Not since I stopped playing football."

"Ah-h. Now, I get it. The infamous head-butting incident? Something triggered it?"

"I was playing a lousy game—getting beaten out, missing my tackles. And it was the anniversary of Tom's death. One of those perfect-storm moments."

"Hence, the psychiatrist's diagnosis of unresolved anger management issues?"

"Hence, indeed." He walked to the other side of the island and rested his hands opposite her. "So now you know."

"Now I know." Then she thought of something.

"Does Tommy know? I mean, your nephew? Does he know he was named after his late uncle?"

"Kind of. Obviously he doesn't yet understand the significance of his namesake. Not that my sister had any choice, mind you. My mother had declared as soon as she found out Basia was pregnant, that it was God's way of preserving Tommy's memory. She was convinced it would be a boy. She even claimed she'd been praying for it the whole time. Truthfully, I think it was more a question that Basia's boyfriend, soon to be husband—and in rapid succession, future ex-husband—in his usual loser ways, didn't bother to use a condom. But don't tell that to my mother."

"Maybe it's better for Tommy to find out when he's older. Less pressure," Mimi responded.

"Meanwhile Basia has had to bear the burden of preserving the sainted legacy. It's not bad enough that she's had to compromise her own ambitions and talents. She's also had to put up with my mother micromanaging Tommy's life." He breathed in slowly. "So, you see, your rosy view of the Golinski family?"

Mimi got up and circled the island. She tucked a hand between his arm and waist and forced him to turn toward her. "I'm truly sorry that things haven't been easy for you. I guess the moral of the story is that no one is spared sorrow at some time. And I understand your desire to move on, to not dwell in the past."

She put her other arm around his waist and drew him close. Heat emanated from his naked torso. She looked up, willing him to lock eyes with her. "But you know, don't you, that you can tell me anything?

He gazed down at her, opened his mouth, hesitated, and then spoke. "About Reunions…"

"Didn't you hear? The Parade is cancelled because of the rain. Leaves more time before the panel, don't you think? For more reflective activity?" She smiled playfully.

"You know, you can really be a distraction when you want to." He smiled back.

The phone on the kitchen counter rang.

Mimi glanced over her shoulder towards the noise and frowned. "You know, if I were paranoid, I'd say your mother has stepped up her surveillance."

VIC RECOGNIZED THE NUMBER that lit up the screen. "You were right to be paranoid. I better get that. It's my parents' house. Who knows what tales Tommy's been telling them."

Still in her clasp, he leaned over and picked up the phone.

"It's raining. I thought it wasn't allowed to rain on Grantham University Reunions." It was Basia.

Vic swiveled back and faced Mimi. *It's my sister,* he mouthed silently.

She made a pointing motion as if to say, "Do you want me to go to the other room?"

He shook his head, adjusted one of her arms on his hip and snuggled in closer. "Is that the only reason you're calling?" he asked his sister.

"Hmm, Tommy did mention something about you having a friend with boobies—a direct quote—but unlike the rest of our family, I figured I'd give you a chance to explain in your own time."

"I always knew you were special. You're bound for greatness—and that includes Carnegie Hall one of these days."

Basia laughed. "Who knows? But, listen, I'm calling because I went on the Grantham website this morning, and not only did I find out the Parade was cancelled, but I also learned that there's going to be a big party in Baldwin gym—in the basketball arena—instead. Everybody's still supposed to come dressed up, and all the bands from the Parade will be there. Like one big party. Doesn't that sound great?"

"Not really. I can think of other things I'd much rather be doing." Vic winked at Mimi.

"Uh-huh, that's too bad because in case you've forgotten, you invited Joe and me and Tommy to be in the Parade with you. I don't know about Joe, but Tommy's not about to let you off the hook."

"Not even with the latest Lego set?"

"Vic," Basia warned.

Vic rolled his eyes. "Okay, okay. When are we supposed to be there?"

"Ten minutes ago."

"Got it. Give me five. I'll text you when I'm in the car and ready to go." He clicked the off button and rested the receiver on the counter. "Duty calls," he announced to Mimi.

She raised her eyebrows.

"The rained-out Parade has morphed into an indoor Un-Parade at Baldwin Gym."

"Goody, goody. My favorite—drunken alums in bizarre class costumes rubbing shoulders in a confined space. Just stick a stake in my heart now." She punched her chest dramatically.

Vic kissed her on the forehead and pulled away. "Gladly, but I've got to first take my sister and Tommy to the festivities. After that, I'll gladly stick whatever you choose anywhere you want."

She rocked her head back and forth at his teasing. "You sure you can't be a few minutes late? I have a few ideas." She wrangled him back with a tug on his arm.

He angled his head, ready to kiss her and more when...

When he cocked his head. "Now it's my turn to be paranoid. I could swear I can hear marimbas playing? Did a Caribbean band suddenly sneak into the house when I wasn't looking?"

Mimi sighed and shook her head. "No, that's the Disney song 'Under the Sea' from the *Little Mermaid.* It's Brigid's ring tone on my phone. She knows how to use speed dial."

"Why am I not surprised?"

"I *also* promised to take her to the Parade, along with Noreen and my Dad, and now she's undoubtedly calling to let me know about the change of plans. If ever there was someone who wouldn't take no for an answer, it's her."

Vic shook his head. "Who'd have thought our sex life would be held prisoner to the youngest members of our families? You don't think we could skip out on the panel this afternoon instead, do you?"

"And have my father on my back—even more than usual—for the rest of my life? No way. But never fear—this is to be continued." She gave him a quick kiss on the lips. "As much as I hate to say this, I've got to get home and change and put on our wonderful class costume. Speaking of which, I can't wait to see you in it." She put her chin in her curled up fist and pretended to study him. "Somehow I can't picture you in a Beefeater's outfit."

"Me? Wear something that ridiculous? I don't think so. I'm prepared to wear a black-and-orange-striped tie, but that's as far as I will go."

"Chicken," Mimi taunted him and started to run from the kitchen.

He grasped her by her trailing hand. "Mimi, before you go. About my not talking about things until you brought them up?"

She pulled away. "You don't need to explain again. I get it. It's a guy thing. We can talk about this at the Un-Parade Parade, okay?" And she scampered away with Roxie trailing right behind.

"Traitor," Vic murmured.

He just hoped she wouldn't think the same thing about him when she found out the truth.

CHAPTER THIRTY-ONE

IT WAS SHEER BEDLAM at Baldwin.

Unlike the Parade, where each graduating class and their family members marched in groups through the university campus and down Main Street of Grantham, the Un-Parade compressed everyone into one massive jumble. The orange battle fatigue outfits in one class mingled with the orange-and-black tuxedoes of another, not to mention the Viking faux-animal skins, Roman togas and yoga mom costumes.

Massive orange balloons bobbed against the netting covering the super-high ceiling and wafted to the floor as the helium escaped. Children scampered underfoot and batted them around in haphazard patterns.

Added to the cacophony of colors and ages was the din of voices and music. The customary bands had relocated to the seating above the basketball court, and it sounded like they were having a face-off. Dixieland competed with a tuba group. New Orleans jazz tried drowning out a swing band. Somehow, the organizers had even managed to maneuver two of the Parade floats into the entrance area of the building.

True to her word, Mimi wore her class's Beefeater's jacket. Only instead of the London Tower's traditional red with gold trim, it was Grantham's school colors—orange with black trim. She drew the line at wearing the oversize black hat, and instead clutched it in one hand. With the other, she held on to Brigid.

"Don't lose me now," she said, bending down.

Brigid stopped lunging for a falling balloon to look at her. "Don't worry. If we get separated I will go to stand next to the Heisman Trophy and you or Mom or Dad or Press will come find me."

"That sounds like a good plan. Wait a minute. You know what the Heisman Trophy is?"

"Dad takes me to see it before every Grantham football game. He tells me it's a shine," Brigid said proudly.

"A 'shine'?"

"She means a shrine," Press explained coming up next to her. "What a zoo, huh? I'm supposed to meet Matt, but I doubt I'll find him."

Brigid tugged on his black shorts.

Press's class outfit was a Tyrolean lederhosen look, and somehow he managed not to appear totally stupid. Mimi couldn't quite figure out why. Maybe it was because he wore a Hoagie Palace T-shirt instead and let the suspenders hang down from his waist.

"I want ice cream," Brigid announced.

"Ice cream? They don't have ice cream," Mimi replied.

"Yeah, they do—Creamsicles. What would you expect," Press answered bouncing on the heels of his boat shoes. Creamsicles were vanilla ice on a stick encased in orange sherbet—perfect for Grantham's colors.

Mimi made head-bobbing motions toward Noreen, who was standing off to the side with Conrad. "Ix-nay on the eamsicle…oh, whatever. I can't figure it out," she said to Press.

He took no notice and waved at Noreen. "Hey, I'm going to get Brigid some ice cream," he announced. Miracle of miracles, Noreen nodded affirmatively. "Ta-ta," Press wiggled his fingers goodbye to Mimi, then hoisted Brigid on his shoulders. "Up we go." He settled her firmly. "You can be the scout and let me know when you see the ice cream, Brig." He pushed his way through the crowd.

Which left Mimi with Noreen and her father, both of whom, she couldn't help noticing, were uncharacteristically subdued for the occasion. Oh, her father was doing his usual glad-handing and superior up-and-down chin acknowledgment of fellow alumni, but his skin was pale, his smile not exposing the normal number of top teeth and gum.

Maybe there were problems with the marriage, after all?

Oh, forget about Noreen and her father. There was only one person she was concerned about seeing. Vic.

Mimi scanned the crowd. Someone knocked into her from behind with a murmur of "Sorry." "That's okay," she heard herself saying. And it was, she realized. She could stand in a crowd, people pushing, and she wasn't afraid.

For once, she wasn't thinking about the past. She was focused on the here and now. And the smile spreading across her face? It hinted at the future.

CHAPTER THIRTY-TWO

PRESS RIPPED THE PAPER COVER off the Creamsicle and passed it to Brigid. "Tell you what. How about I put you down now so you don't drip all over this outfit? It cost me some serious cash." He scooped his sister off his shoulders and lowered her to the floor. "And you better take some of these, as well." He grabbed a wad of paper napkins and held them out.

Brigid was too engrossed with her ice cream to bother to reply.

Press kept the napkins anyway, waiting for the inevitable moment when Brigid would get ice cream all over her black polka dot dress.

"See, Tommy, that girl got ice cream. I'm sure we can get you one, too," a young woman's voice sounded off to Press's right. "Ice cream's much better than an old balloon anytime."

He glanced over. The waitress from the Circus diner. "Basia, right?" he said to her. "My friend Matt and I met you the other morning?"

Basia glanced up. "Oh, right. Press, isn't it?"

He nodded. He looked down at the boy clutching her hand with both of his. "And this is your son?"

"That's right. Tommy, say hello to Press."

Tommy hid farther behind his mother's legs, poking his head around the side of her pants to barely sneak a peek.

Basia looked down. "He's kind of shy with strangers."

"That's okay. He makes up for my half-sister, Brigid, here, who's not shy at all. Brigid, say hello."

Brigid stopped licking. "Hello. Why is he crying?"

"Oh, he's upset because the balloon he had burst. I told him I'd get him an ice cream instead." She ruffled Tommy's dark hair.

Brigid stepped closer to Tommy. "Ice cream's much better," she announced confidently. "How old are you? Are you a baby?"

Tommy stuck his head between his mother's legs. "I'm not a baby. I'm three." He held up three fingers.

Press got down on his haunches. "Well, three-year-olds need to have ice cream, that's for sure." He stood up and spoke to Basia. "If you guard the brood, I'll get another Creamsicle." He looked down at the napkins in his hand. "And you better take these. You're more in the line of fire."

Press moved closer to the table where a couple of students in orange polo shirts were digging through orange-colored coolers, handing out the free ice cream. An orange paper cloth covered the table and two bunches of balloons were taped to the corners. "Could I get another ice cream?" Press called out. "And if you don't mind, I'm going to swipe one of your balloons for a friend of mine." He gave a wink to one of the young women working, and she didn't seem to mind one bit.

"I can get more than one for you," she said, smiling back.

"Oh, that'd be great. Four if you can spare them." He flashed her a killer smile.

"Up to your old tricks, I see."

Press looked sideways, but he already knew it was Amara. She acknowledged him with a shoulder bump.

"Hey, yourself," he responded. "I thought you were working this Reunions?"

"I am. Can't you tell?" She wore the same orange polo shirt as the students working the ice cream table. "I'm in charge of ferrying around one of the old alums in a golf cart, but since the Parade got pushed inside, he's happily ensconced at a table, and I'm supposed to get him some ice cream."

"Here's your ice cream and balloons, then." The female student behind the table held them out to Press. Then she noticed Amara and abruptly turned to help the next customer.

Amara bit back a smile. "Another heart broken by the heartthrob of Grantham." She grabbed an ice cream and spied Press's haul. "So who's the loot for?"

"My new best friend. C'mon, I'll introduce you." Press escorted Amara to where Basia was waiting with the kids. "Here you go, Tommy, one ice cream." He handed it to Basia when she held out her hand. "And two new balloons for you." He separated them from the bundle. The boy clapped. "Why don't we tie them around your wrist so they don't fly away."

"No balloons for me?" Brigid pouted. Ice cream dripped down her hand and forearm.

Press scratched his head. "I guess these must have your name on it." He attached the other two balloons to Brigid's sticky wrist.

Then he regarded the two young women. "I ran into a friend at the table. Amara, this is Basia and her son, Tommy. And you know my kid sister, Brigid."

"How you doin', Brig." She high-fived the girl. Then she looked up. "Pleased to meet you, Basia. Are you a classmate of Press's?" Amara asked coolly.

Press couldn't believe it. How come all his friends acted so weird?

Basia shook her head. "Oh, no. We only met yesterday. I work at the Circus and he came in with his friend Matt. Do you know him, too?"

"Oh, yeah, Matt's great."

Press really didn't need to hear that.

"I go to Rutgers. I should have finished up sooner, but I'm a single mother and…"

"Say no more. My mom raised me alone, too. I mean, I get along with my dad now and everything, but they were divorced. It's a long story." Amara was now all smiles, and she knelt down and played a brief game of peek-a-boo with Tommy. Then she straightened up. "I love kids. If you ever need any babysitting, just let me know."

"That's very nice, but my family usually picks up the slack when Tommy's not in nursery school."

Amara nodded. "So, I bet Press told you how I threw myself all over him last year at Reunions, but he brushed me off because he said I was too young." She scrunched her shoulders forward as she shared the news.

Basia shook her head. "I don't know anything. We barely talked. It was really more about Matt asking me about playing the violin."

"Speaking of Matt. I think that's him now," Press said. He waved toward one of the front glass doors where Matt was coming in.

Matt crossed over, nearly tripping over a double baby stroller with Lion's tails hanging off the handles. "Sorry I'm late. Have you seen what the parking's like?" He gave Amara a quick peck when she offered her cheek. And then he saw Basia. "Oh, hi," he said without much enthusiasm.

"I'm so glad you're here," Basia gushed. "I've been keeping this secret—even from my family, but I just have to tell someone, and you're the perfect person to tell. Our violin teacher—Tina Chang—she helped get me an audition at Juilliard. Can you believe it? I mean, I'm sure I won't be accepted, and I can't even imagine how my family's going to react, but can you believe it? An audition with the best music conservatory in the country?"

"That's great," Matt said.

Press slanted him a look. Couldn't his friend sound

even slightly more enthusiastic? "I'm sure impressed," he said quickly to make up for it.

"Listen, I gotta run before this thing melts." Amara held up her ice cream. "Nice meeting you. Bye, Brigid. Bye, Tommy." She waved, then turned to Matt and Press. "Catch you later, guys."

"I should be going, too," Press added. "My folks will be wondering where Brigid and I have got to. Hey, Brigid, let's rejoin the family." He twirled her around to point her in the right direction. "We'll be seeing you then, but you can stay and talk, Matt."

"No, I need to talk to you about something important," Matt answered. He seemed cross.

"Sure, whatever." He held up his hand to Basia and Tommy. "Great news, again." And he pushed Brigid in front of him. Then he spoke in a low voice that was barely loud enough to be heard above the din. "Couldn't you have been civil at least? She was so excited. And she saved the news for you, for Pete's sake."

"That's exactly what I want to talk to you about. I don't want you pushing me at her."

"Pushing you at her? I'm not pushing you at her. It's more like all the women push themselves at you. Look at Amara."

Matt shook his head. "Amara? I don't know what you're talking about. I'm talking about Basia. I need to stay far away."

"Hold up a sec, Brigid." Press placed a hand on her shoulder and glanced sideways at Matt. "What's so bad about Basia that you would just blow her off like that? Back at the Circus, you looked like you really liked her."

"I did. But that was before the kid."

"What's wrong with that?"

"Like I said before. She's probably married."

"No, she talked about being a single mom."

Matt let out an exasperated sigh. "Even worse."

Press shook his head. "I don't get it."

"You don't know what it's like to grow up with a single mom. All you see is my family now—Katarina, my dad, *Babička*. But it wasn't like that when I was growing up."

"But Basia's not you," Press argued. "Get over your hang-ups. Open yourself up to the possibilities. Let someone in."

"The way you let in Amara," Matt shot back.

"That's different."

"Tell that to Amara. How do you think she feels?" Matt asked.

"Well, you can be there to hold her hand, then?"

"Don't think I won't," Matt answered.

Which was exactly what Press was afraid of.

CHAPTER THIRTY-THREE

EVEN THOUGH VIC TOWERED over most of the crowd, the crush of people made it almost impossible for him to pick out individual faces unless he was right on top of them. He'd arrived at Baldwin more than a half hour ago with Basia and Tommy, and now that they'd gone off to get ice cream, he could concentrate on trying to find Mimi.

He figured she wouldn't be hard to spot, but he was surprised by the number of people in his class who'd come back and felt no compunction about dressing up. They all looked like escapees from *Alice in Wonderland,* and it was honestly hard to keep a straight face when they came up to greet him.

"Yo, brother of mine." Joe came up behind Vic and wrapped his arm around his shoulder. "How come no funny hat?"

Vic stepped back. Basia had texted Joe in the car ride over about the change of leave, so he'd been expecting his brother. But he hadn't expected Joe to be three sheets to the wind. "Whew! It's too early to be hitting the sauce, don't you think?" Vic glanced down at his watch. It was only eleven o'clock in the morning.

Joe removed his arm and gestured dramatically, "What do you mean? I'm merely getting into the spirit of things. You don't think half the people here aren't already a bit tipsy?"

"I'm sure some of them are, but that doesn't mean you need to make a spectacle of yourself." Even to Vic's own ears, he sounded like a stuffed shirt.

Joe tapped his index finger repeatedly on Vic's lapel. "Well, excuse me. And here I thought I was merely bonding with my fellow man. Or should I say *your* fellow alums. After all, not all of us can claim to be so classy." Joe reached for Vic's tie and let the silk slide through his fingers. "I like the stripes, dude. They give you a certain zip—classy but zippy." Joe seemed to find that particularly funny.

If Vic didn't know better, he'd think Joe was feeling sorry for himself. "Maybe it'd be better if you sat down. Can I get you some coffee?"

Joe shook his head vehemently. "Don't need coffee. Don't want to do anything to diminish the great buzz I've got going." He looked around, pleased. "So what's your excuse?"

"I'm just looking for Mimi." Which is what Vic tried to do again, bending to the side to check behind his brother.

"Ah, the elusive Mimi Lodge." Joe leaned in close. "So did you screw her yet?"

"Joe!"

His brother looked as if he'd been slapped. "I don't know what your problem is. I mean, someone might as well get something out of that family, 'cause the business sure as hell isn't. So much for old college buddies looking out for each other."

"Joe, I haven't the faintest idea what you're on about, and I think it'd be wiser if you kept Mimi out of the—"

"And speaking of Mimi Lodge." Joe held up his arm. "Here she is *en famille*—that's French for scum-bags, for you Ivy League types."

Vic swiveled around to see Mimi approaching him. A smile spread across her face. She dragged behind her a couple who seemed reluctant to mingle.

"Vic," Mimi said, sweeping up next to him. "How good to see you again."

"You also." He nodded coyly. "Though I'm not sure I recognize you in your outfit."

"I know. It's horrible, isn't it?" She stared down at the garish costume. "I feel like a drum majorette who's escaped from the Rose Bowl." She gave a tiny shiver. "But enough about me. I don't believe you've met my father and his wife, Noreen. Brigid is off forc-ing Press to buy her copious amounts of ice cream."

Vic laughed. "My sister is also trying to bribe Tommy." He held out his hand. "Mrs. Lodge." They shook hands. "Mr. Lodge. We talked on the phone about the panel."

"Yes, of course. I'm delighted you agreed to partici-pate. It should make for a very interesting discussion."

"As would the state of business at Pilgrim Investments, don't you think, Mr. Lodge?" Joe asked, drawing out the one syllable name.

Vic saw Conrad Lodge's mouth twitch, and his wife subtly, but protectively, slipped her arm through his. "I'm sorry, this is my brother, Joe. I'm afraid he's had too much to drink," he offered.

"No need to apologize. It happens to the best of us," Conrad replied, his eyes darting around the room. He stretched a forced smile to some people passing by.

"So, I hear there's been some excitement at Pilgrim—excitement that is having an impact on the new building contract in Australia," Joe pressed.

"I wouldn't know," Conrad said in a monotone. He looked over at Noreen.

"Perhaps you need some water, dear?" Noreen asked.

"Ah, yes, you Lodges are famous for your water tricks when it comes to us Golinskis. Frankly, it's your business tricks that are more lethal at the moment."

"Not here, Joe," Vic admonished him. "This is about pleasure, not business."

"Sure. I'm just surprised you're capable of enjoying yourself so soon after being let go." Joe wouldn't give up.

"What?" Mimi stared at her father. "What's going on?"

Conrad stared at his feet.

"There was an office coup on Thursday," Noreen spoke up instead. "It seems some of the younger partners decided they wanted to run the show."

Mimi's eyes opened wide. "So…so…that was the emergency in New York. I mean, that's why you went in?"

Noreen grasped Conrad's arm with both hands, a show of support. "Exactly."

"And the reason for the panic attack."

"It would appear." Conrad wet his lips, and Mimi couldn't help noticing his embarrassment, his fear. "Naturally, I'd prefer to keep this all under wraps for now—until I can straighten things out."

"Of course," Vic jumped in. "There's no need to discuss any of this. I'm sure it will all be ironed out soon." Vic thought that was probably unlikely, but he had the good graces to keep that opinion to himself.

Mimi was still shaking her head in disbelief. "And here Press and I thought all the commotion was because Noreen was leaving you."

Conrad looked at Noreen. "You're leaving me?" He appeared stricken.

"Absolutely not." She patted his arm. The relief in Conrad's eyes was obvious, but the worry was not entirely erased.

Joe turned to his brother. "That's all well and good for you to be all noble, Vic, when you know perfectly well Lodge's goose is cooked at Pilgrim." Joe stopped himself. "That may remotely be a pun, but I'll let you figure it out. Anyway." He waved his hand. "Anyway, in the meantime, the new regime has decided to put *our* bid on hold. It seems it's tainted by affiliation with *you*." Joe pointed at Mimi's father.

"Joe, that's enough," Vic said, his voice dangerously low. "There's no need to cause a scene." He turned to Mimi and her family. "I apologize for my brother's rudeness."

"Don't bother apologizing," Joe interrupted. "In fact, don't bother romancing the daughter here anymore. It's not like it's going to do us any more good."

"Joe, why don't you shut up," Vic said under his breath. "You've had too much to drink."

Mimi turned to Vic, confused. "Hold on. What does he mean? It's not going to do *who* any good anymore?"

Joe stepped between them. "The contract for the stone for the new office in Australia. Part of the deal with your father was that Vic here show you a good time."

"Joe! That's ridiculous and you know it." Vic's voice was menacing.

"What does he mean?" she asked Vic again. Then she noticed her father bowing his head. "Father. What did you do?"

Conrad raised his chin.

"I felt that if you could get passionate about something again, it might wake you up from your slumber."

"Slumber? I'm not some Sleeping Beauty. I was suffering from post traumatic stress syndrome!"

"Yes, well, I'm not a psychiatrist. I'm a father."

"Since when?" Mimi shot back.

Joe pushed the sides of his suit jacket back and

stuffed his hands in the pockets of his trousers. He was clearly enjoying the set-to.

"So I tried to think of what would rile you up, what people or events in the past had gotten your goat so much that you couldn't stop yourself from reacting. I'd already been appointed to the Reunions committee heading up the panels, and then it struck me."

She turned to Vic. "And you went along with this?"

"It's not what it sounds like. Your father requested I sit on the panel and at the same time mentioned he might be able to throw some business our way in exchange."

Her mouth dropped open. "This goes from bad to worse. He basically paid you to go out with me?"

"He never said anything about going out with you. That happened all on its own." Vic reached out. "I was going to tell you, trust me. It's just that things kind of took on a life of their own, and when they did, somehow other things got in the way."

"Like sex, you mean?" Mimi laughed. She didn't sound remotely humored.

"Mimi," Noreen said in hushed tones.

Mimi stared at her stepmother, the stepmother she thought she'd understood and admired. "Why so prudish all of a sudden? Weren't you the woman who had an affair with a married man—my father, to be exact? Or was that just a money transaction, as well?"

"Mimi! You apologize," her father ordered.

She held up her hands. "Okay, I take back that last crack. It was a low blow, but at the moment, I'm not feeling particularly charitable toward anyone." She slanted a glance at Vic. "You especially. I thought we had a connection. And all along you were lying to me," she pleaded to him.

"I wasn't lying. I was holding back—just like I do with everything." He shook his head. "I told you things I've never told anyone else." Vic drew his mouth in a hard line. "Listen, I knew you'd be pissed when you found out, that you were bound to take it the wrong way. Your trust in me is still new, still raw..."

"Raw? You want to talk about raw? Well, that's me right now. I'm feeling raw, all right. Raw and used."

Vic grimaced. "Believe me, that was never my intention."

She stared at him long and hard. "Are you sure?" Mimi didn't wait for an answer, but instead addressed her father. "I suppose you still expect me to go through with this panel after lunch?"

Conrad nodded. "Please, you can't back out now. What will people say? I'm worried the rumors are already starting about Pilgrim before I've had time to do some damage control."

Mimi narrowed her eyes. "It's always about you, isn't it?" She breathed in and turned her head to the side. "I can't talk about this anymore. I can't deal with you—all of you anymore." Then she turned back to her father. "But don't worry. Unlike some Lodges, I'm to be trusted. I'll serve on your frigging panel."

Mimi regarded the enormous hat in her hand and kept shaking her head in anger. Then she brought her eyes up and focused on Joe. "Here, you take this. I'm not sure you can fit your big, fat mouth in it, but it's worth a try." She punched the hat in Joe's stomach and took off, pushing through the crowd.

Joe grabbed the hat before it hit the floor. "That beats all." He laughed. "Here, I'm the only one willing to speak the truth, and I get grief."

"Joe, for the love of Pete, would you please shut up." Vic pushed his bottom teeth forward.

"But I was just trying to protect you, protect the family," Joe protested.

Vic slanted him a vicious look. "Yeah? Well, don't try so hard next time."

Joe stuck up his chin. "What? You think you're the only one who knows what's best for our family? For the business? I got news for you. You're just as much a sucker for a pair of tits as the next guy—not that she has much in that department." He snickered.

Vic made a fist with his left hand, brought it up shoulder high and decked him.

The people around them scurried back as Joe lay sprawled on the floor. "What the...?" He tested his jaw, maneuvering it back and forth.

Vic shook his hand to lessen the pain. "I guess I still have some anger management issues, after all." Then he stormed out, too.

CHAPTER THIRTY-FOUR

TWO HOURS LATER, Mimi was seated in a crowded lecture room—ironically, the same one where she and Vic had had the Civil War history course.

She looked around—the place was packed, especially with older men who had that large shoulder, somewhat paunchy build of ex-jocks whose one-time muscle had turned to fat.

"Welcome, everyone, to the Reunions Panel titled, 'A Return Look at the Impact of Title IX on Intercollegiate Athletics at the University.'" Her father, his tortoiseshell half glasses slipping down his nose, read from a note card. Since this morning's encounter at the Un-Parade, Mimi couldn't help noticing that his color was better and he seemed more confident. Being the center of attention clearly put him in his element.

Standing at a lectern to the side of the table of panelists, Conrad made the introductions one by one. The current Athletic Director was seated directly to Conrad's left, and various coaches, the university Provost, Vic and Mimi filled out the remaining seats. Whoever had made the arrangements had stationed Vic toward the middle and Mimi at the far end. Given her suspicious nature, she would have assumed that either her father or Vic had banished her to the nether regions. But she had purposely arrived early, lurking in the back of the auditorium, to make sure there was no hanky-panky on their part.

She also couldn't help noticing that the pitchers of water were placed well out of her grasp.

"Now that we've met all our participants, let me say how grateful I am to our returning members from the original panel," Conrad went on. "It's not often that the university can elicit its members to participate in a second panel twelve years after the original. And this, I believe, is a testament to the loyalty and respect that we Grantham alums feel for our alma mater."

Naturally, his statement received applause from the partisan audience.

"So, without further ado, I thought we'd begin with Athletic Director and Class of '72 graduate, Dwight Reginald. He'll give us a brief update on the current state of intercollegiate athletics at Grantham and the effects of Title IX on the program as a whole. I might ask the other panel members to also keep their responses and comments as brief as possible so that we will be able to get everyone's input as well as answer questions from the audience. We all want to stay on schedule in order not to miss the events of the day. Dwight?" Conrad held out a magnanimous hand.

Dwight Reginald beamed. He had a full head of neatly groomed hair, the requisite Grantham orange-and-black-striped tie and a ruddy complexion that spoke of outdoor sports and a deep familiarity with bourbon on the rocks.

"Thank you, Conrad, and great to see all of you— many familiar faces, I might add." He nodded to the audience. "I am happy to report that once again Grantham had a banner year in sports." Looking at his printed notes, Reginald ran down the statistics of league winners, individual performances and records set.

Mimi found it hard not to zone out. She reached for the water glass in front of her. The coach of the men's squash team next to her slanted her a worried look. She smiled knowingly. "Don't worry, Coach. I'm not in an aggressive mood today," she whispered.

He responded with an unsteady smile of his own.

"It's also important to point out that Grantham regularly meets its Title IX requirements in terms of proportionality. With fifty percent of the student body female, we also have a fifty-fifty split between men's and women's sports." He leaned forward and peered toward Mimi's end of the table.

Mimi was aware that he was singling her out. *Don't bother,* she felt like telling him. *I'm too wrung out from the morning to bother taking on chicken feed like you.*

"Excuse me, Mr. Reginald?" It was a voice seated in the middle of the panel.

Mimi leaned forward, surprised to hear Vic speak up.

"Yes, Vic," Reginald answered. "I'm delighted

to have one of our most successful athletes with us today."

"Well, I can think of quite a few Olympic medalists, not to mention more illustrious professional athletes who graduated from Grantham who might dispute that claim," Vic said modestly. Then he pulled a folded sheet of paper from his jacket.

Mimi rubbed her upper lip.

"I was curious about your figures regarding proportional representation."

The Athletic Director nodded.

"A recent article in the *New York Times* dealt with subterfuges that some colleges are using to give the illusion that more women are participating in competitive sports than is actually the case," Vic mentioned calmly.

"For instance," he went on, referring to his notes, "the coach of the women's tennis team at one university actually encouraged walk-ons to join the team even though their abilities were far below the rest of the roster. They practiced with the team, but were not required to travel, and in fact, never played a match. Nonetheless, these players were included on the official team listing, thus boosting the total number of women players." He turned his head to look at Reginald.

"I can assure you that's not the case at Grantham." He made his remarks to the audience.

Bad move, Dwight, she thought.

Vic shifted in his chair. "Then maybe you could

help me to understand the following. I've been doing research on the web, and I was surprised to see that the women's fencing team regularly has eight members traveling and competing. Yet, according to the records filed with the government, the team is comprised of…let me see—" he peered at the figures "—twenty-five members. When I spoke with the coach earlier in the week—a terrific guy, by the way, and certainly someone who knows how to attract top players—he told me that those twenty-five included eight female players who haven't broken into the top spots—what most of us think of as junior varsity. But that still left nine positions unaccounted for." Vic looked up. "And that's when I learned that the team uses male practice players, and that they are actually reported as members of the women's fencing team, as well. So. You understand my confusion."

The athletic director's neck got taut. "That's all perfectly above board. Federal regulations allow that arrangement."

"But is it right?" Vic pressed him.

Reginald lifted his hand. "With the government, right isn't always the issue."

His response evoked some ripples of laughter.

"You know, I think we can all applaud the impact Title IX has had on our sisters and daughters," Vic continued in his methodical, polite fashion. "Since the law was passed the number of women athletes competing at the collegiate level has exploded by 500 percent." For that number, he didn't need to refer to his notes.

There was a loud round of applause from the audience.

"If I could jump in here." Mimi held up her hand. Vic's arguments had prompted her out of her intended aloofness. "But before I go on, Coach—" she looked at the panelist seated next to her "—could you take this." She held her water glass high enough for everyone to see and handed it to her right.

There were more than a few knowing murmurs.

"As a proud alumna of Grantham University, I like to think we do things not just because we're legally bound to do so, but because we believe it's the just and honorable thing to do." She paused to acknowledge the audience members. She didn't make her living in front of the camera for nothing. "So in listening to this discussion, I can't help wondering, 'Are we morally cheating our students?'"

The athletic director started to speak, but Mimi held up her hand. "Let me finish. After all, I've waited twelve years to say this." She milked the crowd for all it was worth. "The chance to compete at a high level of sport at Grantham is a privilege, a privilege I might remind you, subsidized by tax dollars—all our tax dollars." She made a circular motion with her hand. "When the university—our university—obeys the letter of the law but not the spirit, it not only mocks the purpose of the law, but it also cheats its women students."

Mimi sat back and waited for the onslaught. She saw people whispering in the audience. She tipped her chair back to see if she could get Vic's attention, but he was slanted forward, leaning on his forearms.

Conrad held up his hand. "Before we take questions from the audience, let me ask the rest of our panel members if anyone else care would care to comment?"

"Okay, I'll be brave, but then, maybe it's easier for me to be brave than for others," the Men's Lightweight Crew coach spoke up. A beloved and highly successful figure, he'd won more national titles than any other coach in Grantham history. He numbered twelve Olympic champions as present or former members of his squad, and he himself coached two medal-winning Olympic teams.

"Roster management, the polite term for padding team figures, is the two-ton gorilla of collegiate athletics. In the best of all possible worlds, I know I'd like to see instead an increase in the number of women's teams. I'd even like to see the reinstatement of certain men's teams, such as wrestling."

"Hear, hear," came a cry from high in the audience.

"But achieving equitable opportunities are not easy, especially in light of football—a money-generating sport with large team numbers. And given the current climate of budget constraints, expansion of other sports teams—men's or women's—is pretty much a no-go."

The athletic director nodded. "I couldn't agree more. That's it in a nutshell." He acknowledged the coach, who Mimi saw, crossed his arms and didn't smile back.

"I mean, really, would you rather we cut back on football?" the director asked the audience jokingly. Then he turned to Vic. "I would think that you of all people, in light of your football career and given previous comments on this very panel would argue that's utterly preposterous." He held up his hands.

Vic angled his head and spoke in a determined voice. "I'm very grateful for the opportunities that Grantham afforded me in my career. And I remember—probably better than anyone in this room, with the exception of my classmate at the end of the table—what I said twelve years ago."

Again, the knowing murmurs.

"But Grantham also taught me to be a critical thinker," Vic continued. "And when I was preparing for this panel discussion, I was amazed by the numbers. Five hundred percent increase," he repeated. "I love sports, I loved participating in them at the highest level, and maybe some day I'll have a daughter, and maybe because of Title IX, she'll be able to enjoy sports the same way."

There was thunderous applause.

Reginald sniffed loudly and rifled through his papers. "And are you accusing me of somehow inhibiting your fictional daughter of achieving her dreams?"

Clearly, he'd lost it, Mimi realized. The question was, had Vic, as well?

"I'm not accusing you of anything." He remained unperturbed. "I'm merely bringing up a very real and complicated problem facing intercollegiate athletics today. I don't claim to have the answers."

Reginald shook his head. He leaned toward Vic, sprawling his arm out on the table toward him. "If I didn't know better, I'd wonder about the origins of this whole discussion. True, there've been some articles in the paper. But I also heard from a bunch of people that they saw you two talking early the other morning outside the athletic facilities." He pointed to Mimi. "Not that I'm insinuating anything, but somehow I can't help thinking." He held up one hand. "A football player." Then he held up another. "An attractive woman who we all know is not afraid of controversy…" He weighed his two hands in turn.

"Excuse me," Mimi interrupted. "I resent that."

"I think you'd better apologize to Ms. Lodge." Vic's voice was barely above a whisper, but it echoed to the back row.

Mimi lifted her butt off the chair and leaned over the table to address Reginald directly. "I was going to say you should apologize to Mr. Golinski for implying that he isn't capable of voicing a thought-provoking argument all on his own. I, on the other hand, am perfectly capable of defending myself."

"But you shouldn't have to." The male voice came

from the other end of the panel. And that's when the water pitcher upended on the athletic director.

Only it wasn't Vic.

It was Conrad.

CHAPTER THIRTY-FIVE

MIMI FOUND HER FATHER outside the men's room. He had gone in there soon after the session ended in pure pandemonium. He was still patting down the sleeves of his orange class blazer with paper towels as he reappeared.

"Well, I guess you didn't need to worry about the panel discussion running overtime," she quipped.

He looked up. "I'm not sure we'll be invited for a third go-round, wouldn't you agree?"

Mimi rose and lowered her shoulders. "Hey, your money's still plenty good."

"Just not as much of it, now that I'm no longer with Pilgrim," he reminded her.

"I'm sure you'll bounce back." Mimi found herself in the odd position of having to defend her father. She wasn't sure what to make of it. "Listen, I want to thank you for the noble gesture."

"The little snot was getting on my nerves. And between you and me, the scuttlebutt is that he's due to be replaced by the end of the summer anyway."

Mimi nodded her head knowingly. "I see. An easy target." Why wasn't she surprised at his shrewd calculations. She watched her father wipe his hands. "You certainly didn't miss, that's for sure."

Conrad balled up the paper towel and tossed it into a trash bin. "On a more personal matter, I hope you will one day understand that I instigated your participation on this panel in an effort to help you."

"Father, can we just drop that discussion for now?"

"I'm sorry, but no. And I *am* your father, so you will listen to me."

Mimi bit her tongue.

"Mimi, your ordeal in Chechnya was horrific. And I am not belittling its severity. But it only sped up the detachment you have from the world, your inability to reach out. It had been my impression twelve years ago that there was something about Vic Golinski that awakened a passion in you. I'm just saying, consider my motive."

Mimi breathed in deeply. "Leaving aside whatever you saw and didn't see between Vic and me. I can't believe you're professing a sense of true love and devotion. If you really believed in those virtues, you wouldn't have cheated on my mother. You knew she wouldn't be able to deal with it."

"Your mother couldn't deal with many things. My infidelities were the least among them."

"Yes, she had problems. But that doesn't justify your infidelity. Besides, what about Press's mother, Adele?"

Conrad opened his mouth.

But Mimi held up her hand. "No, don't bother. You

don't need to give any explanations when it comes to that cow. If I'd been married to her, I'd have cheated on her, too—though I hope you know what effect it's had on your son."

"That last remark is for Press and me to deal with—when the time comes."

"I wouldn't hold my breath," Mimi mumbled.

Conrad ignored her comment. "As for my supposed serial unfaithfulness—I'll have you know that I've never cheated on Noreen, nor would I ever. You may not believe me, but I loved your mother—in a fashion. But Noreen?" He paused. "She's the love of my life. I would do anything for her."

Mimi opened her mouth, then hesitated. "Now I get it. This whole asking me to participate on the panel? Your version of shock therapy? Admit it, Father, you didn't do it for me. You did it for you. For you to show Noreen how much you love her. It was probably at her prodding that you did it. She was the one, after all, who was pushing me to see a psychiatrist, not you."

He gave her an unblinking stare. "Think what you like. You've made your opinion clear on numerous occasions. But while you're heaping your scorn on me, consider this. Do you want to end up like me? At my age? Afraid of losing the only thing in the end that matters—people's love and loving them back? Or will you even fail to achieve that kind of fear?"

"How can you even talk about you and me in the same breath? I would never turn my back on my family the way you've done your whole life."

"Are you so sure? Do you send us Christmas and birthday cards? Make sure you or your brother is there for the rest of the family if anything goes wrong?"

"Excuse me. Who held down the fort when you were whisked to the hospital with a panic attack? Press and I?"

"Would you have been there if I hadn't prodded you to come to Reunions in the first place? And do you think your brother has the kind of deep pockets or spontaneous inclination to be in Grantham at the same time as his sister? It's not as if I can count on either one of you. These things don't happen unless I arrange it or foot the bill. Is that the kind of love you want?"

Mimi shook her head in disbelief. No, not in disbelief—in her own stupidity. Her father—her selfish, self-centered father—was all of that. But he was also a sad and disillusioned man. Yes, he'd been a CEO of a financial powerhouse. But that was gone. And what was he left with? A fractured relationship with his older children, the demands of a young one and the fear that his much younger wife, whom he adored, would pick up and leave him.

No, she didn't want to end up like that. And for the first time, Mimi looked at her father—not as a daughter but as an adult. For once, she didn't feel contempt. She felt sadness, a deep sorrow for a lost soul.

NOREEN WAS WAITING OUTSIDE when she saw Mimi run out the side door. A few minutes later, Conrad emerged. She waved and called out to him.

He acknowledged her with a nod of the head, but took a few minutes to chat with some of the audience members who'd lingered. From where she stood, they seemed to be offering support. Conrad shook hands goodbye, there were a few slaps on the back and chuckles, and then he crossed the slate walkway to where she stood by the side of the university chapel.

He gave her a kiss on the cheek, then stared upward at the pointed stained-glass windows. "It was much nicer weather the day we were married here all those years ago." He pressed his fingers around the sleeve of her tight black suit jacket. She wore a large lion pin with a winking emerald eye on the lapel. He had given it to her for her birthday last year.

"I think the audience got their money's worth," he joked.

"I'm proud of the way you defended her. What an eedjit, that man was." She gave an Irish emphasis to "idiot."

"On that we can all agree." Conrad smiled. "Mimi even thanked me."

"Did you talk to her, then?"

"Yes." He looked away.

Noreen used her hand to turn his head toward her. She rested her French nails on his cheek. "Conrad, don't make this any harder. What did she say?"

He pursed his lips. "I think we came to some kind of resolution. But along the way, she said something that struck a chord. She accused me of having done it—the whole panel thing—without her best interests at heart. She said I did it to please you."

"But that's not true."

"Are you so sure?" Conrad inhaled deeply. "Be honest. Are you planning on leaving me? I thought this might happen when I told you about being let go."

Noreen blinked slowly. "Whatever gave you that idea? When I made the appointment for us to see the counselor, it was to help us deal with all the changes going on. I know how much your career means to you."

"Yes, it's important to me. I'm still in shock. But it doesn't mean as much to me as you. And of course, Brigid. The others—Mimi, Press—that's still very much a work in progress. I can't claim to be much of a father to them—but I'm trying—with your guidance. Because I truly love you." He said the last sentence with extra pauses between each word.

"Yes, you definitely are a work in progress. But you pay dividends." Noreen smiled tentatively. "Speaking of dividends, I have some news of my own."

"You'll be traveling more for work? That's all right. I have the time now, not that I intend to retire. I'm already trying to formulate some other plans, put out feelers."

She could see he was attempting to nurture his own ego as much as reassure hers. He wasn't perfect, but then who was? "No, if anything my traveling will probably be curtailed in the future. You see—I'm pregnant. We're going to have another child."

Conrad looked at her wide-eyed. "A baby?" He grabbed both her upper arms.

Noreen nodded. "That should make you feel young."

He breathed in deeply. "Truthfully?" He looked away.

For a second, she feared he was going to run.

But he looked back, a grin spreading across his face. "It scares me to death. But then what doesn't these days?"

CHAPTER THIRTY-SIX

HE FOUND HER IN THE women's locker room at Delaney Pool. "I need to talk to you," he said as he came up next to her.

Mimi turned by her open locker and put a hand to her chest. Goggles swung from her hand. She already had on her racing suit. "Geez, Vic. You scared the life out of me. I thought I was the only one here. You're not supposed to be here. This is the women's locker room."

Vic glanced around. "Like you said. There's nobody else here."

She banged her locker door shut without turning away from him. It didn't close all the way because the sleeve of her Reunions jacket was caught in the edge. "How did you know where to find me?"

He shrugged. He still had on his blazer and button-down shirt, though he'd loosened his tie. "It was either here or Hoagie Palace, and I figured you could probably clear your mind better in the water."

She shook her head. "So you found me."

They stood in silence. The only sound was their breathing, with the smells of chlorine and wet towels permeating the enclosed space.

"I should have come clean right away, okay? About your father calling me and bringing up the whole building contract," Vic finally admitted. "I took the coward's way out. I'm not proud of it, but it's what I did. But I promise you, it had nothing to do with what happened between us. Do you believe me?"

"I don't know what I believe right now." She looked around the locker room. "Maybe it's this place—not here, but Grantham. There's something about it that always seems to rub me the wrong way—like the stupid guy on the panel."

"He's an ass. Everybody thought so, even your father."

Mimi shook her head. "My father…my father…who he is—it's all too confusing. I'd really prefer to leave him out of the whole discussion, if you don't mind."

"I do mind. He's your father. You just can't exorcise him from your being. You have to deal with who he is and move on."

"I can't. I'm too screwed up. Don't you get it?" Mimi picked up a towel and draped it over her arm. She turned back to her locker, closed it properly and locked it. She started to move.

Vic shot out his arm to block her. "Not so fast. That's too easy an excuse. C'mon. You survived an ordeal that would break most people. Don't wimp out now. Why can't you get over your father?"

"I just can't." She stepped forward.

He refused to budge. "Why not?" This time he got right into her face.

"Because…because…" She snapped her head to the side to avoid his gaze. "Because no matter how pitiable or lonely he might be, I can't stop blaming him for my mother's death." She paused. "And because I can't stop blaming myself for her death, too."

Then she peered in his eyes. "Don't you get it? I want my mother back, all happy and healthy and there to love me."

Vic let his arm fall to the side. "But that's not going to happen, is it? No matter how hard you push back. Listen, I can't forgive myself for my brother's death, either. And I wish he were alive and here to love me, as well. But he's not. So that makes two of us in the same boat. That doesn't mean we can't go on, Mimi. I mean, we're the ones who are alive. Don't we deserve a chance to be happy, to love and be loved?"

"I don't know. I just don't know." She sniffed loudly. "I told you I was screwed up. You're better off staying far, far away."

"So now you're an expert on what's good for me, too?" He bent down to be at the same eye level.

She shook her head briskly.

"Tell me the real reason you don't want to see me anymore. And don't give me that crap that you can't trust me. I've explained what happened. I made a mistake, but it's not as if you gave me a lot of chance to explain, either."

She looked down at her towel.

He crouched down more. "Tell me the truth. You owe it to me."

Mimi snapped her head up. "I owe you nothing."

"Oh, I think you do. I didn't open up to you because I wanted a shoulder to cry on. I didn't go out of my way to comfort you because it gave me a cheap thrill. And let me tell you. If I wanted an easy lay, there are lots of easier ways to get that. So, why? Why won't you see me?"

"Because I love you. I love you and I can't deal with it," she practically shouted.

"Well, I love you, too. Shouldn't that make things easier, not harder?" He was breathing heavily, his chest heaving.

She stared at him, her eyes large with wonder. She didn't say anything—just searched his face.

He waited. He hoped.

"I gotta go," she said finally. "I need to get in the water. Like you said, clear my head." She hesitated. "By the way, you were great today—at the panel discussion."

"So, sometimes I do the right thing."

She walked past him, and Vic stood there, watching her go. It was her choice to make. He had done all he could, almost gotten down on his knees to apologize, admitted his feelings.

She reached for the heavy swinging door and pulled it toward her. But just as she was about to step through, she stopped. Looked back.

Vic felt a glimmer of hope. He raised his eyebrows.

Mimi pressed her lips together. Then she lifted her chin. "And when you see Roxie, tell her I'll miss her."

CHAPTER THIRTY-SEVEN

ON MONDAY, PRESS finished packing his laptop into his knapsack and zipped the whole thing up. The carry-on weighed a ton with all the books he had. But he was already worried that his roll-on suitcase was over-weight, and he didn't want to get caught having to pay a hefty fine, or worse-case scenario, having to unpack it at the gate and throw away some of his possessions.

He picked up his phone and glanced at the bed. Noreen had offered to drive him to the airport, and they had better get a move on, especially with the afternoon rush hour traffic.

He looked around the familiar yet somehow distant bedroom. A few things—the Yankees posters, the needlepoint pillows from Noreen, the banner from his sleep-away camp in Maine had changed over the years. But they seemed like remnants from another era, almost another person.

Maybe they were merely false mementoes. Maybe things had never really been that innocent or that simple. Or maybe the memories were no longer fresh enough to conjure up the truth instead of an overly romanticized nostalgia.

"Yeah, well, that's life," he grumbled to himself.

For the umpteenth time, he unzipped the front section of his knapsack and checked that he had his passport and his flight information. Then he reached for his wallet in his back jeans pocket.

He still had some Australian money for the bus into town when he arrived at Melbourne Airport. And he also had a wad of U.S. dollars that hadn't been there before this morning. Mimi had handed it to him as a going-away present when saying goodbye at Grantham Junction.

"Take it." She pushed it toward him when he'd tried to refuse. "I know you could use it. And use it for something fun—a trip, a night out on the town, something you wouldn't normally do. But whatever you do, don't think of it as a bribe."

And then she'd hugged him really hard before she'd made a mad dash for the train. But not before Press had seen tears in her eyes.

I guess her Reunions weren't all they were cracked up to be, either, Press thought.

There was a knock on his door, and Noreen stuck her head in. "There's someone here who wants to talk to you." She glanced down at her watch. "We still have time. Why don't we meet downstairs to go in, say, ten minutes?"

Press nodded. He figured Matt had come to say goodbye.

Noreen opened the door wider, then stepped away. It wasn't Matt. It was Amara.

She hesitated before crossing the threshold, looking

around at the boy paraphernalia that filled the space. "You had the Playmobil pirate ship! I always wanted that, but my mother couldn't afford it."

He glanced over his shoulder at the giant, elaborate model, complete with a dozen or so action figures. "You can have mine now, if you want it. Though I think most of the swords are missing."

"Aw. You don't leave me with any of the fun." She laughed.

Press didn't want to be talking about toys, especially not with Amara. "Listen." He stalled, not really knowing what he wanted to say but knowing he had to say something.

She walked closer. "I'm listening."

That didn't make it easier. "You want to sit down?"

"Not really."

He rubbed his forehead.

"Press?"

He looked up.

"I couldn't just let you leave without saying goodbye in person," she said. "A text wouldn't do."

"You're right. Thanks for coming." He swallowed. "There's not a lot of time, but what I wanted to say is this." He looked her straight in the eye. "You're still in school, and I'm halfway around the world. But would you…what I mean to say is…I won't forget you, and I hope you don't forget me."

"Of course I won't forget you." Amara wrapped her arms around Press's shoulders and gave him a hug like it was the most natural thing in the world.

He tried not to read anything into the gesture beyond friendship—but that was a big ask.

She pulled away and returned his stare. "Don't you get it? You and I are joined at the hip. You'll always be a part of me."

"But what about Matt?"

"What about Matt?"

Press opened his mouth, but then he shook his head. "Nothing. Just remember, if ever you need help—whatever—I'm there for you. No matter how far I'm away."

She nodded. "Same here."

And they stood like that for an awkward moment or two until Press said, "I better get going, then. My flight…"

"Yeah, I know. Can I help you carry anything?" She looked at his bags on the bed.

"Nah, I can manage. Besides, they're ri-donc-ulously heavy." He tried not to think about the bed. The bed and Amara. He smiled at her tightly.

"Press?" she asked.

He raised his head and looked at her through half-slit eyes.

"I'll always remember you here—today—in your room. And I'm not talking about your pirate ship, either." She stepped close to him. "Why don't you lower that chin of yours, Press Lodge, so I can give you a real goodbye—the kind *you'll* remember?"

He did.

And she kissed him. Memorably.

CHAPTER THIRTY-EIGHT

TWO WEEKS LATER ON A Thursday morning, Vic finally made it into the office around ten o'clock.

And found Joe seated at his desk.

Vic looked down at Roxie, who was holding her leash in her mouth. "Attack," he ordered.

Roxie glanced over at Joe, back at Vic, then silently headed for her bed in the corner of the room. She circled the pillow twice and settled in silently.

Vic gave her a dirty look. Ever since that Saturday of Reunions, the dog had been in a funk. "Excuse me," Vic had said to her when she'd rejected her food one morning. "I'm not the one who told her to go away."

"Nobody pays attention to me," Vic mumbled now under his breath, and placed his briefcase atop his own desk. He eyed Joe. "Take over the company while you're at it," he said with annoyance.

"Hey, someone has to run the place while you spend your days moping." Joe tapped his pen—*actually, my pen,* Vic thought. "While you've been wallowing in your grief at losing the love of your life—"

"I never said that."

"Oh, please, it's written all over your face." Joe

didn't seem intimidated at all. "Now, as I was saying, while you've been going around like a hang dog, barely able to drag your sorry self into the office, I've been working my butt off. If it's of any interest to you, your not-so-little brother here has been working the phones, meeting people, wining and dining—"

"You always did know how to run up an expense account." Vic shrugged off his blue blazer and turned to hang it on the coat rack.

"All for a good cause this time, if you please. But ever conscious of your cost-saving measures, I ordered domestic champagne instead of French to celebrate."

Vic turned back. "Celebrate?"

"Yes, celebrate securing the construction account for the new Pilgrim Investments building in Melbourne, Australia."

Vic stood with his mouth open.

"You may thank me now." Joe sprung up from Vic's chair very pleased with himself. Then he patted the seat. "Here, you better sit down. You look like you need to."

Vic circled the desk warily and sat slowly. Then he looked up. "Does Pop know?"

"I called him earlier this morning. He's even coming in to join the festivities."

"He's coming in?" Vic set his mouth in a hard line. "There's something you should know about Dad...and the office. He and Abby have been...ah..."

Joe made a face. "You think I don't know? That's been going on for years. Everybody knows."

"Are you telling me that I was the only one who didn't know about it?"

"I'm pretty sure Tommy's still in the dark. Listen, that's their problem to sort out, not ours."

"No, you don't get it. I'm sure they probably expect me to fix things now—with Mom."

"I'm pretty sure they don't," Joe came back. "They're adults. It's their responsibility, not yours." He waited for Vic to reply.

Vic didn't.

"Okay?" Joe prompted him again.

Vic shook his head reluctantly. "Okay." Then he clapped his hands together. Roxie startled, saw it was only Vic and went back to sleeping.

"So, do you want to have dinner together, then? Celebrate in high style? Break the expense account?" Vic asked, trying to get in the party mood. He was delighted to get the news, but his spirits weren't particularly riding high.

It didn't take a rocket scientist to figure out why. Mimi walking out of his life had been as gut-wrenching as losing his twin brother. No, that wasn't true. He'd lost Tom as a kid. His memories, his emotions were borne out of that time. The wounds he was currently licking were fresh. They made him worry if he was ever going to find happiness, if love would be as elusive as the woman who got away.

"Sorry, Vic. I can't. I'm busy tonight," Joe announced.

Vic frowned. "I can only imagine." The problem was he could.

"No, it's not what you think. I'm taking Basia and Tommy to New York."

Vic was confused. "New York? In the middle of the week?"

"It's kind of a secret. Well, it is a secret. Basia has an audition at Juilliard late this afternoon. And while she's busy, I'm going to take Tommy to the Museum of Natural History to see the dinosaurs. Then afterward, we'll go out to dinner."

"Basia has an audition? She never told me."

"Yeah, like I said. She wanted to keep it a secret. Not put any extra pressure on herself, I guess."

"But why did she ask you?" Vic felt hurt.

Joe held up his hands. "Probably because she realized I was the only member of the family nobody would think to question."

Vic nodded. "You're probably right. But still, I should be there for her."

Joe came over and rested his hands on the other side of Vic's desk. "You've been there for Basia her whole life. Hell, you've been here for all of us your whole life. Why don't you let someone else pick up the slack for a change?" He cocked his head. "And as far as Basia is concerned? Don't you get it—she couldn't tell you because she's going to be there *for* you—and herself, of course." Joe stood up.

Vic regarded him with narrowed eyes. "Who made you so wise all of a sudden?"

Joe put his hands together and bowed. "Oh, great *sensei,* I have learned from the master."

Vic picked up an eraser and threw it at him. It flew wide by a couple of inches.

Joe retreated and turned to see where it landed. "You're losing your touch."

Roxie got up from her bed to investigate the possibility of the projectile being food. She sniffed the pink rubbery square and appeared to shrug her shoulders before settling back on her bed.

Vic shook his head. "It landed exactly where I meant it to land."

Joe rubbed the side of his nose. "And, there's something else I need to say to you." His voice was serious.

Vic raised his eyebrows.

"About my…ah…performance at the Un-Parade during Reunions? I was plastered and pissed about the Pilgrim deal. But that's still no excuse. I shouldn't have acted that way—to you, to Mimi, her family."

"No, that's true." Vic thought a moment. "But if nothing else, it got things out in the open. It wouldn't have been my style, but…" He offered a conciliatory smile.

"That's for sure. And look at the results," Joe pointed out. "You're miserable."

"I'll live," Vic said philosophically.

"There's living and then there's living." Joe pulled a legal-size envelope out of the inside pocket of his suit jacket. He stepped closer and threw it on Vic's desk.

Vic picked it up. "What's this?"

"Open it."

Vic did. He took out a printout from a travel company. "Tickets to Australia?"

"Two tickets to Australia, business class," Joe corrected.

Vic rested them on the desk blotter. "I don't get it?"

"What's not to get? I'm giving you the opportunity to propose to Mimi. From the pathetic look on your ugly face these past few weeks, it's plain as day that you love the woman."

"That's…ah…very generous, Joe, but the woman dumped me."

"And the CEO of our company is going to let that stand in his way? The man who took some of the toughest hits in pro football as well as dishing them out?"

Vic winced. "Let's not mention that, okay?"

"All right. But the man who built up this mom-and-pop business into a stone powerhouse, the man who was able to knock *me* to the ground—*he's* going to just take a little thing like rejection as final?"

Vic mulled over Joe's words. "I must be out of it if you're starting to sound reasonable."

Joe reached over and picked up the desk phone. "Call her. And just remember, Australia is the land of Argyle diamonds. I'm sure you could keep Mimi busy choosing exactly what she wants."

Vic stared at the phone. "I just can't call a woman who doesn't want to see me and tell her I have two tickets to Australia."

Joe slammed the receiver back in its cradle. "Then start with something smaller. Work your way up. What about flowers? A dozen long-stemmed roses? Two dozen? You know—a grand gesture? Ladies love that."

Vic shook his head. "No, not this lady, I'm pretty sure." He paused to think. He rotated his desk chair to study Roxie. The dog was curled so tightly you'd think she was in Anchorage in the middle of winter. She looked pathetic. Almost as pathetic as he felt.

Vic swiveled back to Joe. "I've got a better idea. One she won't be able to refuse."

CHAPTER THIRTY-NINE

SHE WATCHED VIC STAND UP when he saw her approaching across the Allie Hammy plaza.

"You took a taxi," he said in amazement. As usual, he wore khaki pants and a blue blazer.

Why wasn't she surprised?

Mimi stopped three feet away and crossed her arms. "I wasn't about to go traipsing around town in this get-up." She looked down at the ridiculous Beefeater's jacket. "Thank God, I no longer have the stupid hat." Then she raised her head and eyed Vic.

He shook his head. "No, I don't mean that. I mean, you took a taxi—got in a car." He pointed in the direction of the departing cab.

Mimi glanced over her shoulder then back again. "Oh, that. I do a lot of things now. Which isn't to say I didn't sweat like a pig during the ride. But luckily the material on this jacket is so thick you can't tell." She screwed up her face and waited.

He tilted his head and stared at her.

Dammit. He looked so cute. "Well?" she prompted. "Your message said, 'Be there or be square.' Not to mention the fine print about when, where and what I was supposed to wear."

He plunged his hands in the pockets of his khaki pants. "Yeah, it was a dare."

"Hello? What kind of a person in this day and age offers a dare like 'Be there or be square'?" She paused, her mouth open. "Oh, yeah, I forgot who I was dealing with. And that part about Roxie needing me? That was a really low blow."

"I know. I couldn't help myself. But it's true. She won't eat. She doesn't sleep," Vic explained, concern lacing his voice.

Mimi looked around. "So where is she? I don't see her anywhere. She's not at the vet's, is she?" For the first time, she softened.

"No, no, nothing like that," he assured her. "I left her in the car, right on Edinburgh Avenue—just down there." He pointed in the direction.

"You left her in the car?" Mimi was aghast.

Vic held up his hands. "Don't worry. I left the window open practically the whole way."

"The whole way?" Mimi looked skeptical.

Vic nodded. "Yeah."

Mimi brought her fingers to her mouth and whistled loudly.

Two seconds later, Roxie came running to the fountain, skittering next to Mimi.

Mimi knelt down and gave the dog a good rub around the head and ears. "What a good girl. What kind of an owner leaves a dog like you in the car, huh?" Roxie whimpered in agreement. "And he says you haven't eaten. I bet he didn't even think to buy you the special treats like I got you for the picnic."

"You're right. You can see why she needs you."

Mimi gave the dog a final big squeeze and stood up. "What's this all about, Vic? Roxie's fine. Why did you send that text message? I think I deserve the truth." She shot his own words back at him.

"You're right. You do." He peered at her. "The text didn't come at a bad time, did it? I didn't interrupt anything important, did I?"

"As it so happens, I was having lunch in the City with Lilah and her sister-in-law, Penelope, at her fiancé's restaurant—yes, Penelope has finally agreed to marry Nick Rheinhardt. Is that what you wanted to know?" she asked innocently.

Vic opened his mouth, started to say something and stopped.

"We also discussed my future employment prospects. The network offered me a weekend anchor spot. Then of all things, I got a call from the Dean of Allie Hammy. She's offered me a visiting lectureship position on the role of jornalism in international conflicts. Interesting, don't you think?"

"You'd consider coming back to Grantham?"

"It's a possibility."

"In which case..." Vic hesitated, then started all over again. "Listen."

"I'm listening."

"I've got a proposal."

Mimi narrowed her eyes suspiciously. "What kind of a proposal?"

"That we try again. Only this time, we get to know each other gradually—over a longer period of time."

"What? You're proposing we go to a kabuki performance together?"

Vic looked like he wanted to laugh but was way too nervous. "My idea was that we go on vacation," he ventured.

"I never go on vacation," she informed him.

"Neither do I. That's why I suggested it—something new...the start of something new for both of us."

Mimi frowned. "Did you have any place in particular?"

"Joe suggested Australia."

"Australia's nice."

"Yeah, it sounded nice to me, but it has one drawback."

"Oh?" Mimi tapped her foot.

"We couldn't take Roxie. They have strict animal quarantine laws in Australia. I checked."

Mimi shook her head. "Then that wouldn't work at all."

"I agree. See, we're getting somewhere."

Mimi raised a dubious eyebrow. "Go on."

"So, then I thought. What about a road trip across the U.S.—you, me and Roxie?"

"A road trip across America." Now that she hadn't expected.

"We could take as long as we wanted to. No reservations. Maybe take a tent, go camping. I've always wanted to go to North Dakota. I've never been there. Have you?"

Mimi shook her head. "You're crazy. A road trip? We could end up killing each other."

"I'm crazy? I thought *you* had dibs on that?"

She tried to hide her smile by covering her mouth.

"Anyway, who says we'd kill each other. Who knows? It could end up that we actually *like* being with each other—even fall in love again, only this time even more." He raised his eyebrows, waiting for her response. "You want to take the chance? I know that Roxie would love it."

Mimi made a face. "That's…that's blackmail!"

"I know. But I'm desperate."

Mimi regarded Roxie. On cue, she rolled over and exposed herself. "Shameless as usual," Mimi told her. Then she went back to eyeing Vic. "So, say we don't kill each other. Then what?"

"Then I was thinking," he forged on. "If we didn't come to blows driving cross-country, we could then maybe…I don't know…take the trip to Australia?"

"I thought you just nixed that idea?"

"That's true. But I thought it might be a good idea to see if we could function together without the aid of our guardian angel." He looked down at Roxie. "No offence, girl."

Roxie scratched her own tummy with a back paw.

Mimi frowned in thought. "Australia? Maybe that's

not such a bad idea. That way I could check in on Press—see how he's doing."

"You think your brother really wants you to check in on him?"

Mimi looked offended. "Yes…well, maybe, no… Yes and no," she concluded. She smiled brightly.

Vic attempted a smile of his own. It looked pretty feeble to Mimi.

"So what do you think?" he asked. "Should we become travel buddies and then possibly…I don't know…if things go well…see what happens?"

"You're being remarkably inarticulate. You know, the way you're making a muck of this whole 'dare' thing—and now this fuzzy travel plan—I might just have to take a while to think about it." She was teasing, and she was pretty sure he didn't know it.

In fact, Mimi could see that Vic was really desperate, and somehow it amused her in a perverse way. Because she had missed him more than she thought possible.

Well, hell. She knew that she was going to give in even before she put on her stupid Reunions costume and got on the train to Grantham.

"Woman, you're killing me." He shook his head. Then after a moment, he held up a finger. "I know what will persuade you." Vic pushed off his shoes and removed his socks. He passed them to Roxie. "Here, chew to your heart's content."

The dog eyed him warily.

He slipped off his jacket, but didn't bother to fold it,

just dropped it on the marble plaza. Next, he yanked off his tie, undid his belt and tossed it away.

Roxie shifted her head back and forth nervously.

Mimi watched. "It's okay, girl. He's just going crazy."

"Who says I'm going crazy?" He lifted one leg and clambered over the low wall and into the pool. He undid the top button of his dress shirt, then the next and the next. He tore off his shirt and sent it flying.

It slapped Mimi in the face.

She removed it. Her mouth was open as she watched him strip off his pants, leaving nothing but a pair of knit boxers.

Mimi held out her hand. "Vic, no. People might come by. You'll get in trouble."

"It's summer vacation. No one's around. And as for trouble? That's my middle name. Besides, if the police come to arrest me, I'll just give them your father's name. It worked the last time."

Mimi bit her bottom lip. "Actually, it wasn't my father. I was the one who came to the police station and confessed it was all my fault. I said that my father had sent you to rescue me. Then I left before you could see me—I was so embarrassed."

Vic had his hands on the waistband of his boxers. "Really? That's nice to know." He smiled broadly. "Well, this time in a way, he played a vital part—much as I hate to say it. Because the old coot did ask me to come to Reunions to rescue you."

The wail of sirens pierced the air.

"Vic, get out of there," Mimi ordered.

"Not until you agree to travel with me." He started to lower the underwear.

Mimi shook her head, climbed in the pool and waded over to him. "Okay, okay. Enough." She wrapped her arms around his chest. "You made your point. I'll travel with you."

"And afterward?" He held her tight.

"Afterward, we'll see." But she already knew the answer.

The sirens grew louder.

Mimi looked at him, her brow worried. "Who's going to save us now?"

Vic smiled. "Roxie. Just whistle, and she'll come running."

"Just like me, if it's the right whistler."

Then they put their lips together and used them in an even more satisfying way.

EPILOGUE

Late August
Australia

"WHAT?" MIMI SHOT Vic a look.

He glanced at her sideways. They were seated side by side in front of an oversize computer screen.

She followed his gaze, which honed in on the way she was sitting on her hands. "Oh, that. I'm cold. So sue me." True, the damp winter temperatures in Melbourne were a marked change from the tropical climate of the Great Barrier Reef where they'd just come from. But she also knew that the weather wasn't the only reason she'd jammed her hands under her thighs.

"Hello? Hello?" Noreen's voice came over the Skype connection.

"Noreen." Mimi turned to the screen. "Hold up. I hear you, but I can't see you. There's a small window showing Vic and me, but the rest of the screen is blank."

"Geez. You'd think you'd never used Skype before." Press leaned over her shoulder and moved the curser to the icon of a video camera in the upper right corner. Immediately, Noreen came into view.

"Now we've got you," Vic announced. "So how are things in Grantham? And more important, how are you feeling?"

"Enormous." Noreen laughed and rubbed her swollen midriff. "Being pregnant with twins tends to accelerate the bodily changes. Have I mentioned my enormous breasts?" She held up her hands to display ever more burgeoning curves.

Vic opened his eyes wide.

Mimi teasingly backhanded him in the stomach. "You look great, Noreen. Nobody wears a baby bump as well as you, that's for sure." In her sleeveless yoga top, riding high on her rounded belly, Noreen appeared positively radiant. "So do you feel as well as you look? No complications?"

Noreen shook her head. "None really. Thank goodness the first trimester's nausea is over—that's all I can say. Unfortunately, the only downside is that at my advanced age—and with the prospect of twins— the doctor is a little toe-y about me doing too much travel, especially to Africa. So that means that Lilah will have to bear the brunt of traveling to Congo for a while."

"I'm sure Lilah and Justin understand. And speaking of adjustments, how's my father handling the news of twins?"

"Why don't you ask him?" Noreen shifted her laptop, and Conrad came into the picture. He was sitting next to her on one of the stools at the kitchen island in their house in Grantham.

"Hello, Mary Louise. You look well. It appears that Australia agrees with you," Conrad said with a stiff smile.

At the mention of her double-barrel given name, Mimi immediately sat up straighter.

Out of range of the computer, Vic patted her on her leg. "She's a champion snorkler, I can tell you that," he responded to Conrad's comment. "You should have been there. She was the first one off the boat to swim with the manta rays, and they were not exactly tiny."

"I'm glad to hear you are back to your bold self, not to mention enjoying life," Conrad said.

Begrudgingly, Mimi had to admit he sounded genuine. "And what about you? Ready for the changes that come with a growing family?"

"Actually, Conrad has news in that department," Noreen said with a loving smile at her husband.

It may have been the slightly erratic connection, but Mimi could have sworn she saw her father blush.

Conrad reached across the counter and took Noreen's hand. "I've decided I should spend more time closer to home. I'm giving up my commuting ways, so to speak." He gazed at his wife. "Indeed, Noreen, with her altruistic outlook, convinced me that I should consider giving back to the community in some way. So, I talked to several university administrators to offer my services, and we all agreed that the perfect fit would be in the Development Office. I'll be involved with drumming up support from my fellow alumni, helping them to remember their alma mater in the generous manner it deserves. After all, they wouldn't have become so successful if it weren't for the polish and the academic excellence, not to mention the connections, that a Grantham education afforded them. Don't think I won't be meeting with you, too, Vic."

"I look forward to it," Vic replied, carefully keeping his voice neutral.

"So with you teaching at Grantham this coming Fall semester, that means we'll be able to have lunch together at the Faculty Club," Conrad reminded Mimi.

"I look forward to that, too." She swallowed the lump in her throat.

"Prescott is there, I gather?"

Mimi gladly got up from her chair and waved her brother toward the computer.

Press slumped in the chair. He ran his hand through his curly hair, which was much longer than it had been in June, a fluffy Harpo Marx do. "Hello, Father, Noreen," he said formally. He answered politely but monosyllabically while Noreen badgered him good-naturedly about his diet.

"And have you thought about what you'll be doing after you finish up your master's degree?" Conrad asked. He didn't bother with small talk.

"I'm in the process of applying for Ph.D. programs in America," Press answered curtly.

"I hope you've included Grantham among your choices," Conrad lectured.

Press rattled off a handful of universities that were

tops in the field of paleontology, none of which included Grantham. Then he set his jaw, clearly waiting for the anticipated critical response.

Conrad glanced over at Noreen.

The tension in Press's tiny apartment in the South Yarra neighborhood of Melbourne was palpable.

Conrad turned back to speak. "They all sound like top-notch schools. And they will certainly be lucky to have someone of your caliber."

"Thank you, sir," Press said, stunned.

There was a collected exhale of breath in the apartment, during which barking could be heard from the other end of the conversation.

"Is that Roxie I hear?" Vic asked.

"You bet." Noreen turned to Conrad. "Maybe you could get them to come in so Vic and Mimi can see them and say hello." She watched as Conrad rose at her request, then to her computer screen, she said, "I invited Basia and Tommy over to swim in the pool. It's so hot today. Naturally, Brigid insisted that Roxie come along, too. Actually, your sister's been a godsend, Vic. She's a wonderful babysitter, which has really helped me out, especially in the summer heat."

The sound of high-pitched chatter and dog scrambling grew louder as the others came into the kitchen.

Brigid plopped, wet bathing suit and all, on a stool. "Hey, you guys? It's me," she announced.

"Hey, squirt," Press called out. He pulled Mimi over and had her lean down to be in the picture, too. "You look like you're having a good time. But how about you let your mom move the computer down so that Vic can see Roxie? I know he misses her."

"*I* miss her," Mimi added.

"Roxie, how you doing, girl?" Vic cooed.

There was a brief period of voices calling the dog and the screen moving this way and that. Finally, Basia poked her head into view. "Sorry, Vic, she's scared witless of the computer. Why don't I take a picture of her with my phone and I'll email it to you— that is, if she'll let me."

Vic nodded. "It's worth a try. Anyway, it sounds as if she's getting lots of attention. Tell me. Have you started your lessons at Juilliard yet?"

Basia shook her head. "Not until after Labor Day. I still can't believe I'll be studying with the head of the violin program. It'll be a juggling act for sure— going into Manhattan two nights a week and still taking courses at Rutgers *and* waitressing. I gotta admit. I'm scared but excited. Real excited."

Vic frowned. "What did I tell you about the waitressing? I'm happy to help out. If you need money for child care…"

Basia held up her hand. "No, Vic, you know where I stand. Besides, Joe is already turning into a reliable babysitter."

"Joe? Not our Joe?"

"I know. Who would have thought it? I guess we all learn to rise to the occasion when circumstances demand it."

Mimi couldn't help thinking that that statement

just about summed up her topsy-turvy life—in a good way. And if she weren't careful, she'd start blubbering. And there was no way that was going to happen. "Listen, it may be morning in Grantham, but it's late at night here. Maybe it's time to say goodbye, then? We'll be seeing you in less than a week anyway."

"We can't wait," Conrad answered from his end.

And then everyone waved goodbye, including Mimi, who was leaning over between her brother and Vic.

"Hey, something's flashing on Mimi's hand," Brigid blurted out just before Press ended the connection.

Press let out a sigh. "Well, nothing like a family chat to dry out the throat. Can I get you a cleansing ale, Vic? Mimi?" He rose from the chair and made his way to the kitchen.

Vic held up a finger. "Why not?"

Mimi shook her head. "Not for me, thanks." She took over the chair that Press had vacated—he had only two in his sparsely furnished rental. Nothing decorated the walls except for a mounted butterfly in a black frame. A snapshot of Amara was tucked into a bottom corner.

Mimi rested her right hand on her left and admired her new engagement ring. Mike Wilson, a local Melbourne jeweler designed irresistibly elegant pieces with the most beautiful Argyle diamonds. "It's a beautiful souvenir of our Australian travels."

She shifted her hand back and forth to enjoy the

way the canary-yellow diamond glinted in a delicate circle of flawless white diamonds.

Vic took her hands in his. "It's more than a souvenir. It's a keepsake—for life."

Mimi studied their joined hands. She smiled—from the heart. "You're right. But, you know, the ring really isn't what's important."

Vic brought her hand closer to study it. "Does that mean I can return it and get my money back?"

Mimi snatched her hand back. "No way." Then she smiled. "What I was about to say before someone interrupted me—" she glared at him, but couldn't really muster much irritation "—is that the important thing, the really important thing, is the company you keep—for life."

* * * * *